THE LAST BOOK CLUB

THE LAST BOOK CLUB

A NOVEL

JOANNE ROCK

NEW YORK

Books should be disposed of and recycled according to local requirements. All paper materials used are FSC compliant.

Published in the United States by Crooked Lane Books, an imprint of The Quick Brown Fox & Company LLC.

Crooked Lane Books and its logo are trademarks of The Quick Brown Fox & Company LLC.

Library of Congress Catalog-in-Publication data available upon request.

ISBN (hardcover): 979-8-89242-480-6
ISBN (paperback): 979-8-89242-481-3
ISBN (ebook): 979-8-89242-482-0

Cover design by Hayley Warnham

Printed in the United States.

www.crookedlanebooks.com

Crooked Lane Books
34 West 27th St., 10th Floor
New York, NY 10001

First Edition: May 2026

The authorized representative in the EU for product safety and compliance is eucomply OÜPärnu mnt 139b-14, 11317 Tallinn, Estonia, hello@eucompliancepartner.com, +33757690241

10 9 8 7 6 5 4 3 2 1

To my book club, full of amazing, inspirational women bearing no resemblance to the group depicted in these pages! Love you all.

To my book club, full of amazing, inspirational women bearing no resemblance to the group depicted in these pages! Love you all.

Prologue

Present Day, Halloween Night

BLINKING AWAKE WITH a dry mouth and my cheek pressed into the spine of an open paperback, I try to recall whose idea it had been to host a murder mystery-themed game on the night reserved for book club.

Maybe if I can remember, I will be able to figure out why I am here. Because instead of sitting on one of my friends' couches, sipping a perfectly chilled pinot grigio and discussing some fiction (briefly) before launching into local gossip (at length), I'm lying gagged, bound, and blindfolded on someone's cold basement floor.

Not a finished basement, like the one my neighbor just remodeled into a wellness spa and meditation room. No, I'm talking about a dark, below-grade cellar with poured concrete floors and the hint of mustiness that says there's been water damage here.

"Mmph!" I grunt-shout through the duct tape on my face, my situation feeling more and more dire as I try to clear the brain fog that's preventing me from recalling how I got into this position in the first place. Too much wine?

I have a splitting headache. The back of my skull throbs.

Worse, I have no memory of how I got here, and my head is too heavy to move. Only my feet and wrists are bound, but I don't think I can even roll onto my side if I want to because my whole body feels like there's an elephant sitting on me. I had to have been drugged. Our group read a book once where something like this happened to a college-aged girl. Someone spiked her drink at a frat party, and she ended up assaulted with no memory of what happened.

Fear curdles in my belly. I'm still dressed in the same clothes I'd worn to the murder mystery party, so I didn't think anyone had touched me like *that*. Forcing myself to stop and think, to really concentrate, I can definitely remember arriving at Sophie's house on our book club night. I'd been a little miffed that I'd had to come in costume for the mystery game, since my character's backstory was a snooze, and I didn't have much leeway with the outfit.

I had brought a bottle of wine, as usual. Also my favorite murder mystery novel, since I felt a moral obligation to elevate the literary talk among the group even on our theme nights when reading is usually optional. So I remember I rang the front doorbell at Sophie's place with a worn copy of Umberto Eco's *The Name of the Rose* in my hand when someone who wasn't Sophie answered. Her extremely hot husband, Luke. I'd been a little surprised since the spouses normally take off on our book club nights, but I never minded running into Luke. The man was a specimen. Tall, fit, and ridiculously wealthy. It didn't hurt to *look*.

The next thing I remember was drinking a glass of wine. Or maybe a cocktail of some sort? I couldn't recall who'd handed it to me because everyone from book club was dressed up for the murder mystery game. No one looked quite like themselves. There'd been the hotel tycoon and the glamorous actress. A Vegas showgirl and a doctor in surgical scrubs passing out Jell-O shots in syringes. Everyone had a part to play.

Had Luke drugged me? Or Sophie? I'd had my run-ins with both of them in the past, but we're all friends now. I'd been in the book club with Sophie ever since I'd moved into a chichi neighborhood in Saratoga Springs. As for the rest of the book club members, I considered them all friends.

Well, I considered them friend-*ly* at very least. No doubt they talked about me behind my back for things like the Eco book and who knew what else. Who doesn't have at least a little baggage with the members of their social circle? And, let's face it, this particular book club has more baggage than most considering just the quiet backstabbing and public betrayals that *I* know about among my friends. I'm not even in the inner circle, so I've always suspected there is a lot more at play beneath the surface. Not to mention there was that hit-and-run a year ago when one of the members had been struck and killed on the way home from a meeting. Something that seemed accidental then, but in light of my current bound status, I wonder. Is our club turning deadly?

Our themed murder mystery game might hit a little too close to home.

A wave of queasiness grips me, and I worry I'm going to hurl behind the barrier of the tape. Wouldn't that kill me? I'd choke to death. Strangely, that thought prods me the rest of the way out of my drug-induced stupor. My heart rate kicks into high gear, a rapid-fire beat making me breathe too fast as the full recognition of my predicament settles into my brain.

I hadn't been tied up and thrown into someone's cold basement as part of any murder mystery game. Somebody had deliberately hit me on the back of the head, and I was pretty sure I felt a trickle of blood sliding through the roots of my hair. There would be no pinot grigios and bookish discussion with friends this evening. Something is very, very wrong tonight, and I am in real danger.

Panic grips me. I need to move, but I can't.

I might have upchucked then, the swirl of nausea making me dizzy. But at the very moment the bile begins to burn a path up the back of my throat, a scream from upstairs chills me all the way to my duct-taped toes.

CHAPTER

1

Jordyn

Present, Two Weeks Before Halloween

CAN YOU FIND *the killer before another murder is committed?*

Jordyn Lawson fought a shiver at the wording on the glossy black cardstock in her hand. The sentence wasn't meant to be ominous. The elegant invitation had been professionally printed, complete with the outline of a hooded grim reaper.

She leaned a hip against the wrought iron railing on the second story deck of her neighbor's home and trailed a finger over the gold script on the card. Grateful her hostess was too busy preparing drinks to notice how much the card had flustered her, Jordyn reminded herself to be discreet in her response to the invitation.

Today had been major sensory overload. As a certified introvert, Jordyn normally wouldn't have made an effort to meet new neighbors. But her relocation came with an agenda.

A goal that she'd already made sacrifices for. Attending this block party and getting the lay of the land in upstate New York's Spa City—the alternately charming and pretentious Saratoga Springs—was an important first step.

The setting sun burnished Saratoga Lake and Kaitlin Teal's backyard in the rich colors of autumn. Jordyn had only moved into a nearby rental home a few weeks ago, so she was grateful for today's block party that allowed her to mingle with the locals. On Kaitlin's lawn below, a few teens splashed each other with cold water from the lake while younger kids squealed inside a castle-shaped bounce house.

This scene was more relaxed and raucous than at some of Kaitlin's block party cohosts who lived in stuffier, multimillion-dollar mansions all around her. Jordyn had already dropped by a historic Victorian home with catered hors d'oeuvres and a chamber orchestra for the appetizer portion of the day. Then she'd stopped by a French country-style estate where the owners had a full-on luau in progress, complete with fire jugglers for entertainment and a buffet overflowing with poke, poi, and suckling pig. There had been arbors heavy with yellow hibiscus flowers all along the walkways between a temporary dance floor and the pool deck. Even now, almost an hour later, the distinctive sound of a steel guitar and wooden Polynesian drums echoed in Jordyn's head despite Kaitlin's outdoor Sonos speakers blaring a pop tune.

All of this was a world away from her down-to-earth Texas home. Former home. Her live-in lover of two years had given her an ultimatum when she'd told him she was leaving their place in Austin to pursue a quest almost two thousand miles away. Six weeks later, she still didn't regret choosing the quest over him.

"You said this invitation is for your book club?" Jordyn asked Kaitlin, shaking off her unease at the idea of finding a killer as she flipped the card to read the back side. There was an October meeting date and contact details.

Jordyn recognized the street address for the ginormous house with the owners who threw a luau as their contribution to today's event.

"It's probably a bit over the top for your average book club invitation, I know. But you'll get used to everything being a little extra around this town." Kaitlin dipped the rim of a champagne flute into a mixture of cinnamon and sugar as she stood at the stainless-steel countertop of her outdoor kitchen. She had a whole tray of glasses lined up and methodically ran a slice of apple around the edge of each one before coating the rims in the sweet and spicy mixture.

While she prepared enough drinks for a crowd, she settled the last of the flutes on a serving tray before picking up a quart of apple cider and splashing a little into each glass. Kaitlin wore a brown sundress dotted with a daisy pattern, a jean jacket and high leather boots were her nod to the cooler temperatures of an upstate autumn. Every high-end piece of clothing she wore made Jordyn very aware of her consignment store clothes.

At least she'd been careful to keep long sleeves down so that the homemade tattoo on her forearm was hidden.

"Are you reading a crime thriller or something?" Jordyn asked, scanning the invitation once more to see if she'd missed a book title for the meeting.

She was playing it cool, but she definitely wanted to attend the book club meeting. She and Kaitlin had hit it off as soon as Jordyn had made friends with Nala, Kaitlin's fawn-colored American Akita, who had almost knocked Jordyn over with an enthusiastic jump. A conversation about dogs led to one about novels, and, now, here they were. With an opportunity that would really help move Jordyn closer to her goal.

"You would think so, right?" Kaitlin gave a wry laugh as she grabbed a bottle of Prosecco and topped off the flutes with sparkling wine, her collection of silver rings clanking against the glass as she poured. "But the book is optional this month, so I paid no attention to the title. Some of our members gripe about reading too many books each year, so we've started doing a couple of theme nights to space out the reading commitments. This month Sophie decided to do one of those murder mystery games where everyone shows up as a character and we all try to guess who committed a crime."

"And you're sure it's okay for me to just show up at the next meeting? I mean, wouldn't I need to be a character?" Seeing that Kaitlin was ready to start serving the drinks, Jordyn shoved the invitation into her knock-off designer bag and reached to take the tray for her. "Here, let me get this for you at least. I can make the rounds if you want."

"You're so sweet." Shaking her head, Kaitlin kept hold of the silver commemorative platter engraved with a racehorse and the date of a decades-old Travers Stakes. There were horsey touches everywhere in the town famous for mineral springs and a historic race course that touted itself as the oldest continuously operated sporting venue in the United States. Heading for the steps, Kaitlin said over her shoulder, "This way I can greet all my guests while still having a built-in exit strategy for the neighbors I don't want to get stuck talking to."

Perhaps Jordyn's hostess saw her disappointment at being left alone on the deck because she paused to add, "Why don't you walk with me, and I'll introduce you to the people you haven't met yet?"

"Um, yes?" Following her down the steps to the surrounding lawn below, Jordyn lowered her voice for Kaitlin's ears alone. "Assuming I'm not one of those neighbors you need an exit strategy for?"

"Ha! Not a chance. I wouldn't have mentioned book club if you were on my list of people to avoid." Kaitlin headed toward the side lawn first, where a dozen guests congregated around a seating area anchored by a firepit. Before they reached the group, she confided, "And it's probably best you don't mention it to anyone else, either, in case they don't belong. Some people have been lobbying for an invite for years."

OK then.

Jordyn counted herself all the more fortunate to be one of the anointed few. Especially since she didn't exactly blend in with this wealthy crowd. She was renting a carriage house a few blocks down, so it wasn't like she had a splashy home to impress anyone. Maybe no one else suspected her clothes were all consignment shop finds and a far cry from the tees and pajama pants she preferred to wear, but there were other tells that she didn't belong in the same sandbox as the rest of this group. Even Kaitlin, who was a family therapist and lived in a humbler home by Saratoga standards, rocked a Rolex watch and Prada sunglasses.

"Welcome, welcome!" Kaitlin plastered on a hostess smile as she approached the guests by the firepit. Logs shifted in the copper bowl as she drew closer, sending a shower of sparks into the cooling air. "Who's ready for an apple cider mimosa?"

"You don't have to ask me twice." The first one to reach for the tray was an immaculately styled woman in a form-fitting white angora sweater over pale gray leggings. Gold and diamond necklaces lay in the vee of her sweater, glinting in the glow of the fire. Platinum blonde hair swooped over her forehead in an artful roll against her brown skin.

"Jordyn, this is Destiny Griffin. She owns The Ascent, the best gym in town, and lives over on Crescent Avenue." Kaitlin gave a nod in the general direction away from the lake toward town. "Destiny, and everyone, this is Jordyn Lawson. She just moved into the Solomons' carriage house so be your sweetest to her so she'll stick around, okay?"

"Give us a little credit will you?" A soft-spoken, extremely good-looking man in a corduroy blazer reached around Destiny to help himself to a drink. "We're always good to newcomers. I'm Brad, by the way. I just finished up renovations on the white Federalist house two doors down from you."

"Nice to meet you." Jordyn smiled a greeting but didn't have a chance to say more than that when someone spoke over her.

"We're good to the newcomers," echoed a big, athletic-looking guy in chinos who sprawled on a patio lounger with a longneck in his hand. He raised the beer to point it at Kaitlin. "It's the locals we treat like crap."

"That's not true, Nikolai," Destiny crooned, moving closer to him to put a hand on his shoulder. "It's just *you* we treat like crap."

There were a few chuckles from people around the fire, and then Kaitlin was already spinning on her heel.

"There are lots more drinks on the patio when you need to top up," Kaitlin called as she walked away. "Come on, Jordyn, you've got about a zillion more introductions heading your way."

"Nice to meet you all." Jordyn gave an awkward wave at the firepit group before hurrying after her hostess.

"Slow down, new girl."

A voice from behind her made Jordyn pause. Destiny picked her way through the grass in metallic-colored kitten heels.

"You too, Kaitlin." Destiny called as she reached Jordyn's side. She pointed to Jordyn's handbag, her silver-painted fingernail resting on the designer insignia. "What's this all about?"

Confused, Jordyn wondered if she needed to defend her fake Louis purse. "An impulse buy, I guess. Is it that obvious it's not real?"

She lifted the leather to examine the pattern stamped on it more carefully as Kaitlin rejoined them, her tray still half full.

"Not the clutch. This." Destiny withdrew the book club invitation sticking out from the side pouch. She waved it in front of Kaitlin's nose. "You got her in?"

"Well, not in so many words, but I'm going to." Kaitlin shrugged and, now that the sun was almost down, pushed her sunglasses up into her highlighted, honey-colored hair. "We're down a member anyway."

Destiny sucked in a breath before she swore lightly. "And that's what you're going to tell Sophie when you bring Jordyn with you?" She tucked the card back into the open exterior pocket of Jordyn's bag.

"Obviously not, but it's true." Kaitlin tipped her chin as she shifted the tray of drinks onto a patio table near the pool. "And does anyone else think it's in extremely bad taste of her to host a murder mystery game on the first anniversary of—"

Destiny cleared her throat loudly. "Heads up. She just arrived with Luke and the girls."

Jordyn tensed. Was she picking up on apprehension from the others? Or was it because of the subject they'd just dropped like a hot potato?

"Who's here?" she asked softly, even though she was pretty sure she'd followed the gist of the conversation enough to make an educated guess.

She'd been involved with the residents of this neighborhood for all of one day, and she'd already pinpointed the most powerful player on the block. But then, Jordyn had done her homework before she'd unpacked her moving boxes. She'd read about Saratoga's social scene and its new, undisputed queen. The same woman who ran an elite book club and founded a successful podcast that arbitrated sticky break-ups for entertainment value.

"Sophie Durand," Kaitlin muttered as she glanced sideways at a laughing blond woman bracketed by two gorgeous teenage girls. A dark-haired man with a backwards ball cap and a broad smile stood behind the group, his hands on the woman's shoulders. "This month's book club hostess."

Charlotte is the older daughter. She's a carbon copy of her mother. Smart, ambitious, well-rounded. Amelia is the wildcard. Every bit as intelligent as her sister but a little bit of a smart ass. Kind of like you, Jordyn.

Jordyn's gaze roamed over the young women as she recalled the scouting report on them. Willowy Charlotte wore a cropped pink sweatshirt with jeans and white tennis shoes, her attention focused on the young family that had stopped to speak to her mother. She bent toward a sporty leather stroller, covered in horses, to smile at the baby inside. Amelia, the other daughter, a shorter, curvier blonde dressed in a varsity jacket and denim shorts, gave all her attention to her phone. They were both lovely young women. But it was their mother who held Jordyn's attention.

Sophie Durand had the kind of beauty other women only dreamed about. Flawless skin even though she was old enough to have a daughter finishing high school. Wavy golden locks that looked as effortless as her crisp white button down worn untucked over a navy-colored skirt. She had the strong, lean legs of an athlete, and she moved with the confidence and grace of someone accustomed to being the center of attention.

"Now's your chance to tell her that Jordyn's coming to the next meeting." Destiny elbowed Kaitlin as she gave her a sly smile.

Squeals from down by the lake were quickly drowned out by the sound of a boat motor roaring to life.

"That would be great," Jordyn chimed in, determined not to lose the ground she'd gained today in expanding her network in her new town. Sophie Durand was an important player in the social landscape that Jordyn needed to navigate. "I'm excited to meet everyone."

"Careful what you wish for," Kaitlin said, half to herself, before raising her arm to wave over her new guests. Her silver bracelets jangled with the movement. "Here she comes."

Jordyn watched with interest as the two teen daughters peeled off in different directions. One toward the lake, the other toward the house. The man in the ball cap remained in the driveway in an animated conversation with another guy who'd just arrived on a motorcycle.

So they would have Sophie all to themselves.

"The house looks beautiful, Kaitlin." The woman's voice was low and modulated. A good voice for a podcaster. "Thank you for having us."

Sophie Durand enveloped Kaitlin in a quick embrace before turning to Destiny and greeting her the same way.

"Well it's not a luau, but I do what I can," Kaitlin quipped. "I heard your party was amazing."

Sophie shrugged as if it was of no consequence. "It was all Luke's idea. He's so good at event planning." Then her marine blue eyes landed on Jordyn. "I'm Sophie, by the way."

"Jordyn Lawson. I'm a huge fan of your show." She figured a little flattery never hurt the cause. Then, taking a gamble, she withdrew the book club invitation from her purse. "I'm also a huge fan of murder mystery games if you need any help finding a killer."

For a moment, her eyes locked with Sophie's. But it only took a moment for the other woman to smile. "Is that so?"

Jordyn's heart pounded. "Mostly I just really like reading," she admitted. "I may have twisted Kaitlin's arm into telling me about your book club."

"It *is* the best book club in town, hands down," Destiny added, making a show of buffing her perfect fingernails on the shoulder of her sweater. "I mean, she wouldn't *want* to belong to any other."

Jordyn could have hugged her for the endorsement, since it sort of felt like she was on trial. Except she wasn't really of a mind to hug any of the women who belonged to a book club that was—Jordyn was pretty sure—murderous.

Getting into the book club was crucial.

"Right?" Kaitlin reached back to the tray of apple cider mimosas and picked up two, passing one each to Sophie and Jordyn before grabbing two more for herself and Destiny. "It's not like I go blabbing about our group to just anyone."

Sophie's gaze tracked back and forth between her two friends before coming to rest on Jordyn again. Assessing.

"Well I guess that's settled then." She lifted her flute in a toast. "Welcome to book club, Jordyn Lawson."

Relieved, Jordyn clinked glasses with the others, feeling the full import of the day's victory before she indulged in a single sip. She still needed to be cautious. Watchful. But she couldn't resist celebrating this moment after she'd been tense and anxious all day.

And not just because she was a certified introvert trying her damnedest to masquerade as a fun and lighthearted extrovert.

No. Jordyn was a knot of nerves because she really was trying to find a killer.

CHAPTER

2

Tara

One Year Ago

"WAIT UNTIL YOU see the costume I made." Tara Hughes adjusted her video screen to better see her foster sister, Jordyn. Tara sat at a breakfast bar in her friend Sophie's pool house, the de facto office space where they conducted business related to their cocreated podcast.

Sophie hadn't arrived to start the work day yet, so it was a good time to touch base with Jordyn. The foster siblings lived almost two thousand miles apart, but that didn't prevent Tara from trying to reestablish a relationship with one of the most significant people in her life. Tara had only been in the foster system for two years, but she would never have survived that tumultuous time without Jordyn. It still blew her mind that she'd managed to mentally block out that time in her life—and the girl who'd saved her in every way possible—until a bout of therapy three years ago. Tara had explored most of her repressed memories and dealt with the worst of them.

The best of them was Jordyn. It had taken a private investigator to find her long-forgotten foster sister, and she'd broken her promise to her adoptive family never to contact people from that life in order to do it. But secretly defying her family had been worth the risk in order to reconnect. Even if she still kept their relationship under wraps.

For now.

"I'll bet it's fabulous." Jordyn scraped away a curtain of copper curls from her face with one hand while she clutched a coffee mug in the other. She walked through her all-white Austin, Texas kitchen before dropping into a seat across from her screen. She wore a black T-shirt and plaid pajama pants, a perk of working from home as a graphic designer. "Although you have way too big of an advantage. I bet you'll be the only one at your Halloween party in a costume designed by a Fashion Institute graduate."

Tara laughed, enjoying her friend's utter faith in her. How was it that a woman who'd been close to her for just two years as a kid could have such a high opinion of her coupled with zero envy? Meanwhile, the privileged friends she'd made since moving to Saratoga at age fourteen were forever in competition with one another, perpetually ready to backstab.

"Well for all I know I'll be the *only* one in costume since I'm not attending a party, per se. Just my monthly book club meeting." She checked the time on her screen, thinking she should probably wind up her conversation before Sophie arrived at the pool house—the "casita," she called it—to start their work day. "But I ask you, how can anyone host a book club on Halloween night and not expect people to show up in costume?"

"Clearly a costume should be worn." Jordyn slid a pair of reading glasses onto her nose. She looked so different from the stick-thin Goth girl that she'd been in their youth. The old facial piercings were gone, but her self-made tattoo of a labyrinth on her forearm was still visible when she lifted her coffee cup. "Any hints what you're dressing up as?"

Tara couldn't keep it a secret. She was too excited about how the outfit had turned out. "I'm going as Maleficent. The headpiece I made with horns is the highlight of the whole thing. Although the train is something to behold, too."

Behind her, she heard a screen door slam and guessed Sophie had left her main house to cross the courtyard to the casita. Before Jordyn could reply, Tara continued, "Shit. I've got to get my workday started."

"No worries." Jordyn winked at her and reached toward her screen. "Knock 'em dead."

And then she was gone, her sign-off still echoing in Tara's ears, a callback to the days when Jordyn had been like a stand-in mom, even though she was just two years older. It bothered her deeply that she'd blocked memories of someone who'd been so instrumental in protecting her during her time in foster care, but her therapist had assured her that it was common in patients with dissociative amnesia. The last few years of remembering and recovering her past had been painful but healing, too.

Now, Tara's device returned to the open tab showing the day's schedule for *The Clean Break* podcast. The first item on their agenda was to brainstorm their most explosive episodes for a "Best-Of" clip show in the new year.

"Good morning." Sophie stepped into the living area of the casita, dressed in a gray jersey skirt and gray men's button-down, her blond waves in a low ponytail. Her blue eyes were bright as she walked straight toward the wet bar. "It came to me last night what episode to feature in the highlight show."

Frowning, Tara didn't follow. "We need more than one episode though, right? I thought we were going to do a round-up of our best shows."

Sophie spun away from the bar, never bothering to use a laptop when she had Tara around to take notes. Sometimes the uneven power balance bugged Tara, but she also respected that Sophie was the creative force behind the show. Tara had enjoyed working with her over the last few years, getting the show off the ground and then watching it turn into an "overnight success," topping the charts for listens. Success felt intoxicating after years of struggling with imposter syndrome. Her adoptive family was wealthy, and her life with them had felt like an unearned luxury after those two gut-wrenching years in the foster system after her single-parent birth mother had died. But the success of the show had been merited because of their hard work.

Still, getting swept up in her friend's creative vision meant that Tara delayed chasing her own dreams, something Jordyn had helped her realize this past summer when they'd had their first in-person visit since they were kids. Tara had spent her vacation week in Austin with Jordyn, although she'd timed it to coincide with a design conference so she could honestly tell friends and family that had been her purpose for the Texas trip. Not just because she dreaded a confrontation with her parents when they learned how much time she'd spent rediscovering her past, but also because the friendship felt too special to share just yet.

"We'll do clips around one featured episode," Sophie clarified, opening her phone to scroll through whatever it was that was more important than their conversation. "I got inspired for a whole new approach to the best-of format when I recalled the Mark Ribeki divorce. It was so popular, with lots of great sound bites. We can make that the centerpiece of the compilation."

"Oh, Soph. You know how I feel about that one." Her heart sank at the mention of one of *The Clean Break* shows that had left a bad taste in her mouth.

There'd been a handful of episodes that had been problematic for her. But that one was in the top three worst in her book.

NFL star Mark Ribeki and his wife, Evangeline Jameson, had agreed to arbitration via the show, something divorcing TCB guests were occasionally offered to simplify their process. Sophie, who had a law degree that she'd used briefly in her father's prestigious South Carolina firm before she changed career directions, had an arbitrator certification in New York state. She was legally able to make judgments if her guests signed on for the process. Ribeki had been beloved on the field and in his hometown, but had numerous, documented instances of infidelity. The couple had lived in Louisiana, a state where fault-base divorces were allowed, so his wife had assumed the show would weigh in her favor.

But Sophie had shocked her listeners—and Tara—by suddenly announcing her decision on the couple's assets would be swayed by a listener vote. Tara had been stunned at the obvious ratings grab. Ribeki's fans had called in by the thousands, voting to give him almost everything in the couple's split. Sophie had agreed and a judgment was made heavily in his favor. His ex-wife was still trying to appeal the decision through the legal system, but the last Tara had heard she hadn't had any luck.

That had been one of the few episodes that Tara had argued with Sophie about. Normally, Tara did the behind-the-scenes legwork and left the podcast direction to Sophie. But she'd been appalled by her cocreator's sudden decision to pander to listeners.

"And yet, there's no arguing that it's a fan favorite. If we want to keep growing, we need to take risks. Push boundaries sometimes." Sophie gave Tara a sly smile. "Where's your sense of adventure?"

"Should business decisions be based on wanting adventure?" Agitated, Tara stood to pace off some of her frustration. She walked a path between the ivory-colored couches near the fireplace and the eggshell-colored reading chairs near the built-in bookshelves. "This isn't like midnight skinny dipping or hooking up with a stranger. We have a responsibility to take people's break-ups seriously."

"Do we? What do you not understand about the entertainment industry? Because at the end of the day, that's what we're doing. People listen to *The Clean Break* for the entertainment value, not because they want to be sure some quarterback's trophy wife gets a share of his car collection." Sophie swiveled the leather seat of her barstool back and forth, her arms folded over her chest. "We don't need to defend the show's choices, Tara. We get to decide how we want to entertain people."

"Actually, no, *we* don't. You do, Sophie." She stopped in front of her friend's chair, wondering how things had shifted from a partnership to Sophie being in charge. "I don't know how or when you decided that you should call all the shots with the show, but it's my program too."

Sophie rewarded her declaration with a smirk and a raised eyebrow. "Well that puts me in my place doesn't it? Did you put an extra shot in your espresso this morning?"

Tara shook her head. "Don't patronize me. I'm just trying to have a voice here."

Outside the pool house, Sophie's second husband, Luke Sideris, walked through the courtyard dressed for tennis in shorts and a polo shirt. He played three mornings a week, his hours flexible thanks to his consulting work for a tech company.

"And I'm hearing it," Sophie assured her. "Why don't you at least listen to the sample pieces I asked Wynn to put together for us before you nix my idea completely?"

"You already asked Wynn to compile sample audio?" Irritation flicked through Tara.

Sophie was nothing if not committed to having her own way.

"I told you, I got inspired last night. I started hearing how it could all come together. I really think you're going to like it." Sophie rose from her seat. "Let me go grab my laptop, and I'll see if he's sent me a demo yet so you can have a listen for yourself."

Would a stronger person have just said, "Hell no" and been done with the discussion? Tara hated the idea that her kindness and quieter nature could be mistaken for weakness. But she'd been born fair-minded. A nurturer. Even her sun sign said so: Cancer. She knew that because their book club had read something with a main character who was an astrologer, and they'd all done their zodiac charts for fun at the meeting.

No surprise that Sophie was a Leo. A lioness who needed to be the center of attention. Who expected to be worshiped. There were probably positive qualities too, but those characteristics were the ones that had stuck in Tara's mind.

"I'll listen, but I'm making no promises," Tara warned her, all the while remembering Jordyn's advice from that summer visit when she'd encouraged Tara to pursue what she really loved.

Tara's interpretation of that had been that she really needed to step out of Sophie's shadow.

Sophie made a show of compliance, lifting her hands in mock surrender. "Of course."

A moment later, Sophie was out the door and walking across the courtyard to the main house. As Tara watched her through the floor-to-ceiling windows, she couldn't help but feel like she had already lost this battle. But before she could ruminate too much about it, she heard the slide of the patio door opening behind her, on the opposite side of the building from where Sophie had just left.

Tara's pulse quickened. "Hello?"

The housekeepers didn't usually interrupt them during their workday. They knew Sophie used the space as her office unless they were actively recording a show in the soundproof studio she'd had built over the garage.

"It's me." The masculine voice sounded a second before Luke stepped into view.

"Oh, hey Luke," she greeted him awkwardly, anxiety twisting through her. "You just missed Sophie—"

"I wasn't looking for Sophie." He kept coming toward her, his dark eyes locked on her.

She had about a half a second to recall the weird vibes between them the last time they were alone. The fear he'd misinterpreted an alcohol-infused conversation after the anniversary celebration for *The Clean Break*. She didn't know what had come over her to confide in him.

"You know we should probably talk about—" she began.

His mouth was on hers in an instant, hands gripping her waist. The shock of it—the social boundary crossed, the friendship betrayed—froze her for a critical moment. Her brain couldn't compute what was happening because this should *never, ever* be happening. It didn't matter that they'd had an emotional conversation that one time. She'd never wanted this.

Belatedly, she shoved at him. *And he didn't move.*

Twisting away from his lips, she cursed him. Shoved harder.

When he let her go, the smug bastard was smiling. Worse, he didn't even seem to clock her fury because his gaze was trained over her shoulder.

"Here she comes. See you around, Tara." And then he was gone, silent as a ghost, disappearing out the backdoor only a split second before Sophie tugged open the main entrance, all her attention focused on the open laptop she carried.

"Here it is." Tara's friend—her business partner, her neighbor, the woman whose life was inextricably tied to hers—looked up at her with a triumphant grin. "Wait until you hear this. You're going to love the way Wynn edited it." Then her smile faded as she seemed to register Tara's expression. "Is everything okay?"

Who knew what she saw? Cheeks red with anger? Mortification? Lips puffy from being crushed by an entitled man who hadn't sought her consent? Anger seethed inside Tara, clouding her judgement in a haze of red.

Once again, Tara only had a split second to react. To decide whether or not to speak of the colossal betrayal that had just occurred, mere steps away from her partner's marital home. But, as had happened too many times in their friendship, Tara didn't have the courage to take on the lioness.

Not right now when her head was spinning.

"Yeah. I'm fine." Still shaking, she waved Sophie closer. "Let me have a listen."

Later, Tara would have it out with Luke. Make him understand that his behavior was not only inappropriate, it was one hundred percent unwanted. Until then? She knew, once again, that she would let Sophie have her way with the show.

But now more than ever, Tara recognized that she needed a plan to get out of this business and out of this relationship with Sophie. Their friendship would suffer, but it was past time to step away from a work environment that had somehow gone from fun to toxic. The awkward dynamics, the uneven balance of power, and the dogged suffocation of her creativity were slowly killing her.

CHAPTER 3

Jordyn

Present

YOU COULD WIND *up dead.*

Jordyn stared at the most recent text message on her screen.

Enveloped in the scents of eucalyptus and lavender wafting from the nearby spa, she stood at a guest locker in the swanky gym that Kaitlin had recommended. The Ascent was owned by Destiny Griffin, so Jordyn had hoped she'd see Destiny or one of the other book clubbers during a morning yoga session. So far, no luck, but at least the yoga class had been great. Although her grounded-and-centered vibes were fading fast as she reread the message on her phone.

A threat? Nope. Just the latest in a frantic string of eight texts from Ezra, her ex-boyfriend. Scrolling back to the beginning, she tipped her forehead against the cool wood of the open locker door and scanned the content of the thread, if only to determine whether or not she needed to block him. She'd tried her best to end things on an amicable note. It had been his choice to give her an ultimatum, throwing his weight around to coerce her into staying put in Texas.

Which only revealed how little he understood her after two years of dating.

Why are you sacrificing everything we've built to meddle in a police investigation? Leave the case to the experts.

Her spine snapped straighter as she read the words, hearing the dismissive tone he would have used if they were having an actual conversation. Around her, three women entered the locker area, wrapped in white spa robes and engaged in a heated discussion about whether or not someone they knew was pregnant. Jordyn glanced at them just long enough to determine if they looked familiar from the block party. She was on a mission to meet as many book club members as possible before the next meeting.

When she didn't recognize any faces—or overhear any names that Tara had mentioned when she talked about her friends—Jordyn returned to the text thread. She skipped through a few pleas for her to come back "home" even though he'd kicked her out. It was much too late to salvage the relationship. But she wanted to compose a thoughtful response before she blocked Ezra for good. After a childhood full of abrupt goodbyes she had no control over—addict parents who'd lost custody, leaving one foster home for another, losing temporary foster siblings—Jordyn preferred to have agency in how her relationships ended these days. And even though she'd been taken aback by their sudden breakup, she recognized now that it had been for the best. She might miss the comfort and predictability of their life together, but it had been almost six weeks since she'd left Austin, and she didn't miss Ezra. That had shaken her up more than anything. The realization that she'd been going through the motions of a relationship because it had been uncomplicated. Safe.

When had she turned into that person who did things just because they were easy?

Do you honestly believe Tara would want you to risk your life to find her killer? What if she really was mowed down by someone from her book club the way you seem to think?

The more she read, the more she heard the panic behind his words. She regretted sharing her fears with him now that she'd committed to this path of retracing the last weeks of Tara's life. What if Ezra followed Jordyn to Saratoga? Revealed her intentions to the book group in some misguided effort to save her?

One year ago, someone had struck and killed her former foster sister after a book club meeting with the very same group Jordyn hoped to infiltrate. The hit-and-run was unsolved, and Tara's rich adoptive family had been more concerned with protecting their privacy than in pushing the cops for answers. But Jordyn would figure out what happened, if it was the last thing she did. No matter what Ezra believed.

You could be in a lot of danger yourself if someone from that book club finds out who you are and what you're really doing there.

Her anxiety spiked. She'd faced plenty of danger in the six years she'd spent in the foster system. Some homes had been welcoming enough, but others had been fraught with complicated interpersonal dynamics that had been tough to navigate as a kid. She'd grown accustomed to being in fight-or-flight mode twenty-four hours a day. But it had been over a decade since she'd had to be on guard all the time. The ensuing years had taken away her edge. Besides, she'd never faced the kind of peril that she felt in this town. The threat was more subtle with this group of people who pretended to be friends and hid their true faces. How would she navigate that?

She was seized with the need to simply delete the messages and forget all about Ezra, but that might not make him go away. Maybe she should call him. Explain one last time that she did not accept the police investigation into her foster sister's death going inactive after a year of zero results. It was unconscionable.

Of course, this was hardly the place for a private call. Her conversation with her ex would have to wait.

"Look who's here," a familiar voice sounded behind her. "Welcome to The Ascent, Jordyn."

Hurrying to hide her phone screen, she dropped it into her duffel bag hanging on a hook inside the locker before turning to see Destiny. Had the other woman seen anything? Jordyn couldn't recall exactly which message had been open. Something about book club? Or Tara specifically?

But Destiny only smiled, her expression impossible to read. The gym owner looked different today. The platinum hair swoop had been traded in for a posh pixie cut, with precisely curled baby hairs framing her face. She was dressed in garnet-colored workout gear, a bra top and high waisted leggings that showed off lean muscle.

"Thank you. It's a beautiful facility." Her words came out too quickly, her nerves showing. She forced herself to slow down. "I just took an amazing yoga class."

The cost of the trial membership had been eye-poppingly expensive, but Jordyn considered it necessary if she wanted to uncover the truth about what happened to Tara.

People dished in places like this. Well, wealthy, privileged women dished in places like this. So Jordyn planned to spend plenty of time here until she figured out what had really happened the night Tara was killed.

"We were lucky to find Niesha. Everyone raves about the quality of her instruction." Destiny lifted her forearm to scan the face of her smartwatch before scowling.

"Everything okay?" Jordyn asked, discreetly glancing at the smartwatch before tugging her duffel out of the locker. She hitched the straps over one shoulder, needing to shower before she visited a nearby coffee shop Tara had frequented after her workouts. Jordyn hoped that if she walked in her foster sister's shoes long enough, she'd learn about her life in the weeks leading up to her death.

"Just someone not showing up for work today." Destiny waved off the concern while two women entered the locker room behind her, their hair wrapped in towels, skin glowing. "But it's no big deal, I can lead a spin class."

"Excuse me, Destiny, darling," one of the newcomers called. She had wideset dark eyes and plump lips that were either model-perfect or expertly injected. She gestured with black-painted fingernails as she spoke, a diamond on her left hand as big as a disco ball. "You should check the steam room temperature. Your thermostat feels like it's off a few degrees from the steam room at our house."

Destiny didn't turn toward the woman right away, allowing Jordyn to see her eye roll before she spoke. "Nice to see you too, Fatima. I'll get right on that after you meet Jordyn, our new book club member."

There was a leap of speculative interest in Fatima's dark eyes. The friend she'd entered the locker room with, a petite blonde who was already busy combing out her damp hair, turned to assess Jordyn as well.

"I'm just being a good friend," Fatima assured Destiny, all the while looking at Jordyn. "You know how picky some of your clients can be." Then she extended her hand toward Jordyn. "I'm Fatima Chamoun, by the way. And this is Gina Vallot. We took the train into the city to shop for a couple of days, or we would have been at the block party."

So the news of Jordyn's invitation had travelled quickly through the ranks. She could just imagine the group texts that had gone out in the wake of Kaitlin's party.

"Nice to meet you." Jordyn shook Fatima's hand and exchanged nods with Gina, racking her brain for what Tara had to say about these two. "I hope you don't mind me crashing your next book club meeting."

She could recall a couple of mentions of Fatima, the highly educated mother of two who taught at a local private university and was married to an aerospace engineer. According to Tara, Fatima and Sophie were in perpetual competition with one another through their high-school aged daughters, each determined their offspring be the most accomplished.

But Jordyn didn't remember Tara ever mentioning Gina's name.

"You will be a welcome addition," Fatima declared as she pulled her towel off her head and shook out shoulder-length dark hair. "We lost a member last year—"

"Fatima, honestly?" Destiny interjected. "Don't go there."

Jordyn's investigative antennae twitched at the reference to Tara. Who else could it be? Interestingly, Destiny had been the one to shut down the conversation about Tara's death at the block party too, even though she'd done so a bit more subtly when Kaitlin had referenced being "down a member" in their book club. Destiny had artfully redirected the conversation by challenging Kaitlin to say as much to Sophie's face.

And now, judging by the withering glare she gave Fatima, Destiny wasn't pleased to have the dead book club member referenced again.

"I thought *I* was Tara's replacement?" Gina piped in as she worked a silver pick through the ends of her tangled waves.

She seemed to be studying Destiny and Fatima as curiously as Jordyn was.

"No, honey, you were Kit's replacement," Fatima explained. "Remember, your time in book club overlapped with Tara's."

"Only for that one meeting." Gina dropped her robe like getting naked in front of friends was no big deal. Then she reached for a printed wrap dress inside her locker and slid her arms into the sleeves.

But the unexpected peep show failed to distract Jordyn from this first overt reference to her dead friend.

"Who is Tara?" she asked, heart beating harder, silently daring any of these women to speak ill of her friend even as she willed herself to maintain outward composure.

"Sophie's best friend," Destiny explained succinctly. "She died last year, but it really hurts Sophie to talk about it, so we *try* not to bring it up."

Fatima huffed as she tossed her hair towel in a collection basket near the door. Her spa flip-flops slapped against her heels as she walked. "Do you see Sophie here?"

Nearby a hair dryer switched on, the mechanical hum drowning out everything but their conversation.

"What happened to her?" Jordyn pressed, wishing she could observe all of their faces at the same time. She needed to see and dissect each of their reactions.

Could one of them be responsible?

"There was a hit-and-run incident one night after a book club meeting," Gina explained quietly. "It happened the first month I joined."

"The police aren't sure what happened," Destiny cautioned. "It could have just been a terrible accident."

Because she refused to believe anyone she knew was capable of murder? Or because of a need to deflect attention from her role in it?

Fatima picked up the story. Her face showed only concern. Sadness. "Tara was jogging between Sophie's house and her own a little after eleven PM. We never figured out why she'd be out running at that hour. A driver struck and killed her."

Gina tossed her hairbrush into a miniature Gucci backpack before withdrawing her gym bag from her locker. "She seemed like a sweet person," she observed lightly. "I wish I'd gotten to know her."

The words were a gut punch to Jordyn, taking her back in time to when she'd first met Tara, a vulnerable twelve-year-old whose terror of her new foster home was palpable. Jordyn didn't know why she'd felt compelled to protect the scared kid who'd fallen from life circumstances far nicer than her own, but something about her called to Jordyn from day one. Within the first hour of Tara's arrival, Jordyn had gotten two black eyes taking on an older boy who wanted to mess with the new girl. For her efforts, Tara had slid a bracelet into Jordyn's hand that night, just before Jordyn fell asleep. They didn't talk that day. Really didn't speak the whole first week. But Jordyn had kept the twine bracelet with a saint medallion, tucking it into a secret place in the wall behind a broken chair molding where she kept things she didn't want anyone else to see.

These days, she didn't need to hide St. Rita. Jordyn wore her on a leather thong around her neck, a reminder of the friendship that took root that day.

The memory caused Jordyn to miss her chance to ask for more details about the hit-and-run, if only to further ferret out how this group viewed the events of that night. Because a moment later, Destiny pivoted away from them.

"I can't do this now." She held up both hands in protest, calling an end to the conversation and spurring both Fatima and Gina to finish up at their lockers. "I have to honor my own grief, okay? Besides, I've got personnel problems to deal with." She tapped her digital watch as her eyes met Jordyn's, as if she wanted to remind her of the message that had upset her earlier.

Too bad Jordyn had seen with her own eyes that the message on Destiny's watch screen had been from a regional bank, so she seriously doubted the bad news had been in regard to a personnel problem at the gym.

But then, she already knew that Tara's book club had been full of liars. She just needed to figure out which one of them was lying about what happened to Tara.

CHAPTER 4

Gina

Present

THE NEWCOMER WAS up to something.

Gina Vallot recognized the appraising look in Jordyn Lawson's wide blue eyes when they'd been introduced. After all, Gina had infiltrated the snobby Saratoga book club herself when it had served her purposes. She had enough of a social radar to know when someone else was running the same scheme.

The question was—why?

Hastening her step to return to her Mercedes, Gina was glad she hadn't shared a ride to the gym with Fatima. She needed to research this Jordyn Lawson person as soon as possible.

If that was even her real name.

Distracted, Gina nearly stepped into the path of an oncoming e-bike as she crossed Broadway to reach the small parking garage. The biker swore at her as he sped past, but even then, Gina's thoughts lingered on Jordyn.

Something about the woman didn't quite fit. Her clothes were all wrong, for one thing, something Gina couldn't help but notice as a stylist. Even the less fashion-conscious residents of their historic resort town favored certain brands, their clothing announcing their status even if they weren't flattering. But there was a definite recycled-fashion aura around Jordyn from her bag and shoes to her sweater and jacket. She hadn't just adopted one vintage piece among more current pieces, the way most Saratogian conscientious consumers would. It was one thing to make a virtuous nod to the environment by upcycling a key article of clothing. That, she could see. Virtually everything Jordyn had been wearing had been out of date by a few years, even though all of it had been in good repair.

Which made Gina think the newcomer was trying to pass herself off as one type of person while being another. Could she be a reporter?

Fear of being discovered had Gina all but diving into the front seat of her sports car, grateful for the tinted windows that would shield her from any passersby while she pulled up her social media apps on her phone. For good measure, she reached into the back for a sunshade she rarely used and unfurled the silver screen on her dashboard, making extra sure no one could see into her vehicle while she worked.

"Jordan Lawson." She spoke the name aloud as she typed it in the search feature of three different apps, then had to play with the spelling of the name to land on the right one.

And came up with only a couple of profiles set to private. Even the graphic arts contact information for her on LinkedIn didn't reveal a hometown, just that she was located in the U.S.

Frustrated, Gina sent her a follow request on Instagram using a fake account of her own.

"Shit!" She pounded the steering wheel, accidentally knocking into the horn as she did. "Who the hell are you?"

Alone in the privacy of her vehicle, she didn't bother to hide her Cajun accent, letting her Rs roll freely, the way God intended.

The sparse social media presence was a definite red flag. When Gina had changed her name to move to Saratoga, she'd taken the time to create believable social media accounts, covering her tracks to prevent people from learning her real identity. But even then, she could only do so much with the new profiles, since they didn't extend too far into her past. She'd just tried to post a lot on them to keep people from scrolling deeply into her history.

Maybe she would confront Jordyn about her flimsy social media at their next book club. She would be sure to bring up the topic in front of everyone. See how Jordyn responded to the inquiry when her feet were held to the fire.

Until then, Gina would review the photos of anyone and everyone who worked at tabloid media in both New York and Louisiana, Gina's home state, to see if Jordyn matched the image of someone else. Publicly available facial recognition software had advanced significantly recently, so there was a chance Gina could locate the woman even if she'd dyed her hair and grown it out, the way Gina had done. Although if Jordyn had gone as far as Gina had with the plastic surgery on her nose, facial recognition software might not help.

Gina's plan was so close to coming to fruition after a year of hard work. She couldn't afford for anyone to mess it up at the last moment.

Tugging the sunshade back out of the windshield, she started her car. Her hands were unsteady as she pushed the ignition button.

She had to pick up Mario, her Bernese mountain dog, from doggie daycare. Seeing her favorite being in the whole world would help comfort her a little bit. Then, later this afternoon she had a date.

That would help soothe the frayed edges even more. Not because she cared about Luke Sideris. But because of the revenge her affair with him represented. Every time she met him in secret, a wounded part of her soul rejoiced.

Every time she kissed him, touched him, drove him to the edge of sexual fulfillment and beyond, she thought about all the ways his wife had ruined her life. And she hoped with all her heart that Sophie would come to feel a fraction of the pain she'd inflicted on Gina when she'd been someone else.

But that was for a day still to come. Her plan for justice had not been fully meted out yet, but she was close.

So close.

Because a quiet, personal revenge wouldn't be nearly enough to satisfy the gaping hole in Gina's psyche. Sophie had detonated a bomb in her life back when Gina had entrusted her to arbitrate a painful divorce. Sophie hadn't even pretended to care either. Soon, *The Clean Break* host would pay for that. Because Gina wouldn't quit until she'd masterminded a big, public, in-your-face revenge that would humiliate Sophie the same way she'd humiliated so many other people. People who'd put their lives in Sophie's greedy, selfish, backstabbing hands.

Hitting the gas, Gina tore out of the parking garage and out onto the street, reminding herself that nothing would stand in the way of the revenge she wanted. No matter who Jordyn Lawson was, the woman would be collateral damage if she interfered with the very public takedown Gina had in mind for her archnemesis, Sophie Durand.

C H A P T E R

5

Jordyn

Present

AFTER LEAVING THE Ascent, Jordyn walked toward Division Street to find the coffee shop Tara used to hit after her workout. She recalled the quirky place well even though Tara had never mentioned it by name. Tara had video-called twice from the location, and Jordyn remembered the vintage coin-operated horse out front, clearly visible through the glass storefront windows. An internet search had pointed her toward The Right Track, a thoroughbred-themed kitschy spot that had a strong local following because of the quality of their coffee beans roasted in-house.

Jordyn wasn't certain if Tara had favored it because her friends went there or because her friends *didn't* go there. But then, there was a lot about her foster sister that Jordyn still needed to learn. They'd bonded for two years as kids in a rough foster home, then hadn't seen each other for fifteen years. On Jordyn's part because she'd never been told Tara's adoptive family's name, and they'd taken her upstate, far from the Brooklyn foster situation they'd briefly shared. For Tara's part, the long separation was because her adoptive family ensured she had no contact with her former life. And then, somewhere in her teens, Tara had undergone a dissociative amnesia episode that had erased her memories of portions of her past.

But she'd undergone therapy as an adult—to process trauma over her birth parents' deaths, according to her—and had somehow unlocked the buried memories of foster care. And, of course, her close friendship with Jordyn. Tara had seemed genuinely elated to recall Jordyn, locating her at no small personal expense, all without telling her adoptive family.

Now, pushing open the door to the shop where jazz tunes played, Jordyn inhaled the rich notes of coffee, molasses, and something dark and heavenly. Even though drinking a cup would probably keep her awake half the night, she decided to order whatever had been freshly brewed.

Five minutes later, she took a seat at a table near the windows, positioned so she could see down the street to the stoplight that marked the intersection with Broadway. Saratoga Springs was a town of about twenty-eight thousand people, although in the summers during racing season, that number tripled. The rest of the year, like now, it had more of a small-town vibe. Seeing locals come and go wasn't difficult with the downtown area concentrated on Broadway and the few streets intersecting it. Jordyn had gotten acquainted with the lay of the land in the weeks before she'd attended the block party so she could hit the ground running once she'd inveigled her way into the book club.

She was rechecking her makeup to ensure the old holes from her facial piercings were hidden when her cell phone vibrated.

She took her first sip of The Right Track's signature house blend and flipped over the screen to see Ezra's number, then opted to answer so she could put an end to this once and for all.

She hit the button to connect them.

"Ezra, you have to stop contacting me," she said without preamble. "I'm going to block you after this conversation."

Silence stretched on the other end. She ground her teeth impatiently until she prodded him, "Are you there?"

"Yeah, I'm here. Just trying to reconcile the fact that I miss you with that super hostile greeting."

She took a deep breath, reminding herself that smoothing things over with him would be better than drawing an adversarial line in the sand. She hadn't appreciated that last text he'd sent her, the one she worried Destiny Griffin might have spotted over her shoulder back at the gym.

You could be in a lot of danger yourself if someone from that book club finds out who you are and what you're really doing there.

What if Ezra decided to interfere in Jordyn's investigation, telling himself it was for her own good? She'd never imagined her introverted financial analyst ex-boyfriend, who was happiest when surrounded by spreadsheets and data, would suddenly decide to turn overprotective.

"You lost the right to miss me when you told me to choose you or my foster sister." She slid the coffee sleeve up and down on the cup, keeping her voice low even though there was no one seated close to her. The din of the jazz tunes and whirr of the espresso machine helped her keep the conversation private. "The fact that you tried to manipulate me into doing what you wanted only proved how little you understand me. There's no backtracking to fix that, okay? We're done."

"All right then, I guess that's that," he huffed, not bothering to hide his affronted male pride. "Where do you want me to forward this certified mail that arrived for you?"

"I changed my address at the post office." Who would have sent her something certified? "I don't understand—"

"Nevertheless, the delivery lady asked me to sign for it, and I did. Where should I send it?"

Jordyn wanted to argue that he had no right to sign for her mail when she didn't live with him any longer but didn't want to alienate him further. "Would you mind taking a photo of the envelope first so I can figure out what it's about?"

She hated to share her new address even though it probably wouldn't take him long to unearth the details if he went searching for her online. If she'd learned one thing through her investigation into Tara's death, it was that you could discover a ton about people via internet searches. She'd taken that into account before her trip to Saratoga, hiring a data removal service to scrub some mentions of her past before building shiny new social media profiles. Despite her best efforts, her socials were lacking, but at least they were consistent with the story she'd spun about herself.

"It's from some slick Manhattan law firm. Want me to just open it for you?" he offered.

Her heart sank as she connected the dots about who the letter was from.

"That would be illegal, so no thank you." She didn't trust him enough for that. "Just snap a pic." She lowered her phone so she could see the screen when the image came over.

As she did so, a flash of school-bus yellow darted through her peripheral vision from out on the street. When she peered through the coffee shop window, she spotted the vehicle at the corner where it stopped to let a handful of teens out onto the sidewalk.

"What do you think?" Ezra's voice sounded again. "When I hold it up to the light, I can see the words 'cease and desist' in bold, but that's all I can make out."

She swore under her breath. Both at the content, and at her nosy former lover.

"Thanks, Ez. I'll text you a post office box number where you can send it to me, and then I'll be done taking your calls. Have a nice life."

Before she stabbed the disconnect button, she could hear him asking, "You think it's because Tara's family—"

Then the line went blissfully dead. She didn't need his anxieties wound up with her own, knotting her tension tighter. Because she recognized the name of the law firm representing the Hughes family. In particular, Tara's father, who was a retired CEO of a pharmaceutical company and remained a major power broker in the industry. What Randall Hughes wanted, Randall Hughes got.

It bugged Jordyn to no end that he didn't seem invested in finding out what had happened to his adopted daughter. But then, he had biological heirs by his first wife, so he hadn't seemed overly concerned about Tara, the nonbiological child that his second wife had wanted. True to the stereotype for the ex-model turned trophy wife, Lauren had preferred a brief stint at motherhood without wreaking havoc on her figure. Hence, Tara, the fourteen-year-old foster child who was so sweet-natured, she'd never held the lack of love in her adoptive family against them.

Jordyn, however, had been livid with both Randall and Lauren when she'd spoken to them over the phone after the hit-and-run accident. Randall had been more concerned with keeping his name out of the papers, and Lauren just wanted to "move on" by packing up her Saratoga mansion and relocating to their mountain home outside Jackson Hole. Neither of them had shown the least bit of interest in pressuring the police working the investigation.

Recognizing that Tara's parents had no interest in getting to the bottom of what happened to their daughter, Jordyn had briefly hired a private investigator herself at the beginning of summer. That had been the first time she'd heard from the Hughes' family law firm. They'd warned her to let the police handle the investigation and had threatened a cease-and-desist order if she didn't call off her PI. She hadn't fired the guy because of that threat; she'd already quickly realized that his methods weren't effective in obtaining new information from Tara's tight-lipped friends. They would only speak about Tara through their attorneys.

So she'd sacked the PI and figured she needed a workaround. Some other way to unearth information and maybe stir the pot. Like infiltrate the group herself, since none of them knew about Tara's foster sister. The PI hadn't told anyone whom he'd been working for, so the fact that the Hughes' family lawyer had known spoke volumes about how well connected they were. Too bad they hadn't put any of those resources toward figuring out who killed Tara.

And now they were siccing their lawyers on Jordyn again. Had they followed through on their cease-and-desist order threat about the PI, even though Jordyn had quit using his services two months ago? Or did Randall Hughes somehow know Jordyn was in town herself? That she'd even hired a new PI? Finishing her coffee, she was just about to leave when a sudden burst of cool air rushed into the shop, along with bright, girlish laughter.

She glanced up to see two teens just inside the doorway with their heads bent over the same phone, studying something on the screen before they broke out laughing at the same time. She tried not to stare as the pair—perfect visual foils for each other as the sunny blonde was dressed all in black and the girl with glossy dark waves wore pristine white sweats with white tennis shoes—moved toward the barista standing at the register.

One of the teens was Charlotte Durand, Sophie's older daughter, whom Jordyn recalled from the party. She doubted the girl would recognize Jordyn, since she hadn't been around when Sophie and Jordyn were introduced. So Jordyn tossed her empty drink cup and got in line behind the girls to order something else and maybe stretch out her time to eavesdrop. Worst case scenario, she would be bored to tears listening in on teen-girl gossip.

But maybe she'd learn something of interest about Sophie, Tara's friend and business partner. Or about Luke, Sophie's husband that Tara had never wanted to discuss.

"So if this works today, you realize we're going to try it at least once a week for the rest of the semester," the dark-haired girl said to Charlotte after she'd finished giving her order at the counter.

"Of course it's going to work," Charlotte returned, flipping her hair over one shoulder. Her voice shared the same quiet authority and certainty of herself as her mother's. She turned toward the barista then and ordered an unsweetened iced green tea before stepping to one side to wait for her drink beside her friend. "Mom might have spies at school, but if they see my car in the student parking lot, they'll assume I'm on campus."

"What can I get you?" The older woman behind the counter spoke loudly, making Jordyn realize it probably wasn't the first time she'd asked.

"Sorry. I'll have an, um, iced green tea." That didn't have much caffeine at least, and the drink would buy her time to keep listening. She kept her head down, hoping to stay off the girls' radar since she would undoubtedly be crossing paths with Sophie's daughter in the future. Jordyn would rather not be remembered.

After paying for the second drink, she grabbed a chair two tables away from where Charlotte and her friend were seated at a booth, both of them sharing one bench seat so they could look at one another's phones. Their backpacks took up the bench opposite them, while Jordyn sat behind them. It made their conversation a little trickier to hear, but at least the girls wouldn't be able to clock her interest.

For a couple of minutes, the two of them seemed content to comment on makeup trends, every now and then pausing their screen time to discuss the best places for contouring. Jordyn's interest in makeup had died a fast death after an intense Goth phase had her spending any money she scavenged on pale powder foundations and black lipstick. She shuddered at the memory of her attempts to hide her true herself behind a mask, but then her chaotic upbringing bore no resemblance to the charmed lives these girls led.

Jordyn purchased herself a post office box through an online app, then texted the address to Ezra while the girls rattled on about makeup tutorials. Then the dark-haired girl turned sideways on the bench seat to see her friend better.

"Be honest. You're not worried about skipping test prep?"

"God, no, I'm not worried," Charlotte answered. "Mr. Ritter doesn't even notice who shows, and if he did, my mother wouldn't speak to that rat-faced toad in a million years."

Jordyn hid a laugh behind cough. She hadn't expected the vivid visual image. The brunette turned to glance at her briefly before returning to the conversation.

"I know we won't get in trouble that way. But you aren't like, worried your test scores will be worse for skipping the classes?" The girl's voice sounded sincere. Anxious.

"Sareena, isn't your mother already pushing you to your personal breaking point on this shit?"

"You know she is." Something about the way the girl spoke, a tilt of her head or the emphasis of the words reminded

Jordyn of Fatima Chamoun, and she wondered if this was one of the woman's daughters. "I lost two points on an English essay last week and Mom lost her mind. She had a ninety-minute-meeting with Mrs. Volk about it. *Ninety minutes* about two points."

Tara had mentioned Fatima and Sophie were locked in a weird, reflected glory competition through their daughters' successes. If her guess was correct that Sareena was Fatima's daughter, it appeared the competition between the mothers didn't extend to their offspring. Sareena and Charlotte appeared close.

"Of course she did." Charlotte tipped her drink in Sareena's direction, pointing at her. "So you tell me if you think *more* stress in your life will help you in your pursuit of a perfect SAT score, or if maybe an hour of friend time mixed in your week will serve you better."

"As long as we're back for lacrosse practice." Sareena tilted her wrist and must have checked the time. "Brayden better be here soon."

"You worry too much," Charlotte added breezily. "It's bad for your skin."

Jordyn tuned out again, telling herself she was wasting her time eavesdropping. No need to learn the ins and outs of teens skipping classes to defy their parents. Nothing unusual there. She checked her phone to see if she had any messages from the attorney she'd consulted for help in learning why Tara's estate hadn't entered probate nearly a year after her death.

She'd read online about possible hold-ups if an estate anticipated a wrongful death claim, but Tara's family hadn't made any such legal assertion as of yet. For that matter, she had reason to believe that Tara had a will based on a conversation they had when Tara had visited her in Texas. Yet no will had been filed and a representative at the surrogate court had suggested the estate might be administered under intestacy.

That in itself had made Jordyn suspicious.

Had the police investigated who stood to benefit from Tara's death? She'd had generous trust fund payouts ever since she had turned twenty-five, not to mention her partial stake in *The Clean Break* podcast. But of course, the police didn't share their notes when an investigation was ongoing, even though the case grew colder by the day. So Jordyn would turn to other sources for help figuring out what happened. While she infiltrated the book group to find out which one of them might want Tara dead, she had hired a probate attorney to look into what was happening with Tara's estate. And even though the first PI she'd hired hadn't worked out since he'd been unable to finesse any new independent witness interviews, she had hired a new one to assist her with a case review. She understood that she couldn't see the police files, but there were a few clues that had been made public: a paint chip and a call for information for anyone driving a banged-up dark-colored SUV.

Plus there'd been an anonymous noise complaint to the cops from the neighborhood where the accident had happened, and it had been phoned in an hour before the hit-and-run. The police had asked that person to come forward after Tara's death, but Jordyn didn't know if anyone had done so.

So Jordyn had her work cut out for her. What she refused to do, though, was cease and desist.

Opening a chat window for the probate law office where she'd already left a voicemail, Jordyn took another sip of the horrible iced green tea, then requested a call back. As she tapped in the message, the nearby conversation snagged her attention again.

"—and Mom has been operating at Defcon 2 ever since Tara died," Charlotte was telling her friend with more animation than she'd shown earlier. "It's like she expects some psychotic to mow me and Amelia down every time we step out of the house. It's insane."

"While, yes, that sucks," Sareena acknowledged, her attention still fixed on her phone as she scrolled through an endless page of dresses. "Don't you think it's legit creepy the cops never arrested anyone?"

Charlotte made a huffing sound as if to protest, and Sareena quit her scroll to grab her friend's wrist before continuing.

"Seriously, listen to me. If I was your mom, I wouldn't want you to get run over by some maniac targeting hot young women on our block."

"Yeah, no one is targeting hot girls in the neighborhood. Someone just hated my mom's best friend." Charlotte shrugged in a gesture that looked forced to Jordyn's eye. Like she wasn't as tough as she sounded, and beneath the teenage bravado she worried about what happened to Tara, too.

But Sareena didn't catch the emotion in Charlotte's voice because her attention was fixed on a white Land Rover rolling to a stop outside the coffee shop, a rap tune thumping bass so hard it made the store windows vibrate.

"Could Brayden look like more of a tool?" she asked Charlotte as she jumped to her feet and collected her backpack and empty cup. She was all smiles now, clearly a little enamored with Brayden—tool or not. "Come on."

Sighing, Charlotte followed her friend more slowly, her expression still troubled as she hitched her leather backpack onto one shoulder, her sweater drooping off the other.

Jordyn cursed Brayden's timing, wishing the girls' conversation hadn't been cut short. Yet one good morsel of news had come out of it. After all the news articles and interviews she'd read speculating Tara's death could have been a genuine accident caused by a stranger to her, Jordyn was glad to know that someone else in Tara's sphere shared her suspicion. That her foster sister's death wasn't an accident at all. It had been a murder committed by someone who knew her well.

CHAPTER

6

Tara

One Year Ago

NEEDING A FRIEND-TALK to bolster her spirits after a rough week of podcast drama, Tara stood on Fatima's front porch amid the potted mums and pumpkins and rang the bell. She had a bottle of cabernet tucked under one arm, her surefire ticket to an invitation inside.

A few moments later, after continuous barking from her two shih tzus, Poppy and Milo, Fatima herself flung open the door. Dressed in a belted silk gown that could have been a night robe or a swimsuit coverup or a designer original, Fatima lived in dramatic, colorful clothing. Her high-heeled green mules were probably her version of house slippers.

Tara tried not to feel underdressed in her athleisure separates that seemed sufficient whether she was going to the gym or the market. Despite her adoptive mother's admonishments to dress more fashionably, Tara still gravitated toward simple silhouettes. For Tara, it was more fun to make *other* people stand out with fashion. Not herself.

Halloween being a notable exception.

"Is it wine o'clock yet?" Tara held up the bottle.

"Darling, you can count on it at my house." Fatima opened the door wide while Poppy and Milo raced excited doggie circles around Tara's feet. "I just finished teaching my afternoon class online, and the girls won't be home for two more hours. Leyla has violin lessons and Sareena is at lacrosse practice."

Tara wasn't surprised. Fatima ran her kids as hard as Sophie did hers, insisting on extra tutoring, endless extracurricular activities, and volunteer work, all in a bid to get them into the best college programs. Tara couldn't help but empathize with the teens, since her adoptive mother had been every bit as demanding for Tara to distinguish herself at school. That hadn't been easy for her since—even before she'd gone into foster care—Tara had never attended the kind of rigorous academic programs that Lauren Hughes enrolled her in. She'd worked her butt off to earn her adoptive mother's approval, a perpetually elusive goal.

Minutes later, Fatima had the bottle open, and they were just settling into the barstools at her kitchen counter when the doorbell rang again.

"That'll be Mei or Sophie," Fatima guessed after a glance at her smart watch. "They both wrap up their work days around this time."

Tara's heart sank at the possibility that Sophie could be here now, when venting about Sophie had been a large part of her mission. Sophie was her friend, yes. But the greatest hits podcast was driving a wedge between them. Not to mention the drama with Luke.

But then Mei Kita entered the kitchen, a blue bottle of Riesling in her hand. Pausing, she held it up to show it off. "Great minds?"

Relieved that it was Mei, Tara enveloped her in a hug. Was it her imagination, or was it only half-heartedly returned? Mei was a hard-working, independent CPA who had been in their book club for years. She'd had a long struggle with infertility and the fact that she was here with wine in hand surely meant this month had been another heartbreaker. But Mei was also intensely private about her journey, so Tara only reached for the battery-operated opener to uncork the white wine that was Mei's preferred pour.

"Well now it's practically a party." Fatima picked up her television remote and tapped a button to connect a music playlist, upping the happy hour vibe. She did a shimmy-shake in her floral silk robe as she moved back to the bar and picked up her glass of red. "What shall we make a toast to now that we're together?"

Tara met Mei's gaze across the tops of their glasses, suspecting Mei hadn't come to celebrate but to commiserate. Really, it was the same reason that had brought her here, even if the underlying cause was different.

"To friendship," Tara offered, lifting her glass a little higher.

"I like it!" Fatima agreed, clinking both their glasses with hers.

Mei's small smile was fleeting before she took a sip. "I'm mostly here to drown my sorrows for an hour before I start dinner, so I'm just glad to hear the latest gossip. Since I missed last month's book club at Kaitlin's house maybe you can tell me how life is among the Real Housewives of Saratoga?"

"Ha." Tara shook her head, not feeling remotely like a suburban diva. "I can't answer since I've never been a camera-ready housewife."

"Now, now," Fatima admonished, striking a pose complete with a pout. "We are as glamorous and as accomplished as ever. Although we aren't doing a book this month for book club, so we won't win any prizes for being culturally aware."

"Pretty sure that's never been a concern for the TV housewives," Tara offered, hoping they wouldn't devote much time to discussing the previous month's meeting.

Her memories of the gathering weren't exactly happy. Kaitlin was still nursing her grudge against Tara and Sophie for having her role cut out of *The Clean Break*. She'd threatened a lawsuit twice in the past few months and their friendship had gotten downright uncomfortable. Kaitlin had barely spoken a word to Tara all that evening.

"So we're meeting at Sophie's house on Halloween?" Mei asked, spinning a crystal charm around the base of her stemware. Hers was blue, Tara's was pink, and Fatima's was—as always—a red dragon.

"Correct. Although Sophie warned us we might get underway a little later than usual as she's recording some extra promotions that day for *The Clean Break*," Fatima observed dryly before turning to Tara. "No offense, of course Tara. I know she's the one who makes those kinds of decisions."

Tara ground her teeth together, frustrated that everyone believed Sophie ran the show and that Tara was some kind of underling. Well, everyone except for Kaitlin, who seemed as if she would be quite happy to sue both Tara and Sophie equally.

Even Luke treated Tara as some sort of hapless show intern that he could manipulate, rather than Sophie's colleague. Her blood boiled every time she recalled the way he'd taken advantage of her shock that day in the pool house. She needed to have it out with him at some point. But how could she find a time to speak to her partner's husband alone without it seeming super awkward?

"Well I, for one, will be glad not to have to suffer through some tedious historical tome that I fall asleep trying to finish." Mei smiled as if to soothe the barb of her different opinion. "No offense."

"Oh, touché, Mei." Fatima mimed silent applause at the comeback. "Someone's come to happy hour with an edge."

"You're not kidding," Mei muttered. "Our next toast ought to be to sharp edges."

Fatima and Tara exchanged glances.

"That sounds like more than the usual wine-o'clock grievance—" Fatima began.

"I'm pretty sure Nikolai is cheating on me."

Mei took a long drink of her wine, finishing the glass, while Tara and Fatima gaped. Nikolai was an investment banker whose work was his life's passion, frequently travelling out of the country to visit businesses that might be worthy of investment. Tara had never heard Mei utter a word about that being a hardship for her. She'd always seemed happily independent while remaining steadfastly devoted to her husband.

The only mentions Mei had made of him seemed positive. He'd been committed to her IVF efforts, rearranging his travel schedule to be with her for appointments.

"What makes you think so?" Fatima lifted the Riesling bottle to refill their friend's glass with a generous serving.

"A colleague saw Nik at the bar in the Adelphi Hotel last week during a time he told me he had meetings in Manhattan."

Tara frowned. "Is your colleague sure it was him? Hanging out at a local landmark doesn't sound like the act of a man with something to hide. He must have known people would see him."

Shrugging, Mei withdrew her phone and tapped through a few screens before sliding the device across the white marble counter toward them.

"My friend snapped a photo after she texted me. That's definitely Nik walking out of the hotel with another woman."

Fatima tipped the phone toward her to see the image from a better angle while Tara craned her neck to view it.

"It looks a little like you, Tara, from the back," Fatima observed, lifting her attention from the screen to study Tara with an intent gaze. "Same color hair."

"I thought the same thing," Mei seconded in a hard voice. "Right down to the dress."

"Of course it's not me." Alarmed, Tara scrambled to take the device from her friend. "Let me see."

Scanning the image that Fatima had enlarged, Tara took in the details for herself. Even from the back, Nikolai's likeness was hard to deny since he was six-foot-four and built like a professional athlete. His palm rested possessively on a woman's hip, a signet ring of some kind visible on his right hand.

As for the woman, the auburn updo definitely resembled Tara's on a very good hair day. And the forest green dress was a simply cut ribbed knit that skimmed the woman's subtle curves. Tara had the same one—or at least something very similar—in her closet at home. Though she'd never appeared so svelte in it.

Didn't they see that?

"This isn't me," she protested quietly, as much to herself as to her friends.

Or would that be her *former* friends? Even she knew how bad the optics were.

"Oh please." Mei snatched back her phone and slipped it into the taupe-colored statement bag that announced her wealth and status despite her dark jeans and T-shirt that were her everyday staples. "There's a photo of you on *The Clean Break* website wearing that exact dress."

Tara's throat went dry, envisioning the picture from a promotional shoot for the fall show line-up. She looked the other woman in the eye. "Mei, I swear to you, that is not me in your friend's photo."

Mei's mouth flattened into a disapproving line, but her gaze searched Tara's. Looking for the truth?

Fatima cleared her throat before adding, "Forest green is a popular choice for redheads. And it's not like Tara buys all designer originals. Someone else could have that same dress."

When Mei didn't reply right away, Tara jumped in again. "Plus photos can be altered so easily now with AI—"

"Are you suggesting my colleague took this photo and then altered it before sending it to me?" Mei slid off her barstool, shouldering her bag. "Look, Fatima, I've got to go. We'll catch up some other time, all right?"

"Mei, let's talk about this," Tara protested as Mei started toward the foyer. "Have you asked Nikolai? He can tell you I wasn't with him—"

Mei spun around fast to face her. "No, Tara, I haven't." She blinked rapidly, the only sign that she might be rattled since she spoke with the same even tone as always. Of all the book club members, Mei always seemed the most grounded. The least likely to get dragged into drama. But right now, the tension practically vibrated off her. "And I don't plan to talk to him about it either, so you're not going to get your alibi that way. Whatever Nik is up to, I *will* have his help while I try to get pregnant, so I'll find another way to deal with . . . whatever he's doing on the side."

Without another word, she walked out of the house, the door closing softly behind her. Tara was mortified. She had no desire to sit around and bemoan her rough week with Sophie and *The Clean Break* drama now when she had a new crisis to handle. Starting with searching her closet for that green dress.

Because the strange coincidence of that photo gave her the creepy feeling that someone had purposely impersonated her. Which was probably a farfetched idea . . . right?

Her counselor had warned her that the old case of dissociative amnesia could cause problems forming new memories. But there was no way in hell Tara had been with Nikolai that day and did not recall it. Not just because she trusted her own memory more than that, but also because she was not the sort of woman to stick a knife in a friend's back by making a play for her husband.

A message she needed to get across to Luke Sideris as much as Mei. Why did it seem like her whole friend group was imploding?

She needed to get to the bottom of whatever was going on. Maybe, just maybe, she'd even confront Mei's standoffish spouse herself. Because she wasn't going to sit back and quietly accept another woman's accusations of cheating with her husband and risk losing a whole set of friends.

The book club circle might have the occasional drama, but what friend group didn't? The members were her neighbors and confidantes. It was one of the reasons she'd put off a difficult talk with Sophie for so long about their weird power dynamic at work. She hated to upset their friendship.

But enough was enough. Tara needed to start advocating for herself. With Sophie, yes. With Luke. Also with whoever could help her clear up this misunderstanding about Mei's husband. She needed to do something soon before Jordyn, her recently rediscovered secret sister who lived eighteen hundred miles away, was the only person left standing in her corner.

CHAPTER

7

Jordyn

Present

AFTER A LONG day, Jordyn pulled into the driveway of the carriage house she'd rented and saw a man standing on the front step. He held a covered plate in one hand and a bottle of wine in the other. He turned to look at her as she parked on the gravel outside the white-washed brick building, and she recognized him from Kaitlin's block party.

Brad Reynolds.

She might not have recalled his name if she hadn't written copious notes about every single interaction she'd had with members of Tara's book club since she'd arrived in town. While she hadn't had enough time to speak to him at the block party, she recalled him saying that he lived two doors down from her.

"Looking for me?" she called over the hood of the silver coupe she'd bought the same week she'd moved into the carriage house. She hadn't wanted out of state license plates to raise questions about her time in Texas. Instead of transferring the registration to her old car—a well-used compact that would have stood out like a sore thumb—she'd traded it in for something a little newer and scored New York plates in the bargain.

"Hello, neighbor. I come bearing gifts." The man lifted his hands to show his offerings. He wore a navy-blue sweater with honest-to-goodness leather patches on the elbows and tan corduroys. Between the outfit and the perfectly coiffed light brown hair, he looked like an elite New Englander on a country weekend outing. "We met at Kaitlin's house. I'm Brad Reynolds from—"

"The white Federalist house." Jordyn pointed toward the house just visible through a boxwood hedge on the far side of the Solomon's neighbors. "I remember meeting you. I happen to love the kinds of gifts that come with a cork."

Locking her vehicle, Jordyn left her box of files about the hit and run accident on the floor of the backseat, safely out of view.

"Excellent. I didn't know your wine preferences, so I went with a white they recommended at Putnam Market." Brad stared dubiously at the label. "I'm not a connoisseur, so I have to trust others. The cookies, however, I stand behind one hundred percent. No one has ever not liked my salted caramel chocolate chips."

"Brad, you're already my favorite neighbor." Jordyn took the plate before gesturing to two loungers near a firepit. "Do you have time to sit for a minute and join me in a glass while I sample these?"

At his nod, Jordyn hurried into the carriage house to search for a corkscrew and glasses, things that came provided in the furnished rental. Whoever had done the remodel had taken care to preserve the character of the structure with reclaimed wood flooring and white shiplap walls. Pockmarked wood beams ran the length of the living area, and painted black sliding doors leading outside maintained the feel of a converted barn. Old horseshoes hung over every arch and doorway. Her art supplies had been scattered haphazardly since she'd only worked on the most pressing client projects to finance her mission in Saratoga. A small safe held more of her notes on Tara's case, the one thing she'd taken care to secure at all times.

A few minutes later, after another trip inside to retrieve a log to toss into the firepit for an atmospheric flame, Jordyn claimed one of the outdoor Adirondack chairs and Brad took the other.

She helped herself to a cookie from the china plate that looked like an heirloom and then passed it to him. For a few minutes they exchanged the usual pleasantries. He was divorced from an actor on a popular daytime soap opera who spent his weeks filming in New York City but came to Saratoga on the weekends as part of their custody arrangement. They had two small children, a boy and a girl, whom Brad didn't get to see enough. Brad was working on a literary novel.

For her part, Jordyn dodged more questions than she answered but shared the rough outline of her cover story. That she'd ended a relationship (thanks to Ezra, that part was true enough) and needed a change, so she'd left an apartment in the Bushwick neighborhood of Brooklyn to check out upstate. The foster home she and Tara had shared had been two neighborhoods over from Bushwick, so Jordyn had a working knowledge of the area if anyone quizzed her. Brad did not.

"It's easy for me to move since I can do my graphic design jobs remotely." Another true point, though she tacked on a fictional detail as she reached for the pinot grigio to top off Brad's drink. "I did some design work as a subcontractor for the racetrack a couple of years ago and thought the photos of Saratoga looked beautiful. I figured now was as good a time as any to check it out for myself."

"Thoughts now that you're here in person? Having experienced your first block party?" Brad asked, lifting an eyebrow as he gave her a sideways glance. "Still beautiful?"

She sensed a man ready to dish some gossip, but she sure wasn't giving away *her* impressions as a means to get him to spill his own. She needed to play this diplomatically.

"Honestly, there wasn't anything about the block party that wasn't gorgeous. What you're all calling homes are more like mansions in my mind, so it was fun getting a peek behind the facades."

Brad tilted his wine glass toward her, his hazel eyes narrowing. "Right. Easier to see inside the houses than the people."

"Do tell," she goaded him with a smile. "Are you suggesting the locals might not be as lovely behind closed doors?"

"I said no such thing," he protested, lifting his feet to rest on the stones surrounding the firepit. "But talk to me a month from now after your first book club and then tell me what you think about Saratoga's most glamorous residents."

"Seriously, Brad? I thought we were friends after you brought the salted caramel chocolate chips. You can't leave me hanging now." Shifting in her seat, she tucked one foot under her thigh so she could turn to see him better. "Tell me more about book club. What are they like?"

"Cliquey." He tipped his head back against the wooden slats of the Adirondack chair and seemed to admire the orange and marigold colors of the sky as the sun set. "And that's not giving away any big secret. Sophie would say we're exclusive, but isn't that just another way of saying the same thing?"

"I'm surprised I got in," she admitted, even though she'd done her level best to connect with Kaitlin as soon as she walked onto the other woman's property.

"They like artsy types," he said candidly, gesturing with the wineglass again as he seemed to indicate her outfit. Something in the looseness of his gestures suggested he was feeling the wine. "The vintage clothes and quirky style would appeal to them. One of our former members was a Fashion Institute grad. Your style reminds me of hers. A little, anyway."

Jordyn tried not to show her interest even though her whole body went on high alert, tension making her muscles go taut.

"You mean Tara?" She lowered her voice. "Her name came up the other day, but I noticed Destiny shut down discussion of her in a hurry."

"She would." There was an edge to his tone, but he seemed to catch himself then and softened the remark with a smile. "She knows that talking about Tara upsets Sophie, so she tends to stifle all discussion of her. But I like remembering Tara. She brought a lot of life to our group, and I, for one, really miss her."

A few bats chased through the yard as the twilight fell, and Jordyn tried to choose her words carefully. She didn't want to push too hard and end the conversation prematurely.

Or raise suspicion.

"You don't think the others miss her much?" Reaching for the wine bottle, she tipped the last of it into the glass that he had emptied once more.

"Maybe they do, I don't know." He shrugged apologetically. "Don't mind me as I drift into a melancholy wine-haze. I'm sure everyone loved Tara, but since she worked on *The Clean Break* with Sophie, she was bound to ruffle feathers too."

Meaning Sophie was the great feather-ruffler, and Tara was secondarily to blame. Jordyn appreciated his take.

"But I assumed everyone enjoyed the podcast. Sophie's sort of a local celebrity, isn't she?"

"Oh, that's a whole other bottle of wine right there." He shook his head as if to dismiss the question. "I'm not touching that one tonight, but I'm not the only person who has been hurt by *The Clean Break*."

"How so?" She knew from Tara that Sophie had shut Kaitlin out of a creative credit on the show when they'd first developed it. As a family therapist, Kaitlin had offered ideas on how to interview guests in a sensitive way, so she'd been a little involved in the early days of hammering out the production's style and approach.

And angry to be excluded later on.

But if the podcast had hurt anyone else in the group, Jordyn was in the dark.

"My ex-husband and I were two of the earliest guests on the show," he admitted, swirling the newly poured wine around his glass a little too aggressively so that a bit splashed out onto his hand. He hardly seemed to notice. "It was foolish of me to assume maybe Sophie would take our friendship into account when she helped Carlo and me with our split. I signed off on the arbitration option, naively thinking Sophie would at least be fair about it. But now, Carlo has the day-to-day care of the kids while *I'm* the weekend dad."

Could that be a motive to kill Tara? Revenge for stripping Brad of the larger share of parental rights? Tara was cocreator of *The Clean Break*, after all. Brad could blame her as much or more than Sophie, no matter what he said about missing her.

She made a mental note to dive deeper into the old podcasts and review the content more closely. Had she missed anyone else who might have an axe to grind because of *The*

Clean Break? She had her reasons for believing Tara's killer was a book club member, thanks to an exchange with her foster sister the night before she died. But what if there was an outsider holding a grudge about an unpopular decision made on the podcast?

That sounded like motive to her.

"I'm really sorry that happened to you." She couldn't imagine the pain of missing your kids. Though she did understand the pain of losing parents.

Her mom and dad might have been addicts, but she'd loved them. Or maybe she'd loved the consistency of having a single home. By contrast, the uncertainty of the foster world had rattled her, even when she'd landed in a good placement. She'd never known how long it would last.

"You know, Tara said the same thing to me afterward." He leaned forward in his chair as if ready to stand. "But she also claimed to have no power to rein Sophie in once she made her mind up, so . . . who knows?"

Jordyn would have liked to have continued their conversation, but Brad drank the last of his wine and placed his glass on the edge of the firepit before getting to his feet.

"But I should get going now. I made a New Year's resolution not to dwell on things I can't control, and since it's only October, I still have two months to try and actually accomplish that."

Jordyn rose to say good night. "Well now that I know about the resolution, I will ask less provocative questions the next time you join me for wine at sunset."

The lights had come on in the sprawling Victorian mansion belonging to the family who'd rented her the carriage house. The security light over the driveway illuminated Brad as he backed up a few steps, his hands in the pockets of his corduroys.

"Don't you dare. Although next time, maybe it will be my turn to do the question-asking."

Did he suspect her of not being the person she claimed? Her personal radar beeped mildly, but she dismissed the comment as something he'd said to reciprocate interest.

"I'm far too boring," she insisted. "You'll be asleep two minutes into my life story."

He laughed quietly before turning. "Night, neighbor."

Jordyn waited until he was out of sight before returning to her vehicle. Unlocking it, she pulled out the box of files related to Tara's death and then carried it inside. She had a lot of work to do, starting with reviewing a list of *The Clean Break* episodes.

Who else had Sophie and Tara ticked off with that show? The box felt heavier with each step toward her front door.

CHAPTER

8

Gina

Present

OPENING THE FINANCIAL manager app on her phone, Gina tried to put her time to good use while she staked out the downtown offices of Luke Sideris's tech consulting company. She'd left the Mercedes in a nearby garage and switched over to the unmemorable—and frankly, ugly—SUV crossover that Luke had bought her for driving to their trysts. While she appreciated his commitment to secrecy, she had to laugh at herself for accepting the crappy offering from her married lover. Some other woman in her position, taken to the cleaners by an ex-husband, might have sought out a boyfriend who could support her in the style she'd grown accustomed to, back when she'd been a professional athlete's wife.

But Gina was far more interested in revenge than money at this stage of her life.

So, to ensure Luke wasn't hiding any surprises up his cheating sleeve—like a secondary mistress that would only interfere with Gina's plans—she'd taken to staking out his office this week. For one thing, he'd told her he was going out of town for business for a few days, yet the data from the handy GPS tracker she'd put on his car told her he was very much still in town, and that raised red flags for her. As did the used syringes she'd found in his glovebox the last time they'd gone away for a weekend together.

She'd never seen him use drugs before. So where had those needles come from?

As a woman who'd already been cheated on, she wasn't getting fooled by a man ever again.

Hence the stakeout. She knew he enjoyed office hook-ups. Maybe someone was going to meet him here. Gina had been on high alert for trouble on every front ever since she'd met Jordyn Lawson. Gina's antennae were up and constantly twitching, searching for any threat to her plans for revenge. The October book club meeting was just around the corner, and she'd slated that date for the big reveal of her affair with Luke. Along with a few other surprises to ensure her nemesis's world was as devastated as Gina's had been back when she'd been living another life.

Thankfully, the heavily tinted windows on the hideous little SUV allowed her to remain anonymous while she watched who came and went from his office this week. The baseball cap she wore helped.

For now, however, no one was going out of the office entrance to the three-story brick building, built to blend with the more historic structures surrounding it. Luke's suite had a dedicated private entrance on the less-travelled side street, and it was this one that interested her more. Luke had given her the key to that door early on in their relationship, and she suspected it wasn't the first time he'd arranged for women to meet him there.

While she waited, she scrolled through her account information on her financial aggregator app. Her learning curve about money had been steep after her divorce. Prior to that, she'd been excellent at spending it. She'd had a lot to learn about saving it. About setting aside enough to finance her plans to make Sophie pay. The plastic surgery hadn't come cheap. Not to mention the wardrobe she needed to continually update in order to blend in to Sophie Durand's world.

Today, Gina's account balance was stabilized. But not large enough to finance the digital forensics tech she'd hoped to hire to uncover the story behind Jordyn Lawson's arrival in Saratoga. Gina's digging online only revealed a brief mention of Jordyn's existence during her college years. Gina had learned Jordyn had been a student at Brooklyn College but couldn't find a record of a graduation or a home address. Gina knew it wasn't cheap to maintain such a low profile online, but she herself had managed it even while married to a professional athlete. Gina's wealthy father had always been vigilant about his family's digital privacy for safety purposes, which she'd despised as a teen but had grown to appreciate later in life, recognizing how competitive it could be for young women. All of which went on to help her now. Because if there had been more photos of her online while married to her ex, she might not have been able to pull off her revenge plot now. But there weren't many people who were as careful with their socials. Jordyn Lawson must be hiding *something.*

A sound outside the car made her look up in time to see the side entrance to Luke's office bang open in the fall breeze. Out stepped her lover himself, his attention fixed on his phone as he shut the door behind him.

Damn it.

She scrunched down in her seat and pulled the baseball cap lower on her head. The liar. What was he doing on the street right now, at half past two in the afternoon in the middle of a work week when he'd said he was out of town? Her brain scrambled to concoct an excuse to feed him if he spotted her.

Luckily, he headed up the street toward Broadway instead of turning toward her, making it easier for her to track his progress until he rounded a corner.

"What are you up to?" Drumming her nails against the steering wheel, Gina only waited a few seconds before deciding to follow him.

Hopping out of the car, she slid a pair of big sunglasses onto her face and hoped she wouldn't see anyone she knew. By the time she rushed toward the intersection, Luke was already in the crosswalk at the next block up near the post office. How would she catch up without making it obvious she was following him?

Gina dodged a few shoppers sipping from paper coffee cups as they maneuvered strollers in front of a store window full of kids' books. She kept her eye on Luke's retreating figure as he walked out of view up Church Street. Speed-walking into another gear, she was almost to the corner when a familiar voice called her.

"Gina! Over here!"

Her gut sank at getting waylaid in the middle of the chase. She tried to mask her disappointment as she slowed her step and turned to see Kaitlin Teal hurrying toward her, a yoga mat under one arm. Just before Kaitlyn reached her, Gina tapped the earbud in her right ear as if shutting down whatever she'd been listening to.

"I thought that was you, but you were walking so fast I had to speed up to see for sure." Kaitlin threw one arm around her for a side hug, the ends of her cashmere wrap swatting

Gina in the face and making it feel like a hug from a cat. "Where are you off to in such a rush?"

Shadowing the man I'm cheating with to make sure he's not cheating wasn't a good answer in any world, so Gina shook her head and gave a wry laugh.

"I'm in this fitness club online, and if I don't get ten thousand more steps in the next seventy-five minutes, I lose my gold badge streak." She made a show of tapping her watch screen a couple of times before putting her hand in the pocket of her cropped hoodie. "But real-life friends are more important than bragging rights with a bunch of women I don't even know."

"Well I can walk with you," Kaitlin offered, nodding toward the street ahead of them. "Want to loop around Woodlawn and back down? I'm going to The Ascent but my class doesn't start for twenty more minutes."

"Sounds good." Gina pretended to restart the fitness app she did not have on her watch and hoped there was still a chance she'd catch sight of wherever Luke had gone. "So are you off today? I thought you usually see clients in the afternoons."

As Kaitlin and Gina rounded the corner, Gina scanned the buildings up ahead. It was quieter here, with only a handful of other people walking, none of them Luke.

"I try to give myself late lunch breaks on the days when Sophie drops new episodes of *The Clean Break* so I can listen." Kaitlyn tilted her phone screen toward Gina, showing off the logo of a red heart broken in half and a push broom leaning against one side of it. "Have you been following the split between the former boy band member and his influencer girlfriend?"

Her stomach lurched, and Gina had to steel her body against the physical effects of just seeing the stupid logo of the show that had cost her everything—dignity included. The subject of the podcast didn't come up all that often at book club, thank goodness, which Gina had found a little surprising at first. Over time, she'd come to realize that lack of discussion was in deference to Tara Hughes's involvement in the show. Sophie's friends all danced around mentions of Tara, so it seemed like that habit extended to *The Clean Break*, Sophie and Tara's joint venture.

"I don't really tune in much. I realize Sophie provides a kind of public service for a lot of the couples who appear on her show, but personally I find it tough to listen to other people's heartache for entertainment." She realized belatedly that her words might sound judgy about Kaitlin's enjoyment of the show. "I mean, I totally see the appeal—"

"Oh my God, don't apologize for speaking your truth." Kaitlin shoved her phone back in her pocket before eyeing Gina with renewed interest. "And cheers to you for honoring your boundaries. I'm sure all that talk about break-ups could be very triggering if you've gone through a rough one yourself."

Gina mustered up a vampish smile, leaning into the Gina Vallot character she'd created for herself. "Lucky for me, my mama taught me to be the one who does the walking away."

How she wished that were true.

The truth was that her divorce had gutted her even before the harrowing final blow of the appearance on *The Clean Break*. Finding out that her husband couldn't turn down any opportunity to cheat on her hadn't just been humbling. It had been humiliating. Infuriating. And it had made her question every single one of her life choices. As if it had somehow been her fault, when of course it wasn't. She'd been her husband's loyal supporter ever since he was a college football star. She'd invested in their relationship and told herself that her low public profile would benefit him since their private life together would never detract from his feats on the field. And she'd been rewarded by having all the foundations of her world crumble beneath her feet.

No, they didn't just crumble. They *disintegrated.* She didn't even have the rubble of her old life to stand on since her family had never liked her choice of husband. They didn't need to say "I told you so" when the words hung like a chill in their Garden District mansion.

As they drew even with the parking garage behind the post office, a familiar-looking ugly SUV came into view as it exited onto the street. The vehicle wasn't Gina's, of course, but snagged her attention because of the similarity to the one Luke had purchased for her to help hide their trysts.

The driver of the other SUV was only visible for a split second. But it was long enough for her to get a good look at him.

Luke Sideris sat behind the wheel.

What the hell?

He was obviously the owner of a second incognito vehicle as well. One that didn't have her helpful GPS tracker attached, so she'd have no idea where her treacherous lover was headed next. Out of town with another woman? The one who used the needles she'd found in his other car?

She had no answers. But one thing became perfectly clear to her then. If Luke didn't want her to know where he was going, that meant her shady lover could only be up to no good.

CHAPTER

9

Tara

One Year Ago

"LET'S FACE IT, ladies. We all know when the man in our lives has got to go." Sophie read the script for the promotional spot with pitch-perfect intonation. "Isn't it better to just make a clean break?"

Tara listened to her partner work her audio magic for a few more minutes before removing her headset, ready to excuse herself from the sound booth. She wasn't technically needed today for the promotional recordings since Sophie was the voice of the program, but Tara was working harder lately to make her presence felt around the business. Especially since Sophie thought nothing of going off script to say whatever she pleased once she got into the sound studio.

But Tara didn't think that would be the case today for the promo spots. Sophie respected that Tara had a strong marketing background, so she tended to follow through on projects like this that could help extend their reach on a variety of audio platforms.

"I've got a few calls to make," Tara said softly to Wynn, the sound technician. She pantomimed the act since Wynn had his headphones on.

He simply nodded, barely lifting his eyes from the laptop where he monitored the sound quality and tracked any ambient noise as Sophie continued to speak on the opposite side of soundproof glass.

Freed from work without Sophie even noticing she was gone, Tara slipped down the stairs and out the side door of the two-story garage that doubled as their studio. This was about the same time of day that Luke usually left the house to play tennis, and she hoped to run into him so she could clear the air.

Her life felt like it was running off the rails the last couple of weeks. First, there'd been Sophie's maneuvering to have the larger say in their business, dismissing Tara's concerns about taking *The Clean Break* in directions that made her uncomfortable. Then, there'd been the unwelcome kiss from Luke, and the fear that someone had impersonated her to make Mei think Tara was involved with Nikolai. That last one had gone from being frustrating to being downright creepy.

She'd checked her closet when she got home after that tense confrontation with Mei. And that green dress had still been in a wrapper from the dry cleaner's, exactly where she'd remembered hanging it the last time she'd been in her dressing room. No one had stolen the garment.

So for right now, the only problem she could figure out how to fix was the matter of Luke. His car remained in the driveway, so she hadn't missed him, but she didn't see him outside yet. Following the path of pavers from the studio toward the pool house, her phone vibrated in her pocket. She withdrew it to read a text from Luke.

Looking for me?

Pausing, she glanced around the property, wondering if he could be nearby. The phone buzzed again.

Go through the back gate toward the garden.

Tara returned the device to the pocket of her sweater and headed toward the wrought iron fence behind the massive pool. The heavy decorative bars of the fence were woven through with rambling roses, the vines empty of flowers but still green enough to hide the garden beyond. She glanced behind her as she approached the gate, already feeling guilty for entering a space that she normally never visited.

Still, she slid through the archway and into the half-acre space that Sophie had turned into a small cottage garden surrounded by decorative perennials. Even now, past the midpoint of October, there were still squash plants with ripening fruit on the vines. Tara saw a raised bed of Swiss chard and mustard greens that looked barely harvested. Two bee pollinator towers hung on a decorative fence in the back of the garden, although there wasn't any activity near them now.

"Do you have time to sit for a minute?" Luke called to her from a bench seat tucked under a weeping willow.

She hadn't even noticed him there at first. But then, Sophie had designed the outdoor space with three little nooks off of it so that visitors could enjoy views of the garden from different vantage points. Tara had watched the whole project come together from one of Sophie's many vision boards. Her friend really was a creative talent, even if she occasionally irritated Tara to no end.

"For a minute," she agreed, pivoting toward the willow and then entering the nook where pavers gave way to white crushed stone. Two benches sat across from one another, a small fountain between them.

Tara sat on the bench that faced Luke's. Through the vine-covered wrought iron fence nearby, she could see the woods that provided a thin barrier between Sophie's French Country megamansion and a much smaller home. She could hear two kids in that backyard, their raised voices and cheers making it sound like they were playing a competitive game of some sort.

"I've been wondering when you would make time to see me again." Luke's gaze wandered over her while birds chirped in the trees overhead, a happy counterpoint to the uncomfortable conversation.

"Only because I need to clear the air between us. You caught me by surprise earlier this week, and I was too stunned to set things right." Even now, her heart beat too fast at the awkwardness of the conversation.

She hated confrontation.

He raised dark eyebrows. On an objective level, she recognized that Luke was a very handsome man. He ran a successful business and seemed like a good stepdad to Sophie's girls. But Tara had never been attracted to him for a minute, mostly because his wedding ring was a giant "do not touch" sign in her point of view.

"You were surprised? By what? The fact that I took you up on what you were so clearly offering during our conversation at *The Clean Break* party?" He leaned back in lazy sprawl, one arm draped along the bench seat next to him.

"Luke, at no time did I make an . . . offering." She found the choice of words distasteful but wasn't sure how to paraphrase. "I may have made the mistake of oversharing something personal with you, but at no point did I suggest an interest in anything between us."

The conversation felt so cringey she already wanted to go home and shower.

Luke shook his head, a wry smile lifting the corner of his mouth. "You just happened to overshare a personal story about the guy who dumped you to go out with Kaitlin. You weren't looking for an ego boost from me or anything."

Of all the narcissistic things to say. How could he believe that interaction was about him?

"Excuse me for mistaking you for a friend." Tara wouldn't have mentioned it to him but she'd been standing right next to Luke when Kaitlin chose that moment to arrive at *The Clean Break* anniversary celebration with the very same guy Tara had thought would be attending the party with her. "Next time something shitty happens to me, I'll know better than to vent to someone who thinks the world revolves around him."

She jolted to her feet, finished with their conversation and certain she'd gotten the point across that she wasn't interested. She moved toward the arch to reenter the main garden.

"I am your friend. And you should think twice before you alienate me, Tara," Luke's voice, low and easy, tugged her to a stop again.

"What are you talking about?"

He shoved to his feet, lifting his tennis bag from the ground beside him and looping the strap over one shoulder.

"I just thought maybe you'd want to keep your connection to someone who has a relationship with Sophie now that things are coming to a head between the two of you." He stopped a foot in front of her. Too close.

"Why would you say that?" She hadn't told anyone beside Jordyn that she needed to create some space between herself and her business partner, and she knew for a certainty that Jordyn would never share that. "What makes you think there is any problem between Sophie and me?"

"Because my wife is ten steps ahead of you, Tara. Hasn't it occurred to you that maybe there's a reason she acts like *The Clean Break* is all hers? That maybe she's setting you up to steal the business right out from under you?"

"She wouldn't do that." She protested automatically even while she ran over the possibility in her head. "She couldn't."

"No? What makes you think that? Do you have a contract that spells out your partnership?"

Her stomach sank. The sounds of the birds and the kids playing in the next yard over all faded away until the only thing she could hear was the anxious beat of her own heart.

"We had a handshake agreement." They were friends, after all. She'd known Sophie since they'd been cochairs at a summer charity gala right after Sophie had moved to Saratoga five years ago. They'd made such a good team that they'd gone from working on that gala to brainstorming ideas for the next year's event. After that was an ever bigger success, they started talking about doing a podcast.

"Ah. I'm sure that will be a valuable asset in a court case when you need to sue her after she wrests away full control of the show. I'll just leave you be since you seem to have things well in hand." Luke walked away at his unhurried pace, not caring that he'd just turned her life upside down.

Could he be serious?

Was Sophie really making plans to oust her from the business they'd started together? She didn't want to believe it. But Sophie had done the same thing to Kaitlin though, hadn't she?

Panic clawed its way up her throat. She'd thought about ways to get out from under Sophie's thumb, but she never in a million years imagined Sophie could be scheming to take over Tara's half-ownership of the program.

"Wait." She caught up to Luke, fearing she'd have to make a deal with the devil if she wanted to know more. "You honestly think she's plotting against me?"

Part of her hoped that this was just another one of Luke's manipulation tactics.

He crossed his arms and rocked back on his heels. "If you really knew my wife, you wouldn't have to ask me that."

Something about the way he said it convinced her he was telling the truth.

She had witnessed the way Sophie could turn on other people before. She cut Kaitlin out of the creative credits on the show without so much as batting an eye.

Yet Tara hadn't ever considered that she could be next. Because she was naïve? Because it was just easier to bury her head in the sand? Her father had warned her that if she went into the podcast business with her friend, she should formalize the relationship. Maybe that was part of the reason she hadn't. She loved her adoptive dad, but Randall Hughes was the most cynical person she'd ever met, and she didn't want to share his life view.

Now, she could only feel foolish that she hadn't listened.

"I don't want to be kept in the dark," she admitted stiffly, the words sticking in her throat when she really wanted to have nothing more to do with this man. "If you learn anything concrete about Sophie's plans, I would appreciate it if you'd tell me."

Luke paused just before the gate that led back to the main yard and the swimming pool. He scanned the grounds for a second before taking a step backward, closer to her.

"Excellent." He nodded, satisfied. "I'll call you. Soon."

Tara swallowed hard, hating the sound of that. Had he just played her? Either way, she would stay close to Luke for now. Because she wouldn't allow Sophie to strongarm her out of the business she'd helped to grow. People might view Tara's kindness as weakness, but she knew the truth.

Her therapist had helped her to recover her memories of foster care, and all the strength she'd mustered to get through the difficult teen years that had followed her adoption. She'd shoved those thoughts away and locked them into a box to forget them for almost two decades. By now, she'd recovered most of it. She certainly recalled a stronger facet of herself that had always lurked in the back of her psyche, protecting her. And she wouldn't hesitate to tap that inner strength again in order to hang onto the new life she'd built for herself.

CHAPTER 10

Jordyn

Present

"I think we'll avoid attention if you park just before the end of the cul-de-sac." From the passenger seat of Jordyn's car, private investigator Natalie Ramos indicated a spot on the opposite side of the road where no houses were visible.

Based in Glens Falls, a neighboring community just north of Saratoga, Natalie had only been helping Jordyn for the last week, but she'd moved quickly when Jordyn had called her. She was the very same PI that Tara had hired to locate Jordyn in the first place, so at least the woman had met Tara and knew something about her. Soft-spoken but steely, Natalie had become a private investigator at forty-five years old. She'd been incensed that local cops hadn't collected enough evidence to arrest one of her neighbors for killing his wife despite multiple domestic violence calls. Because of

Natalie's relentless efforts, the guy was now serving a life sentence.

Just like Jordyn hoped Tara's killer one day would.

Jordyn had offered to drive them both to the scene of the hit-and-run, hoping to attract as little attention as possible from the locals. Three book club members lived close by: Gina, Fatima, and Sophie. However, all of their homes were set back from the street, as the multiacre properties were deliberately built for maximum privacy. Jordyn had visited the spot once before, when she'd first arrived in town. She hoped getting that first emotional visit out of the way would give her the detachment required to think like an amateur detective as opposed to a best friend.

Pulling to the side of the road to park, Jordyn switched off the engine and passed Natalie a real estate flyer for a property two streets over. "Here, take one of these. If anyone sees us, we can fake like we're just checking out the neighborhood because I'm thinking about that house, okay?"

"Nice cover." Natalie withdrew a paper of her own from an interior jacket pocket of the leather jacket she wore. "Just take a look at this first to get oriented before we step outside."

Jordyn glanced at the sketch of the street with details from the accident, startled to see a crudely drawn figure with limbs lying at an awkward angle. Oh God. Had she really thought she could remain detached? The thought of her vibrant, kind-hearted friend here, on this very street, broken and alone, sucked the air from her lungs.

She licked her dry lips. Tried to steady herself as she focused on the need to find the person responsible. "Is this from the police files?"

"No. Sorry. They wouldn't let me view anything official since they're still saying the investigation is active." The PI met her gaze across the console. "Are you sure you're okay with this?"

"I'm—yeah. I'm okay."

Natalie continued. "I have contacts on the force, and I convinced one of them to talk me through their crime scene photos enough to recreate quite a few of the details."

"That's good." Jordyn nodded, swallowing the lump in her throat. Tamping down the fury that Tara had no justice for the violence that had taken her life. "So she was facing that direction?"

Refocusing on the place as a crime scene that needed decoding, Jordyn tucked her emotions away in a box.

"Correct. The street runs roughly north–south, and Tara's body was in line with the road, her head to the south and her feet to the north." Natalie pointed out the directions on her drawing, her silver rings and black nail polish aesthetic the kind of thing that Jordyn would have envied as a teen. "Based on her injuries, we know the vehicle hit her head-on. Also based on the tire marks, police experts have determined the car was headed south, so that means Tara would have been running north."

"Towards Sophie's house." Jordyn lifted her gaze from the drawing to the road, trying to appreciate the scale. Through the windshield, her attention drifted to a white cross stuck in the ground about a tenth of a mile down the road. The sight was another gut punch, one she hadn't worked up the nerve to approach the last time she'd been out here. "Although someone placed her memorial marker closer to Gina's place."

"Which was Tara's home at the time," Natalie reminded her, flipping over the paper to consult a list of names and addresses on the back. "My notes show that Luke Sideris purchased 51 Daybreak Hill to live in while he and Sophie were building their megamansion at the end of the cul-de-sac.

After construction was completed, they moved out of the smaller home and Sideris rented it out to Tara for almost three years. Then, about two months after her death, Gina Vallot moved into the property. She still rents 51 Daybreak from him."

Mind. Blown.

Jordyn hadn't realized that at all, and she grounded herself in facts to distract from the white cross near the road. She knew Tara had lived in the home that Gina later moved into, but she'd had no idea that Luke's name was actually on the deed. Whether it meant anything or not, she couldn't be certain, but she was grateful for the information.

The more she learned about this group of friends, the more she recognized how deeply intertwined their lives had all become. She envisioned a giant spider web, with *The Clean Break* podcast and its cocreators at the center.

"Did your police contact say whether they have any evidence that suggests Tara intended to return to Sophie's house that night?" She'd asked herself hundreds of times what had made Tara venture out for a late run at that hour on Halloween night. She hadn't even worn a reflective vest, which seemed particularly negligent on a road with little ambient light.

"That remains unclear. She could have been just running laps on this street, sticking closer to home since it was late and there was no moon that night."

Another detail that Jordyn hadn't known.

"So she could have just been running off excess energy," Jordyn mused. "As if she was upset."

"Or she could have met up with someone outside her house and gotten into an argument. That would explain the noise complaint that police say happened before the hit-and-run."

"Unless someone called that in as a decoy." Jordyn's thoughts were firing quickly, possible scenarios flashing through her brain.

"*Before* the hit-and-run even happened?" Natalie frowned, already shaking her head. "As if someone planned ahead of time to hit her?"

"Maybe whoever hit Tara that night initially hoped the police would put in an appearance at Tara's house, and that would settle things down. But things escalated too quickly—"

"You're saying you think the hit-and-run was premeditated?"

"It might have been." Jordyn shrugged. "Since we're low on facts, we might as well try to look at this from all possible angles, right?"

"Spoken like a good investigator." Natalie nodded her approval. "But I'd suggest saving any theories until after we walk the scene for ourselves."

"Fair enough. So we know the vehicle hits Tara and somehow spins her around one hundred and eighty degrees so she winds up facing in the opposite direction." Pausing, Jordyn ground her teeth together as her attention returned to the drawing Natalie had made. This was so much tougher than she'd imagined. "All right, I think I've got it. Let's take a look."

A minute later, they were outside the car, walking the perimeter of the accident site. Despite Natalie's cautioning words, Jordyn's brain still ran a mile a minute, trying to make the assorted facts fit together.

"Did you learn anything more from your inside source?" she asked, hoping for a nudge in the right direction.

"So far, I only know what was shared in the official press releases to the media, but I do have more sources I can tap so I'll keep digging. The cops were looking for a dark-colored

SUV, a description that fits a third of the vehicles around here." Natalie kept her focus on the bushes, her brown eyes scanning. "And we know the noise complaint was logged about twenty minutes before the incident."

"But it was weird that it was an unknown caller, right? I've read that in most municipalities you need to identify yourself. You can't just make an anonymous call to lodge a complaint about someone."

"You can if you hang up fast enough," Natalie informed her wryly. She consulted her notes again. "In this case, the call wasn't entered into the system as an official complaint because the person didn't give their name, but a record of the call still exists. A woman phoned to say there was a lot of shouting coming from Daybreak Hill, making it sound as if she wasn't a resident of the street, but maybe a street close by."

"And the call wasn't recorded?"

"No. It came into the front desk of the police station, not through the 911 system."

Jordyn paused to listen to the neighborhood at midday, wondering how far sound might carry at night. Right now, she could hear the high-pitched whine of a leaf blower from somewhere in the vicinity. The incessant hammering that characterized a roofing job. The occasional shrill shouts of children playing in a backyard somewhere nearby. But none of that activity was visible amid the tall pines that lined Daybreak Hill. Whoever developed the street full of high-end homes had made sure to maintain the mature landscaping, making the lots feel private from the street and even from one another.

"I hadn't expected this spot to feel so isolated," Jordyn observed finally, remembering her first impression of the spot from her earlier visit. "I had looked at the Google maps of this street and from the overhead views, it looked much more like a traditional neighborhood. But once you're standing here, it's less surprising that no one saw what happened that night."

Her PI companion folded her arms and stared up the street before adding, "Or so they say. But consider that the people who saw might have a reason to keep quiet."

"Are you thinking of Sophie and Fatima?" Jordyn tried to envision the well-heeled Saratogians that she'd met witnessing a murder and not saying a word.

It wasn't all that difficult to imagine.

"Or anyone in their families. We haven't talked about who else lives in those houses with Tara's fellow book club members. But you mentioned they all socialize together, so there could be interconnections outside the book club. Extramarital affairs. Jealousy."

That was a good point. Jordyn had told Natalie about the block party, and it stood to reason that the significant others could play roles that Jordyn hadn't yet considered.

"Plus there seems to be plenty of ill will generated by *The Clean Break*." Jordyn couldn't forget what Brad had told her about the show costing him primary custody of his child.

"You think Tara could have suffered for that, even though Sophie seems to be the public face of the podcast?" Natalie began walking toward the white memorial marker.

Jordyn followed, wishing she'd brought an offering of some kind. Tara had been a fan of daisies and sunflowers, which suited her sunny nature. Jordyn had incorporated the bright blooms into a tattoo that commemorated their friendship.

"Possibly Tara was an even more enticing target than Sophie because Tara was behind the scenes. Someone looking at the program from the outside could surmise that Tara ran the show, and Sophie just acted as the talent."

"But the members of their book club would know differently, wouldn't they?" The leather sleeves of Natalie's jacket creaked as she shifted position to check her phone screen before pocketing it again.

No doubt they'd spent enough time out here. They were lucky no one had driven past them.

"That's the thing about the book club. I can't say how well any of them really know one another. The secrets and scandals are so deep, I'd need hip waders to get through them all."

"That doesn't surprise me." Natalie laughed. "There's a reason I moved out of this town after my marriage fell apart."

Surprised, Jordyn wondered about the woman's connection to the community. "You used to live here?"

"Back when I cared about appearances and still bought into the idea that a husband and wife could be a team." She met Jordyn's gaze with a hard stare. "Before I learned I was all alone operating under that delusion. Yeah, I lived in a neighborhood like this once. And every woman I knew on that block was killing herself to maintain the illusion that she was living the dream."

Jordyn mulled that over as they reached the white cross stuck into the dirt along the road. She understood what Natalie was saying about the suburban utopian ideal. Maybe the stereotype still appealed to people in this storied town with a historic past and wealthy roots.

"As a single woman, Tara didn't have that kind of conformist pressure. She was independent. Artistic." Jordyn's hand went to the saint medallion she wore around her neck as she remembered her friend.

There were a few chrysanthemums in pots behind the cross, and a woven friendship bracelet in a rainbow of colors hung from the wooden marker. The sight of the bracelet surprised her a little since it seemed like something a younger person would leave. Almost a year had passed, but the spot was still being maintained.

"No pressure from a husband, maybe. But from what I've read about the adoptive parents, the Hughes family wrote the book on conformity. It couldn't have been an easy transition for Tara to be plucked from a foster situation to begin a new life with Randall and Lauren Hughes."

"That tracks with things she told me," Jordyn admitted, hating that she hadn't offered more moral support or encouragement when Tara expressed frustration with her life. Tara had talked about her relationship with her dad feeling fraught.

Natalie said nothing, but something in her shrewd gaze suggested she guessed there was more to the story.

Jordyn took a deep breath, knowing she should share as much as possible if she wanted this woman's help finding answers. "But I'm sorry to say that it was tough for me to empathize with some of her problems, even as an adult, because I still carried—still *carry*—the old baggage of being the kid who didn't get picked."

It stung to admit out loud. Jordyn had her personal demons under control, but that didn't mean they didn't occasionally behave badly. She'd done her friend a disservice.

If she'd been more supportive—if Tara had felt fully accepted and understood when they spoke—would Tara still be alive today? Maybe she would have confided more. Maybe Jordyn could have helped. The thought haunted her.

"Even among the wealthy elite, the Hughes family is exceptionally well off." Natalie backed up a few steps to get a better look down the driveway that wound toward Gina's house. The house that Tara called home in the years before her death. "From the outside, Tara's life looked pretty perfect."

The two-story rental property combined cedar shake siding with brick, the effect homey and welcoming. The three-car garage and extensive landscaping underscored that this was no average place in the suburbs, however. Home prices here were hefty.

"That was all smoke and mirrors though." A bolt of fury heated Jordyn's blood to think about someone ending Tara's life without a second thought. Speeding away in an expensive SUV as Tara took her final breaths alone in the dark. "The more I learn about Tara's life, the more I see it was far from perfect. And, no matter what her killer might think, the crime that silenced Tara wasn't perfect either. Which means we're going to find out who did this to her and make them pay."

CHAPTER 11

Tara

One Year Ago

SUNDAY DINNERS WEREN'T a custom in the Hughes family.

So Tara had to ask herself why she continued to try and turn them into a ritual when no one—her included—enjoyed them? No doubt it had something to do with the hopes and dreams of an orphaned little girl. Dreams that were never fully realized despite the glamorous world she'd been adopted into.

Standing on the front step of the home where she'd spent her teen years, Tara rang the bell and listened to the deep, resonant chime from inside. She wondered how many other adult children were too intimidated by their parents to simply walk into their childhood homes, but not in a million years would she have taken it upon herself to enter the elegant Victorian mansion unannounced once she'd moved out to attend college.

For one thing, there was the ever-changing door code security. For another, there was her father. Randall Hughes was not a man you wanted to catch unaware.

A moment later the door swung wide. A young woman in a neat gray dress stood back to admit her. "Hello, Miss Hughes. Your mother is still upstairs."

The scent of furniture polish and fresh flowers hung in the air as Tara stepped onto the marble floor of the foyer. The bouquet that rested in a massive vase at the base of the curved staircase was changed twice a week. Today's flowers were autumn-themed, heavy with golds and reds as canna lilies and sunflowers took center stage. High ceilings with crown moldings and elaborate woodworking details characterized the home built in the American Gilded Age. Tara recalled thinking it looked sort of like the Addams Family home when she'd first set eyes on it as a teenager.

With a brighter paint job.

"That's fine, Callie." Tara had met the maid for the first time the week before. Tara's mother enjoyed being waited on, but didn't keep staff for longer than a few months, so there was always someone new. "I'll just wait for her in the front room."

"May I take your wrap?" the woman offered after shutting the front door. "Or can I get you a drink?"

"No, thank you. And I'll keep my sweater." The house had never been warm, and it certainly wasn't because her father couldn't afford to heat it. Tara had lived in hoodies and slippers growing up, much to her fashionable mother's disapproval.

She'd been a part of the Hughes family for almost twenty years, and yet she still felt like a guest. For the last year or two since she'd recovered some of her memories through therapy, she'd toyed with the idea of quitting the

Sunday dinner ritual all together since her parents wouldn't miss it. But tonight, she had questions that only they could answer.

"Tara!" Her name boomed through the house like someone had shouted it through a megaphone, the noise making Callie jump as she walked away. "Come through already."

Unable to shout to the same effect as her father, Tara merely hurried past the stairs toward the west wing of the house where her father kept an office. He paced irritably in front of the French doors that led out to a courtyard, his phone attached to his ear, his golf attire his only nod to the weekend.

"—and I wouldn't have to get involved at all if you put half as much time into making money as you do on spending it. I'll be in the office tomorrow and there'd better be answers by the end of day." Yanking the phone from his ear, Randall Hughes stabbed a button and then tossed the device on a nearby wingback as he turned to Tara. He was in his early seventies but had the vitality of a much younger man. His hair was silvery white, but he'd retained an enviable amount of it. "This really isn't a good time for me, Tara. I need to get to the city tonight."

Before Tara could answer, her mother arrived in a cloud of White Linen perfume, still fastening an earring into place.

"For God's sake, Randall, you just got here, and you haven't spent time with Tara in weeks." Lauren was almost twenty years younger than her husband, and she was every bit as elegant and intimidating as she'd been when Tara had first met her as a fourteen-year-old. Lauren's long dark hair fell in a glossy sheet, and a figure-skimming ivory sheath dress showed off the hours she still spent in the gym. She spared a smile for Tara. "Hello, darling."

"Hi Mom." She approached her mom to hug her, having learned long ago that her mother's love language amounted to tasteful displays of affection she didn't necessarily reciprocate.

Lauren Hughes had spent two years in Paris and Milan working as a model but had cut her career short to marry Randall. For their first date, he'd flown her to Louisville for the Kentucky Derby, where a horse he co-owned had won. They still travelled to thoroughbred races around the world, one of their few shared interests. Photos from the Dubai World Cup and Epsom Derby dotted the office walls. Tara had rarely accompanied them on those trips, relegated to nannies right up until she'd turned seventeen, and her father had deemed her old enough to "man the fort" alone.

She'd really missed the company of a nanny that last summer under this roof before she'd left for college at the Fashion Institute in New York City.

"Evander is going to make a mess of a deal I hand-delivered to him with a goddamn bow," Randall explained, shutting down the open laptop on his desk before sliding it into a drawer and locking it. He frequently butted heads with the oldest son from his previous marriage. "I can't stay for dinner."

Tara's skin chilled at the mention of her half-brother. Evander and his full siblings had never been kind to her, openly antagonizing her as much as they could get away with. Their enmity seemed rooted in events before Tara came into the family, along with a deep resentment at having to share any of their inheritance with her. Thankfully, she'd never spent much time around them. Perhaps her mother had glimpsed the tension, because she made an effort to keep Tara apart from them.

"Well that's a new record for cutting the weekend short," Lauren remarked mildly. "You've been in town for what, thirty hours? Less?"

"I think we both know it was *your* decision to live so far away from my business and my heir." Randall's icy words made Tara want to run from the house and the confrontation.

But she couldn't hide from tough discussions forever.

"Dad, I had a quick question to ask you before you go." She shuffled into his path to forestall his exit. "Can I have five minutes?"

It was difficult enough to get an audience with her father, and she'd already invested emotional energy bracing herself for an awkward conversation.

Randall stopped short, huffing out a breath, but his tone was kind once he refocused on her. "Of course. How can I help?"

Her stomach clenched and then her words came out in a rush. "Suppose I wanted a lawyer to help me draft a partnership agreement—"

"Are you thinking about starting a new business?" His blue eyes narrowed. "We should discuss viability—"

"It's actually for my partnership with Sophie and *The Clean Break*," she explained quickly, twisting a ring around her finger before realizing she fidgeted like a teenager. "The podcast."

Her father swore. "We talked about this a long time ago, Tara. Please don't tell me that you went into business with that woman—a lawyer with an arbitration license, I might add—without the protection of a partnership agreement."

"Oh Tara, that was not well done." Her mother shook her head as she moved closer to join the conversation, the three of them standing just inside the office while the grandfather clock in the foyer chimed the dinner hour. "Sophie Durand is a shark in high heels. Remember what I told you about the permits she filed to get approval for that nouveau atrocity she calls a home? She pulled a fast one with the zoning committee that was for sure."

Tara had heard the story about Sophie and the zoning board more than once but never gave it much credence. Still, she could admit she'd been wrong not to listen to her parents' advice on this.

"I read that it's never too late to put an agreement in place." She'd done a deep dive on the kind of language used in those sorts of documents and realized how helpful it would have been to have something that spelled out participation expectations, dispute resolution, and dissolution arrangements. At the time, she hadn't wanted to offend Sophie by bringing it up, figuring their friendship was solid enough to help them navigate any bumps in the road. "I just wondered if you had any recommendations for an attorney that could help me."

"Tell me this first." Her father clapped his hands on Tara's shoulders and looked her in the eye. "Are you doing this now because you suddenly see the wisdom of an agreement? Or are you really just angling to get out of the partnership?"

"I don't necessarily want to end things now, but I want to make sure my interest is protected." In case Luke was right and Sophie was ready to oust her somehow.

"It sure sounds like you're starting to worry that you can't trust her," her mother guessed, rearranging Tara's hair and frowning a little as if she spotted split ends.

At least Tara had worn an outfit her mother had bought her for her birthday, a sleek red angora sweater dress that was too formal for virtually anything but dinner at her parents.

No matter how much money accumulated in Tara's personal bank account, she had never morphed into the kind of person who wanted to jet to Fiji or Monaco for long weekends. She appreciated people more than places.

She also appreciated a work-from-home dress code.

"Let me call my friend Arnie, and I'll have him give you a ring." Her father huffed another irritated sigh and then stalked toward the foyer. "You're going to be working from a position of weakness, obviously. This should have all been spelled out before your first episode aired."

"Thank you, Dad. I really appreciate it." Tara figured it had been a good thing Randall was already so preoccupied with whatever was going on with her half-brother that he didn't bother to lecture her further for neglecting the partnership agreement.

He waved a hand in acknowledgement, but he was already hurrying up the stairs to pack whatever it was he needed for the trip downstate.

Beside her, her mother looped an arm through hers. "Come sit and tell me what's really happening with Sophie while we have dinner. I heard she financed Destiny Griffin's new gym."

"Maybe?" Tara shrugged, uneasy as she let her mother lead her into the dining room where Callie was filling the wine glasses at three place settings.

Destiny had asked Tara for a loan as well, so she was surprised to hear that she'd needed financing from Sophie too. Was Destiny in financial trouble?

"Well I hope it's a good investment," Lauren explained before telling Callie to clear Randall's place. When they were alone again in the round dining room that seated twelve, her mother continued, "Is Sophie overbearing to work with?"

Yes.

But she didn't say that. There'd been a time when Sophie had felt more like a friend and less like someone trying to manipulate her. Even now, it felt disloyal to complain about her. Especially when the gossip mill in their town could be swift and brutal.

"Not at all," Tara lied, sipping the white wine that accompanied the salad course and wondering how she could maneuver the conversation around to what she really needed to ask her mom. "I think we complement each other creatively. She has a lot of great ideas, and I help her refine her focus to shape the best of them into actionable steps."

"Ever the diplomat." Her mother sat up straighter as she said it, and Tara knew that the comment wasn't intended as praise.

They meandered through their usual safe topics over a meal of Icelandic cod francese. The social missteps of the first Mrs. Hughes. The Seychelles trip Lauren had planned for the holidays. Randall's poor diet and lack of commitment to Lauren. By the time Lauren refused the offered dessert and suggested Callie bring them hot toddies instead, Tara realized she couldn't put off the topic she needed to discuss with her mom any longer.

Following Lauren into the den where she'd asked for the drinks to be served, Tara rolled out the admission she'd been practicing in her head.

"You remember how one of the things I was working on with my therapist was to explore that dissociative amnesia episode I had after we moved here?" Tara had been in and out of counseling ever since her parents had adopted her.

In her teen years, her mother had told her that therapy would help her navigate the changes in her life. Yet Lauren had pulled her out of treatment once she learned that Tara had asked the counselor to help her recover her lost memories, convinced that recalling past trauma would only be damaging to Tara in the long run.

As soon as Tara turned twenty-one and could call her own shots, however, she'd quietly gone back into therapy. For a while she'd been content simply to gain more perspective on her life and all that she'd experienced at a young age. But eventually, she'd come back to the key question that had haunted her for years. Why had she blocked out almost two years of memories?

"And you remember that *I* told *you* I think your mind almost certainly gave you the gift of disassociation to protect you from whatever horrors you endured before you joined our family."

Lauren chose her favorite seat on one end of a white sectional sofa in the room at odds with the rest of the carefully restored Victorian home. She had never particularly liked the historic structure with its overly fussy features and elaborate woodwork, preferring minimalist lines and neutral colors. But despite her personal preferences, Lauren also believed in supporting the architectural integrity of an area, which was why Sophie's new home irritated her.

The drinks had already been delivered on a wooden tray that rested on the corner table between the sofa and a buff-colored leather occasional chair. Sitting, Tara grabbed one of the warm glass mugs from the tray. She didn't really want the heavy beverage when her stomach was already in knots over a topic she dreaded discussing, but she appreciated having something to hold in her nervous hands.

"I understand that's how you view it, Mom." The last word had never flowed off her tongue easily, but she'd always felt it was one she owed this woman. Randall hadn't wanted any more offspring, particularly not one who didn't share his blood. But Lauren had lobbied for a child she could call her own and because of her steely determination, Tara's life had changed in an instant.

Though it was an instant she couldn't recall with clarity thanks to the amnesia that had stolen details from so much of that transitional time in her life.

A long-suffering sigh hissed from her mother's lips as she collected a drink for herself, her weighty pear-shaped diamond clanking against the glass handle of the delicate mug. "Okay, so how is your *exploration* of the *episode* going?"

"Not great," Tara admitted, knowing she needed to circle back to that. But first and foremost she wanted to confess the secret she'd kept from her parents for two years. "I'm still working to figure out what caused the episode in the first place. But I have had better luck recovering older memories. Things from my time in foster care."

Her mother froze for a moment. Then, she carefully returned her drink to the tray. Leaning forward, she looked directly at Tara.

"Your older memories are the ones that caused you to lose time in the first place. Your experience in foster care is the whole reason your brain had to create an elaborate system to protect you. Why are you doing this, Tara? Why do you insist on picking through the biggest pain points of your life? Just to hurt all over again? To hurt your whole family?"

And there it was.

The idea might be wrapped in different language tonight, but beneath the words lurked the same old accusation that she wasn't grateful enough for being plucked from her former existence. That she had dragged past baggage with her and made her adoptive family suffer for it.

"I never want to hurt you or Dad—"

"Yet you *do*. Every time this comes up it's hurtful to both of us." Her mother flipped her long hair behind one shoulder impatiently. "You're an intelligent woman. I know you must see how this . . . *fixation* on your past drives a wedge between you and your father and me."

"I'd hardly call my efforts to heal a fixation."

She just wanted answers. A cohesive understanding of her past. Unlike her friend Jordyn, Tara had been raised in a warm and loving home before her single-parent mother died of ovarian cancer. Before she'd gone into the foster system, she'd known what it felt like to be loved unconditionally. The relationship she had with her adoptive mother had never felt that way.

"And what exactly are you trying to heal? The winters we spent in Aspen? The private tutoring and riding lessons? The graduation trip to Capri along with a ring from Cartier to celebrate?" Lauren shook her head. "Because clearly none of that was good enough for our artsy, complicated daughter who was too busy navel-gazing to see she had everything in the world a girl could ask for."

Stunned at the outburst, and at this perception of her as overly entitled, Tara wasn't sure how to react. She scrambled to summon her therapist's suggestions for dealing with confrontation. Stay calm and composed. Focus on the issue and not the feelings.

"You did give me everything a child could have wanted," she assured her mother quietly, knowing it wasn't true. She would have traded the ring and the trips and the riding lessons she secretly despised for a genuine sense that she was valued for herself and not as an imperfect reflection of her glamorous mother. "But I'm not a child anymore. And I don't think it's uncommon for people to want to understand their pasts."

She needed to account for that missing time. To know if she'd formed any other relationships like the one she'd discovered with Jordyn. Or to find out what kind of trauma she'd faced to make her memories shut down.

"Okay then. Since you want to discuss this—what great things have you learned about your foster care experience now that you've recovered some memories?" Lauren stretched her lips into a mask of a smile. "You might as well share now that you've already shredded a layer of my skin." She retrieved her cup again and this time, took a long swig of the drink before settling back into the corner of the sectional.

The ticking of the grandfather clock seemed to count down the seconds until Tara admitted what she'd done.

"I connected with a friend that I remembered from that time. Her name is Jordyn Lawson, and she lives in Austin. I visited her last summer when I attended that design conference." She'd made really happy memories there, feeling like she was doing more than just rediscovering a friendship.

She'd rediscovered herself. The adolescent girl she had been before she became a Hughes.

Her mother's face fell.

"Meaning you broke the promise you made to your father and me not to have anything to do with those people."

The accusation hit a sore spot, and Tara couldn't seem to find her composure or any distance from her feelings. Which hurt.

"The promise you coerced from me when I was a fifteen-year-old? I'm not sure you can enforce it for a lifetime. I did keep it while I lived under your roof." She couldn't stop herself from defending Jordyn. "And Jordyn is leading a successful life, something tougher to achieve without millions of dollars backing her every move."

Lauren sat up again, putting both of her taupe high heels on the floor and smoothing her skirt to where it ended just above her knee. "You may not live under this roof, but you still enjoy the privileges of a trust fund, don't you?"

Tara blinked. Her mouth went dry. "And you view that money as some kind of payment to ensure I only behave the way you want me to?"

It was the first time either of her parents had suggested such a thing. While she wasn't nearly as motivated by money as her parents were and could surely forge a good future without that generous bank account balance, she had also never conceived of her life as bought and paid for because of that money.

"I'm saying a broken promise isn't very honorable, Tara. And you might have just forced me to admit something your father has been trying to convince me of for twenty years." She pursed her lips. Her eyes narrowed. "Maybe the old adage is true. Blood will always out."

Shooting to her feet, her mother walked toward the door.

Tara stood more slowly. She felt herself trembling. The conversation had gone every bit as badly as she'd feared.

Worse.

"Mom, wait." She'd risked her mother's wrath and now fully incurred it. She might as well go for broke. "Sooner or later, I'll remember what happened to me to cause the big hole in my memory. Because I know it happened *after* you adopted me. Are you sure you don't want to just tell me what you think happened before I recover that memory on my own?"

Her mother's shoulders tensed visibly. When she turned around again, her voice was cool. Calm.

"Has it ever occurred to you that maybe your brain isn't protecting you from something that happened *to* you, but from some awful thing *you* did?"

The words echoed inside Tara. Rebounding. Reverberating.

Rewriting her whole concept of self.

Could it possibly be true? Or was her mother's accusation simply a new form of deflection?

Tara didn't even notice when Lauren walked away, her high heels hammering home what Tara had suspected all along.

She would never discover the missing pieces of her past from her parents. Tonight would be the last time she would ever try.

CHAPTER 12

Jordyn

Present

A*RE WE DOING the Witch Walk this year?*

Seated at the small island inside her carriage house rental, Jordyn had to reread Kaitlin's text a second time before she realized it wasn't just to her; it was part of the book club group text thread.

She'd invited Natalie to the carriage house today to go over the information they'd each gathered so far about the hit-and-run. She didn't feel comfortable meeting the PI publicly in case someone recognized Natalie. No sense having anyone think Jordyn was in town for any reason other than exploring a cool new place to live.

They'd only just taken their seats at the kitchen island when Jordyn's phone vibrated with the text.

"Do you know anything about a local Witch Walk?" she asked Natalie as she put the phone down, assuming she didn't need to reply yet.

"Oh, it's pretty fun. It's a fundraiser for shelter pets, and everyone dresses in costume to parade around town. There are special dances, themed foods and drinks, plus the businesses all get involved."

"Cool. Guess I'm in the market for a pointy hat." She wouldn't miss an opportunity to hang out with the book club friends before the Halloween meeting. "So I'm dying to know what you've unearthed since we spoke last."

Because everywhere she turned lately she felt like she was pounding her head against the wall. The probate attorney still hadn't gotten back to her about the status of Tara's estate. Neither Randall nor Lauren Hughes would return her calls. Plus she'd listened to podcast after podcast about people's heartbreaks and betrayals. Although she had a whole list of individuals around the country who could potentially have a reason to hate Sophie and Tara, the content of the shows made Jordyn feel incredibly depressed.

Why were people so heartless toward one another? Particularly people they used to love? Every break-up the show covered was painful.

Natalie flipped open the top of the stainless-steel water bottle she'd brought along. She was dressed in another leather coat today, this one a dark brown bomber jacket with jeans. "I found out some juicy stuff. But first, let me tell you that I did most of my online digging while staking out Daybreak Hill."

"Really?" Jordyn frowned, silencing her phone that was starting to vibrate, probably with group text replies about the Witch Walk. "Why?"

"Checking how many vehicles use that road that don't belong to people who live on the cul-de-sac. I took the day shift, and I hired someone to take night shifts for the hour when Tara would have been struck."

"I wonder if the cops thought to do that as part of their investigation." Jordyn wished she'd thought of that months ago. It would have been a good assignment for the investigator she'd originally hired to look into the hit-and-run.

"My contact on the force didn't mention it. I made a list of the vehicles, plate numbers, and how long they spent on the street." She tapped her phone screen and pulled up the electronic version of the document to show Jordyn. "Granted, this was only over the course of three days, but in that time every single person had a connection to one of the houses on the street. Nannies, tutors, other parents dropping off kids from sports practices, a couple of contractors, lawn care, and deliveries. But after nine PM, there was zero traffic except for residents."

"That fits with what I've thought all along. I always figured it had to be someone from the book club who hadn't gone home yet. All the members told police—at least according to the information released to the press—that they were at Sophie's place until things broke up around ten forty-five. Shortly afterward, someone calls in a noise complaint. Then twenty minutes later Tara's dead."

"Meaning we're on the right track looking into the group." Natalie nodded as she withdrew a sleek silver pen from an interior pocket of the jacket she still wore. "I've spent most of my time digging into everyone's financial situations and trying to figure out who would benefit from Tara's death. But I also dug deeper into everyone's backgrounds. I can just go through each member and tell you what I learned."

"Perfect. Who's first?" Jordyn had some notes of her own, but she wasn't sure there was anything that she hadn't already shared with the PI in their initial call.

"I say we start at the top, since it's Sophie's book club." Natalie flipped open an old-fashioned notepad with a purple cloth cover that looked like something a junior high kid would make. Inside, the note paper was covered from top to bottom in notes in—

"Is that shorthand?" Jordyn asked, surprised to see the squiggles she vaguely recalled reading about in a book.

Natalie nodded as she scanned the page. "You'd be surprised how helpful it is in my job. Anyway, Sophie divorced Amelia and Charlotte's father seven years ago, and eighteen months later she married Luke Sideris. David Durand had money, but Luke had more." Shrugging, she paused to meet Jordyn's eyes. "I'm not making judgments, I'm just going to blast through facts."

"Blast away." Jordyn pulled out a sheet of paper and a ballpoint so she could keep track of what she learned.

"Sophie still works remotely for her father's South Carolina law firm. Her family has money, but again, not to the degree that Luke does. I can't find any kind of partnership agreement regarding *Clean Break* between Sophie and Tara, so there's no way to know if Sophie technically took over the business before Tara's death or after."

"Wait." Jordyn put her pen down. "You're sure that Sophie has full ownership of *The Clean Break* now? Even though I haven't heard anything from the probate court about the status of Tara's estate?"

Natalie shook her head. "Sophie filed the paperwork early this year to restructure the business as an S Corp, and she's the sole owner."

"Guess who just shot to the top of my list," Jordyn muttered, wishing she'd paid closer attention to Tara's discussion of her work.

Had Sophie killed her partner to gain control of the business?

"Maybe hold off on that until you hear the rest because I'm just warming up." Natalie flipped the page of her notebook with a flourish.

"Kaitlin Teal's financial situation is sound. She inherited that lake house from a great aunt, and she's never been married. But the scuttlebutt on her is that she was cut out of the podcast even though she was instrumental in coming up with the premise."

"And you found that out how?"

"Social media griping in groups she thought were private." Natalie made a face. "Never put anything on the internet that you wouldn't shout out your front window for the whole neighborhood to hear. Because that's what you're doing."

"Right." Jordyn was impressed. She'd hunted through the social media accounts of all the book club members and hadn't found those posts. "Can you screenshot some of that?"

"I've already created a secure shared file with all of this information in there. I'll give you the sign-in after we finish."

In short order, Natalie had also learned that Destiny owed both Tara and Sophie money since they'd kicked in the funds necessary to open The Ascent. Sophie had filed a promissory note but Tara had just handed over the cash as far as Natalie could learn.

So that gave both Kaitlin and Destiny motives.

Brad nursed a grudge about losing primary custody, which gave him one.

Fatima Chamoun didn't seem to have anything against Tara, at least not that they'd uncovered so far. Although Fatima and Sophie had been locked in a competitive war to see whose daughters achieved more, she couldn't see how that could be related to Tara. And after summarizing both Brad's and

Fatima's financial situations—neither seemed like they would benefit from Tara's death—Natalie flipped another notebook page.

"Now, here's when the motives might turn less financial and more emotional. Because I learned there is some evidence that Tara was having an affair—"

"With Luke?" Jordyn guessed.

Natalie swung her head to face her. "Well, wow. That's not where I was going. Have *you* heard that?"

"No. But I sensed a weird vibe between them." Jordyn wasn't totally sure why Luke had been her first guess. Maybe because she rented the house from Luke? "But I wondered if there was something between them based on a conversation I had with Tara. What have you heard?"

"A waitress at the Adelphi Hotel told me she saw Tara with Mei Kita's husband, Nikolai Moskal. And apparently I'm not the only one who went to the restaurant asking about it. Mei briefly hired a colleague of mine to follow Nikolai, so she must have been suspicious of him too."

"Do you know if that person uncovered any proof?"

"My contact wouldn't say more than that. I just know he tailed Nikolai for a couple of weeks last year because Mei hired him to." She clicked the push button of her pen back and forth a handful of times while she seemed lost in thought. "So that's a potential motive for Mei if she heard the same rumor as me, that Nikolai had been with Tara."

"Maybe you could find out more from that colleague? Do you think if I offered to pay this other PI for the information he would let us know definitively one way or another what he shared with Mei?"

"It's worth asking." Natalie made a note in her phone then set it aside again. She paused to take another swig from her water bottle, which was covered in stickers from visits to national parks. "But I saved the best for last."

"We've covered almost everyone in the book club." Jordyn frowned. "You know that Gina Vallot had only just arrived in Saratoga a few weeks before Tara's death, right?"

"I do know that." Natalie leaned closer, her eyes alight with whatever information she hadn't yet revealed. "But what if Tara was the whole reason Gina moved to this town in the first place?"

Jordyn felt her eyebrows shoot up. "Okay, I'll bite. What did you find out?"

"Have you been listening to *The Clean Break* backlist?"

"I have. Gina's name didn't come up in any of those though."

"It wouldn't. Because she didn't go by Gina then."

"She appeared on the podcast?" Jordyn couldn't believe her ears. It didn't seem possible. "Wouldn't Sophie and Tara have recognized her?"

"They don't necessarily see the people since it's all done with audio recordings."

"But they must check out who their guests are. Put together bios and backgrounds on the guests. There are show notes on each episode where you can find out more about the people." She'd scanned through a lot of those herself.

"In this case, the woman not only changed her name, she changed her whole look. Dumped her Cajun accent."

"And you don't think the book club members know who she is?"

"There's no way in hell they know who she is." Natalie retrieved her phone and scrolled through some tabs before turning the screen toward Jordyn. "Gina Vallot is Evangeline Jameson Ribeki, wife of the two-timing NFL player who went on the program for divorce help and wound up being the victim of a publicity stunt."

There, on the screen, Natalie had photos of Gina side-by-side with one of Evangeline, who had a notoriously scrubbed online presence. For being married to a very public figure, Evangeline had scrupulously avoided the media and had stated on *The Clean Break* that she found social media harmful toward women. She made a habit of appearing in sunglasses and a hat in public, but Natalie had a blurry photo of her as a younger woman in a picture that looked like it might have been taken from a high school yearbook.

"How can that be?" Jordyn's hand went to her lips as she compared the faces. The eye color and hair color were different now. She'd almost certainly had some cosmetic surgery on her nose, which changed the look of her face. But the shape of her mouth was the same. "Evangeline was furious about that show. She's *suing* Sophie. I don't understand how she could do all of that without ever coming face-to-face with her nemesis."

Natalie took back her phone. "Her lawyer has been the one to handle the case, so Gina doesn't necessarily need to appear in front of a judge. I'm texting you the sign-in information for the digital file with everything I shared today."

"Should we call the police with this?" Jordyn was reeling, trying to process the news about Evangeline/Gina. "In light of who she is, there's no way that it's a coincidence that Tara died the night of Gina's first book club. She obviously moved here to exact her revenge."

"Maybe. But why would she kill Tara right away and not lift a finger to do anything against Sophie when she obviously holds Sophie more accountable, based on the statements her legal team made to the media?"

Jordyn hadn't spent much time reading about the football player's wife or the lawsuit she'd brought against Sophie and *The Clean Break* because she had assumed there was no connection between that episode and the killer in the book club.

An oversight she would remedy as soon as possible. Finding out that Evangeline had slid right into the lives of her enemies changed everything.

"Because Sophie has deeper pockets and more influence? Maybe Evangeline figured she would kill one of the partners and sue the other one?" Jordyn grabbed her phone again, needing to confirm that she had the right sign-in information from Natalie. She needed to go over all of the information they'd gathered with a fine-tooth comb. Double check everything and figure out what to do next. "Thanks for sending that. But what do you think I should do as far as sharing this with the police?"

She didn't want to involve law enforcement. Yet she couldn't deny feeling a renewed sense of danger now. How far would Gina go to protect her secrets?

"It's your call." Natalie slid off the barstool and tucked her notepad into her handbag before shouldering the strap. "But I suspect they would just confront Gina and start asking questions of all the book club members, so you'd lose the advantage of knowing a key piece of information that no one else in the group does. Maybe see what you can find out on the Witch Walk before you decide either way?"

"You're right. The whole reason I'm here is to feel out the situation for myself. Get to know the players in the group." She said it to herself as much as Natalie, appreciating the reminder of why she'd traveled across the country, ended a relationship, gave up a home, and possibly risked her own neck to get to know the women in Sophie Durand's book club.

The Witch Walk was a public event, so Jordyn would be safe enough.

She would leverage her access to Tara's former friends. Rattle some cages. See what happened. Starting with the woman who called herself Gina Vallot.

CHAPTER

13

Gina

Present

On the day of the Witch Walk festivities, Gina drove into the same public garage where she'd spotted Luke driving his secret vehicle that day she'd been staking out his business. She arrived late to catch up with the rest of the book club, since she had a mission to take care of before she joined everyone else.

A group of laughing teens raced past her in matching Day-of-the-Dead-style makeup. Had no one taught them about cultural appropriation? But then, who was she to judge, dressed like a pagan when she'd been raised to attend Mass twice a week.

Driving slowly up the garage levels, she finally found Luke's SUV parked on the roof. Luckily, there were still open spots, so she drove into a vacant place at the other end of the building to put some space between their vehicles, then walked back to Luke's car. She double-checked the plate number before she stopped to withdraw a small mirror from her handbag. The cool October breeze blew her crimped hair in every direction, so she tucked a few extra strands beneath the black satin witch hat that she'd decorated with dried flowers. In the mirror, she could see the purple spider webs she'd painted around her eyes, but she wasn't using the mirror to check out her reflection. She was more interested in making sure no one was coming before she crouched beside Luke's secret second vehicle and tucked the magnetized GPS into the wheel arch.

Straightening, she closed her compact and stepped away, making sure the tracker remained hidden from various angles.

Once that was done, she slid her mirror back into a flat waist pack that fit under her black satin corset. Broom in hand, she followed the sounds of Celtic music played in fiddles and uilleann pipes, down the stairs and out onto the street. The roots of the festival were more German, but Gina had noticed the year before that there was a blend of pagan traditions represented. And the event was intended to raise money for a variety of animal rescue organizations, so the point wasn't authenticity so much as fun.

Twilight settled onto the street, halogen lamps flickering to life. The scent of fair food staples like popcorn and fried dough mingled with specialty offerings from local restaurants. A smoke machine billowed purple clouds into the air, and orange fairy lights had been strung in the trees.

Gina hurried toward Broadway, even though her black lace-up boots were a bit clunky to walk in, mainly because they were cheap. She hoped to run into Luke before she found the book club ladies, but any hope of that was dashed when Jordyn Lawson suddenly appeared in front of her, her copper-colored hair twisted into uneven pigtails tied with purple velvet bows. She wore eyeliner that would have scared a small child, her makeup trending toward ghoulish.

"I almost didn't recognize you." Gina held out her arms for a friendly hug even though some sixth sense warned her that this woman spelled trouble. Stepping back, she admired Jordyn's black lace dress decorated with spiders and lizards. "Kudos to you on going all in on the theme."

Jordyn gave her a half smile. "I may have dabbled in some Goth trends in my youth. Putting on the eyeliner felt like old times."

"Oh, do tell. I love it when skeletons come falling out of the closet." Gina pointed south at the intersection. "And we might as well walk that way to find the others. Fatima messaged me a little while ago that they were having drinks in front of the distillery."

They approached a witch stirring a giant cauldron with what looked like dry ice inside, the contents bright red and smoking. Beside her, another woman dressed in a billowing green skirt wound with gold tassels and a belt of tiny skulls held a tray full of bright green drinks that were labeled "Kiss of Death."

Jordyn paused to buy two of them with cash and passed one to Gina.

"Well now that you know something about my secret dark side, you owe me a little bit about yours." Jordyn clinked her plastic cup with Gina's before trying her drink.

"I guess there's no better time to share the feminine dark side than at a Witch Walk." Gina sipped the beverage and found it tasted better than it looked. "But I'm not sure that you being a former Goth girl counts as a big reveal. That would be like me telling you that I used to work as an exotic dancer."

Jordyn coughed, spluttering a little as if she swallowed wrong. "Were you really?"

"No, that was more of an example." Gina's gaze scanned the crowd, still wondering if she'd see Luke tonight, or if he was going to claim he was still "out of town." She could hardly pull off her big revenge scheme at the Halloween book club if Luke broke up with her beforehand.

"You're not very good at this game." Jordyn twirled around in a quick groove move as they passed a trio of musicians playing instruments that looked like they came from another century.

The street overflowed with witchy revelers now that the sun had set. Different music poured from each street corner and bar. Hard rock gave way to modern pop. Another group of street musicians danced around them playing wooden pipes and homemade drums while they chanted something about new moons and love potions.

If Gina hadn't been stressed out of her mind between trying to unravel what Luke was up to and worrying that Jordyn wasn't who she pretended to be, she might have enjoyed herself tonight.

"Sorry, I'm just trying to come up with something appropriate. How about this. During my last break up I went literal scorched earth on the guy and burned the word 'cheater' into his perfectly manicured front lawn."

Jordyn gripped Gina's elbow, her eyes going wide. "Now we're talking. That's some dark energy right there."

"Yes, well. No getting on my bad side." She hoped Jordyn would take it as a warning. She didn't trust the newcomer with almost no social media footprint.

A sharp whistle pierced through the musical cacophony and street noise.

"Gina! Over here." Destiny stood near the old-fashioned clock on Broadway. Dressed in a black cape and form-fitting black tulle gown, she waved at them with extreme stiletto nails painted bright red.

The whole group had gathered in front of the bank. Brad was there, dressed in a wig that made him look like the David Bowie character in *Labyrinth*. He had an arm slung around Mei, while she tasted a drink he held for her. Fatima, Kaitlin, and Sophie were channeling the Sanderson Sisters from *Hocus Pocus*, just like they had for the Witch Walk the year before.

Sophie's blond hair curled in perfect imitation of Sarah Jessica Parker's character. Fatima's dark hair hid beneath a black velvet cap, and she held the leashes of her two Shih Tzus, Poppy and Milo. Kaitlin wore a red Bette Midler wig as she tried to keep her American Akita, Nala, from jumping on Jordyn, who had rushed over to greet the dog like an old friend.

"The gang's all here," Gina observed quietly to Destiny when the gym owner gave her a quick side hug.

"As if anyone in this group would miss a chance to let their witch flag fly." Destiny's gaze seemed to land on Sophie as she said it.

Then again, maybe Gina was seeing what she wanted to see. Because her attention went to Sophie also. And at that very moment, Luke suddenly appeared behind her, wrapping his wife in his arms and kissing her on the cheek. He wore a black jacket and dark jeans, his only nod to the dress code a pin on his coat that showed a figure in a pointy hat, flying in front of a full moon.

"Me included," Gina assured Destiny, lifting her broomstick made of willow branches and tied with a purple ribbon. It happened to point toward her treacherous lover. "I wait all year for a night to cast spells and call down my minion demons."

"Well, don't get too carried away, Demon Girl." Destiny gently pushed aside the broomstick before leaning against the metal post that bore the clock. "Tonight is a family event."

"If you say so." Sighing, Gina finished the rest of the drink Jordyn had bought for her.

She would have to wait until after the Witch Walk festivities to confront Luke about where he'd been when he'd said he was out of town.

Unless . . .

An idea came to her as the friends agreed to stroll toward Congress Park to see what else was happening along the walking route. They would go right past Luke's workplace. What if she slipped away from the group and used her key to let herself into the side entrance of Luke's office? Would she find any evidence of whatever business he'd been conducting in secret?

"Besides," Destiny continued as she looped one of her arms through Gina's, careful not to catch her extreme-length nails on any fabric. "The real night for witch work is Halloween. You should save your spells and demons for the murder mystery game we're playing at book club."

Knowing what she had planned for that evening, Gina couldn't have agreed more.

CHAPTER

14

Jordyn

Present

As much as Jordyn genuinely enjoyed the momentary stress-relief of greeting Kaitlin's fluffy dog, she could have kicked herself for getting so distracted that she lost track of where Gina had gone.

The book club members walked toward Congress Park, some paired up in conversation and some strolling with their families. Sophie's oldest strode beside her while the younger daughter, Amelia, seemed to be wheedling extra spending cash from her stepfather. Fatima's husband was nowhere in sight, but Jordyn recognized her daughter Sareena from that day in the Right Track coffee shop. Sareena ambled along between Charlotte and her mother, her attention fixed on her phone screen until Fatima palmed the device and stuffed it into the teen's jacket pocket.

"Did you see where Gina went?" Jordyn asked Brad who brought up the back of the group.

His silvery white mullet wig had a scattering of glittery hairs, while the high neck of his white puffy shirt made him look like an alien pirate.

"She said something about finding another one of those green drinks." He pointed with his thumb in the direction they'd just come from. "Back that way."

"Maybe I'll get something too." Jordyn pivoted on her heel, eyes already scanning the streets for signs of Gina. "Would you like me to pick up anything for you?"

"If I take one more sip of any of those weird cocktails, I'll go into a sugar coma." He patted her arm. "Thanks though."

"Sure thing. I'll catch up with you." She walked swiftly toward the clock, wondering if Gina had slipped into one of the buildings.

Most of the restaurants were open and a few of the shops, all doing a brisk business from the evening crowds. Jordyn peered into a bookstore and a bar. Then, at the next intersection, she glanced up and down the side streets.

Just in time to see a feminine figure slip into a side entrance a few hundred feet off the main road.

Could it be her?

Jordyn wouldn't be fast enough to identify the woman with any certainty. But once she reached the door for herself, she turned on her phone flashlight and spied the business's name on a call button mounted to one side of the entrance.

"Sideris Enterprises." She read the name aloud, hoping she wouldn't get caught on a security camera.

But her cover story was that she thought she saw Gina go inside here. Backing into the shadows further down the street, she told herself to wait a few minutes to see if the person exited again.

"Come on. Come on. Come on," she urged the figure inside, occasionally visible as the glow of a flashlight spinning across one of the windows. "What are you doing in there?"

The fact that the space must be the office for Luke's business probably increased the likelihood that it was Gina inside. After all, the two of them knew one another through Sophie. And Natalie had made a point of stressing that Luke was the greater source of Sophie's money. Maybe Gina wanted proof of the man's net worth to hand to her legal team while they sued Sophie.

Moments later, the door swung open again, and Gina Vallot stepped outside. Jordyn tucked deeper into the shadows, dragging in deep breaths of cool night air. Gina locked the door from the outside with a key before rearming the alarm system on the digital touchpad near the entrance. Then, after glancing in either direction up and down the street, she pulled out her phone and spent a couple of minutes reading whatever was on her screen.

Messages from her friends? A lover? Was she looking at photos taken while she'd been inside the building? That she had a key to the office and knew the code was interesting. What if Luke had evidence of Gina's involvement in Tara's death, and she'd tried to steal it back? She was reaching at straws maybe, but she'd been reeling ever since she'd learned that Gina had a hidden identity.

If the police had been more interested in solving the mystery of the hit-and-run in the first place, Jordyn would have been inclined to contact them now with her suspicions. But Natalie had raised a good point. What if the police simply confronted Gina with what Jordyn had already learned? There was no way to ensure the cops would protect Jordyn's privacy, and the whole truth about her connection to Tara could come tumbling out. Any edge Jordyn possessed by befriending the book club group would be lost, and they would close ranks.

That being said, she couldn't deny that she was starting to feel the full import of how dangerous her mission had become. Someone in Tara's book club or, at the very least, someone close to her, was responsible for her death. If anyone found out about Jordyn's past, would she be next on their list?

Surprised that Gina still hadn't made any move to rejoin the book club, Jordyn began to fidget in her hiding spot between two buildings. It was quiet down this side street, even though they were only a half a block from the festivities on Broadway. Jordyn didn't think there was an outlet behind her, the narrow alleyway completely dark. So she couldn't move without Gina seeing her, since her place of concealment was almost directly across the street from where the other woman stood.

A moment later, Jordyn heard quick footsteps heading their way. She held her breath, hoping the newcomer wouldn't notice her. As the footsteps drew closer, Gina pocketed her phone and stepped into the middle of the sidewalk as if to intercept them.

"You sure took your time," Gina greeted someone that Jordyn still couldn't see.

From the sultry tone of her voice, Jordyn suspected the person was a romantic interest.

She didn't have long to wonder. Because a moment later, Luke Sideris stepped into view, wrapping Gina in his arms and greeting her with a kiss that practically devoured her. By the time they were done, he had her backed up against the building, and he murmured words too muffled for Jordyn to hear.

But a minute later, Luke had the code deactivated again, and he opened the door with his own set of keys. He tugged

Gina into the darkened interior with him, his low growl giving way to her delighted laughter for a moment before the door slammed closed behind them.

Jordyn had no idea what to make of what she'd just witnessed, but at least she had one more piece of the puzzle that kept eluding her. Luke Sideris was an adulterer. And Gina—who had surely hated Tara as much as she must hate Sophie—seemed only too happy to lead him astray.

But what reason did Gina have for spying on Luke too? Was she using him to find dirt on Sophie to leverage for revenge? Could she be cultivating Luke as an accomplice in whatever scheme she had cooked up?

Now that the street was quiet once again, Jordyn stepped out of her hiding place and hurried to rejoin the others. Even though she had unearthed a juicy new clue about Gina, she wasn't done with her work tonight. She wanted to use this event to get closer to the book club members. Strike up conversations. Ferret out secrets.

Next up on her list? The grande dame herself. Tara's closest friend in Saratoga. The woman whose husband was busily undressing someone else.

Sophie Durand.

CHAPTER

15

Tara

One Year Ago

"SOPHIE, ARE YOU almost ready?" Tara checked her watch for the third time in as many minutes as she paced her business partner's kitchen. She was already dressed in her costume for the Witch Walk, her face painted green and a prosthetic nose in place. Sophie had greeted her at the front door five minutes earlier but said she needed a few minutes to put on her costume. "We're going to be late for the zombie flash mob dance if we don't get out the door soon."

Instead of a response from Sophie, her friend's younger daughter walked into the kitchen wearing turquoise-colored leggings and a long ivory sweatshirt. Amelia had one eye on her phone, but she must have caught sight of Tara in her peripheral vision because she did a double-take.

"Auntie T, you look terrifying." The girl had started calling Tara her "aunt" the same year Tara and Sophie had started hanging out.

At first, Tara had assumed she must do the same with all of Sophie's friends, but she'd been all the more flattered when she'd realized that somehow she was the only one given the title.

"Thank you." Tara preened, spinning on the heel of one black lace-up boot to show off her outfit. "I was inspired by the classic Bugs Bunny cartoon character Witch Hazel."

"Hmm." Amelia pocketed her phone to touch one of the "flying" bobby pins that Tara had attached to an invisible hair net. "You realize you're playing right into the patriarchy's attempts to depict powerful women with knowledge as grotesque creatures?"

Tara pouted as she smoothed her hands over the purposely tattered blue fabric of her long dress. "I created this in protest of all the sexy witch costumes I saw online."

Amelia quirked an eyebrow at her. "Damned if you don't. Damned if you do. Welcome to womanhood."

"Spoken like a fifteen-year-old going on forty-five." Tara leaned her broomstick against the massive stone fireplace built into one wall of the kitchen. "And why aren't you dressed for the Witch Walk?"

"Have you met my mother?" The teen scowled as she tugged open one of the huge side-by-side refrigerator doors in Sophie's spotless kitchen. "She's letting Charlotte dance in the flash mob, but apparently she doesn't believe people *my* age should have fun. Our time is better spent studying for trigonometry exams than developing social skills."

"Oh. Sorry." Tara checked her watch again to hide her expression in case her face had turned judgy. She had no business weighing in on anyone's parenting, of course, but she'd witnessed plenty of occasions where Sophie expected her daughters to excel at everything.

From the hallway, Sophie chimed in a moment before she breezed into the room. "Dearest daughter, you had too much homework tonight, and you know it. You will thank me in your valedictorian speech."

Dressed in a ruby red lace gown with lipstick to match, Sophie appeared camera-ready. It was the most colorful garment that Tara had ever seen her minimalist friend wear.

"You look gorgeous." Tara held her arms out to give her friend a hug.

Thankfully, Luke was nowhere to be seen tonight. Tara had avoided two of his calls since their conversation in the garden, hoping he would just leave her voicemails, but no such luck. She knew she couldn't avoid him forever. Especially since she'd told him she would appreciate any warning about Sophie's maneuverings with their business.

"You look every bit as frightening as I'm sure you intended." Sophie smiled at her as she stood back to take in Tara's outfit. She gave no notice to her daughter as Amelia stomped out of the room. Instead, she bit her lip before saying, "In my rush, I forgot my cape upstairs. Tara, would you do me a huge favor and grab it off the back door of my closet while I find Luke to give him some instructions for Amelia's study schedule? I know we're running behind."

"Sure thing. I'll be right back." Tara walked lightly on the marble floors, always convinced she'd leave a scuff mark no matter what shoes she wore.

Sophie's mammoth primary suite loomed at the top of the stairs, a sanctuary even larger than Lauren's huge bedroom. Sophie had left the closet door open and the lights on. Not that Tara needed help finding the way. She and Sophie had gotten ready for events together in the ensuite bathroom before, trading makeup advice like they were still Tara's daughters' ages.

Back when she'd still trusted her friend.

At first, she didn't see the cape that Sophie mentioned. She pulled one door partway closed to see if there was a hook on the other side but found no cape there either.

Hurrying, she walked to the chest of drawers in the center of the closet, where a clear glass top allowed her to look down at all of her friend's jewelry inside a locked drawer. Deeper in the closet, she spotted a small gray chaise lounge with a dark purple garment draped over it. She picked it up and shook it out to make sure she was really looking at a satin-lined velvet cape.

The wide hood and silky ribbons assured her she'd found the correct piece. She reached for a small lamp on one of the built-in dressers, switching it off out of habit, since she'd never been able to leave a room with all the lights on.

As she turned to leave, a unique shade of green caught her eye in Sophie's closet that mostly consisted of camel, taupe, gray, or navy. The garment was somewhere between moss and olive, a shade friendly to redheads like Tara. But a hue she couldn't ever recall seeing on neutral-loving Sophie.

Her heart beat faster as she moved toward the padded hanger at the far end of the rod. Tara's hand went to the fabric, knowing even before she touched the dress exactly how it would feel against her skin. She already knew how it was cut.

Because Tara had a dress exactly like this at home.

The same one that a mystery woman had been wearing in that incriminating photo with Mei's husband, Nikolai.

CHAPTER 16

Jordyn

Present

BY THE TIME Jordyn rejoined the book club members at Congress Park, the festive atmosphere had kicked up a notch. The group congregated in a cobblestone area around one of the park's fountains. Kaitlin and Destiny were engaged in a friendly argument over the correct moves for some kind of line dance, while Brad monopolized Mei's attention as he related the long and convoluted storyline of a sci-fi thriller he'd just finished. Fatima and Sophie were discussing the odds their daughters' lacrosse team would make it to the state finals, while also critiquing which of the student athletes had the most difficult parents.

If Jordyn hadn't had an agenda tonight, she would have joined the dance discussion since she happened to have watched a handful of TikTok videos on that very subject last spring. But single-minded in her mission, she joined Sophie and Fatima instead. Sophie had proven the most difficult book club member to get to know. And no matter that Gina Vallot had pulled into the front runner position in Jordyn's suspicions about Tara's death, Sophie remained high on her list too.

That meant Jordyn had work to do.

"When does the lacrosse season start?" she asked, hoping to insert herself into the discussion.

The Witch Walk revelers were thinning out in the park, but a small group held a drum circle nearby, providing a backdrop of thumping and chanting.

"The season never stops," Fatima informed her at the same time Sophie said, "Late winter."

"Ah. I'm not much of an athlete, so I give them a lot of credit for keeping up with a sport." Jordyn tugged her black scarf closer as a cold breeze chilled her. "But I've been meaning to ask you about the next book club. Do guests typically bring dishes to share? Or should I just come armed with wine?"

Sophie waved to someone walking past before answering. Jordyn wondered if it was another parent of school-aged kids, since Fatima stepped away to speak to the couple.

"No need to contribute anything at all. I'll have everything covered. The costume assignments were all generated at random by the company that created the murder mystery game. Even I won't know who is coming as what character."

"Oh really?" Jordyn had opened the email with her costume assignment two days before and had spent half an hour trying to find the right clothes for her character, who was described as a "nerdy scientist." "I've never played a game like this."

"This will be a first for me, too." Sophie gestured with her hands, spreading her fingers in a show of innocence. "I wasn't sure how it would go over with the book club, but everyone is excited about the idea."

"I am, too," Jordyn enthused, even as she privately marveled at the way women like Sophie seemed to take praise and admiration as their due. Jordyn hadn't really dealt with a Queen Bee personality since her days in the occasional foster group home where the reigning characters were tough and streetwise as opposed to wealthy and privileged. Yet there were similarities. Both liked having their egos stroked. But Jordyn wasn't here for that. "You're not worried that the murder aspect will be triggering for some of the members? What with Halloween being the anniversary of your friend's death?"

Sophie's attention was focused on the couple still speaking to Fatima, so Jordyn didn't have the benefit of witnessing her reaction head-on. But even in profile view, she could see the slight narrowing of Sophie's gaze before her expression cleared. Then she turned to face Jordyn.

"I think it will be an act of self-care for us to spend the evening together, distracting one another from our grief." The woman seemed to take Jordyn's measure anew, reassessing her.

Wondering, perhaps, if she could disinvite her?

Jordyn decided to dial it back.

"I'm sure you're right. As an only child, I didn't have anyone to grieve with when my mom passed. I'll bet it is comforting to have a friend group to share memories with."

If she had feared Sophie might ask her questions about her mother or her personal background, she needn't have worried, because Sophie merely gave an imperious nod. Affirming Jordyn's opinion while maintaining distance.

"I should probably find Luke—" Sophie began.

"What was she like?" Jordyn blurted over the other woman's words, unwilling to end the interaction just yet. "Your friend Tara?"

Sophie peered at her silently, as if trying to decide whether or not to dignify the question with an answer. In the quiet between them, Jordyn heard the drum circle slowing their rhythm. Nearby, an event tram rolled to a stop to ferry pedestrians back to parking lots. Closer to them, Destiny and Kaitlin were now demonstrating line dance moves for Brad and Mei, who clapped their approval.

"She was a beautiful soul," Sophie said finally, holding Jordyn's gaze. "That rare friend who has a generous heart and absolutely no agenda."

The words sounded so sincere, so truly reflective of Tara's character, that for a moment Jordyn couldn't even reply. A pang of loss clutched at her chest.

"I had a friend like that once. I felt fortunate to have her in my life, even though it was only for a short time," she said, her throat closing with grief. She felt a pain she couldn't quite push through. Regardless, Jordyn suspected she wouldn't obtain any more information from Sophie this evening. Clearly, she wasn't the sort of woman who shared confidences more easily after a few drinks.

Sophie Durand exuded icy control at a time Jordyn struggled to blink away the threat of tears.

A burst of laughter interrupted their strange stare-off, and Kaitlin ambled over to link an arm through Sophie's.

"Are you ready to head back, Soph?" Kaitlin had pulled off the red wig she'd been wearing earlier, and she spun it on one finger like a top, her movements loose and a little wobbly. "Mei said Nikolai will be our designated driver. He's just up the street."

"That sounds good since Luke seems to have disappeared." Sophie's face remained a mask. Her tone even.

Did she have any clue what her husband got up to when he vanished on occasions like this?

"Gina never came back either," Brad remarked blithely, tugging off his David Bowie glitter wig. He ran his fingers through his own hair before he winked at Jordyn as if they shared a secret. "I wonder why?"

His musings could have been lost in a sudden exchange of hugs as the group broke up for the night. But Jordyn hadn't missed the words, and she would bet that Sophie hadn't either.

Clearly Brad got his jabs in where he could.

"Did you need a ride?" Brad asked Jordyn, while the rest of them followed Mei toward her husband's waiting vehicle.

Traffic was already thinning out on the access road around the park. They'd stayed later than most of the revelers, or maybe the hardcore partiers had moved onto the bars.

"No thanks. I'm in the parking garage. How about you?"

"I rode my bicycle." He pointed in the opposite direction of where she was headed. "But I'm happy to walk with you—"

"That's okay. I'll be fine." She would keep one eye out for sightings of Gina or Luke on her way back. "I'll see you at book club?"

He was already backing away toward the bike stand. "I wouldn't miss it. Something tells me this next meeting is going to be full of fireworks."

Was it her imagination or had his grin seemed momentarily vengeful?

Alone again, Jordyn was glad for the time to think through what she'd learned tonight as she retraced her steps back up Broadway. Brad had more of an edge than she'd realized. If he still nursed a grudge against Sophie, had he been equally angry with Tara?

As for Sophie, no matter what glowing admiration the woman expressed about Tara, her aspect hadn't matched the words. Maybe that had more to do with the fact that she hadn't appreciated Jordyn asking questions about her friend than any old resentments she had toward her one-time business partner.

A partner she no longer had to worry about.

How much had Sophie's net worth increased when she went from owning half of *The Clean Break* to the whole thing?

Reaching the intersection where she'd witnessed Gina and Luke kissing like the survival of the human race depended on their immediate coupling, Jordyn saw the Sideris Enterprises building remained dark. No sign of Sophie's husband or his mistress on the street either.

She continued toward the parking garage, keeping pace with the other pedestrians headed in the same general direction. She withdrew her phone from her pocket to keep her occupied while she walked behind a couple of older witch-women. They each used canes, but they were dressed to the nines for the event. One of them wore black satin pants with wide swathes of purple fabric sewn around her calves in decorative flounces. Jordyn hoped she dressed that well when she was their age.

Scrolling through her messages, she ignored two new ones from Ezra before she spotted a voicemail from the probate attorney.

Finally.

She brought her phone to her ear to hear the message privately.

"Hello, Jordyn; it's Emily. We can talk more tomorrow, but I knew you were anxious to learn as much as you could about Tara's estate. Her assets have been frozen while the investigation into her death continues, which you already knew. But I learned definitively that a portion of *The Clean Break* was not included in the list of her assets. Most of her income came from a trust fund that paid out monthly, with the payments halting on her death. She didn't own a home, so a couple of cash accounts represent the bulk of her estate. I'm sending you a secure link to access my notes. Call me in the morning if you want clarification on anything."

She still couldn't conceive how Sophie had wrested full ownership of the business away from Tara right before her death.

Or had it been right after?

She needed to research partnerships more to understand the legalities better.

The street had cleared by the time she neared the parking garage, and she played the second voicemail message from a number she didn't recognize.

"Jordyn, it's Lauren Hughes," a low feminine voice began. "I'm in Manhattan for three days with Randall. If you still wish to speak, you can call this number to set up a time to meet when my husband is out. I'm not comfortable speaking over the phone. He wants no part of what you're doing, so this would be strictly confidential." There was a protracted pause. "As in, I'll deny ever having spoken to you."

The message ended abruptly.

Tara's adoptive mother was ready to talk?

Jordyn would be on the first train to the city tomorrow if it meant an audience with one of Tara's tight-lipped parents.

By the time Jordyn arrived back at the parking garage, she was still guessing what kind of information Lauren might have about her daughter's death. Jordyn climbed the deserted stairwell up to the top level where she'd parked her vehicle. As her footsteps echoed in the dark, she momentarily wished she'd accepted Brad's offer to accompany her to the car.

Because her little silver coupe sat all by itself, half of it in shadow, the security light busted out. It definitely hadn't been like that when she'd parked earlier. She would have noticed the glass on the concrete, especially since it fanned closer to her driver's side tires.

Anxiety skittered up her spine.

Mindful of her surroundings, she dropped her phone back into her pocket and retrieved her keys. She adjusted her hold on them, sliding a key between each of her fingers so that she had a makeshift set of spikey brass knuckles if someone approached her. It wasn't much protection, but it was something.

She walked carefully around as many of the shards as she could but in the end had to step on some of them to open the driver's side door. Old survival instincts kicking in, she grabbed her phone again to turn on the flashlight feature and peered into the backseat. *Empty.* Her heart still raced even as she breathed a sigh of relief. She bolted into her small coupe and locked the doors behind her.

Only then did she notice the piece of paper stuck under the windshield wiper. The torn scrap was pinned facing her so that she could see the writing in black sharpie.

Go home before you end up like her.

CHAPTER

17

Tara

One Year Ago

By the time Tara and Sophie arrived at the Witch Walk, they had just missed the zombie flash mob dance in Congress Park. The event was so busy, they'd had to wait for one of the small buses to transport them from the parking area to the grassy area near the fountain where the zombie antics were to take place.

But even as they hurried over they heard the dance music come to an end and spontaneous applause break out among the gathered onlookers.

"Don't let on that we were late," Sophie warned Tara quietly as the dancers melted back into the crowd. "Charlotte would be disappointed if she thinks we didn't see her." Then, raising her voice, she waved to a tall blonde, the teenage version of herself. "Charlotte, darling. Over here."

Tara schooled her features into a happy greeting even as she wondered if all mothers told lies to keep the household peace. She could envision Lauren doing so with ease, of course. But her memories of her birth mother long ago were much different. She'd been warm and kind though she hadn't sugarcoated the truth when it came time to share her cancer diagnosis with Tara.

"Hi, Mom! Hi, Auntie T." Even through pale face makeup, Charlotte's cheeks were flushed from pleasure or maybe exertion. She wore a tattered dress with ripped stockings and high boots. "What did you think?"

"You were wonderful," Sophie assured her, enveloping her in a hug. "The best zombie out there."

Tara took a turn hugging her friend's daughter. Unable to bring herself to tell an outright lie, she stuck with something innocuous. "Such a fun song to dance to."

"Right? Mom, we're going to walk down Broadway then go to Kennedy's house for a few, okay?" Charlotte beamed while a handful of friends surrounded her to offer congrats and show her photos they'd taken.

"That's fine, but be home by ten," Sophie reminded her. "You have morning sprints."

Some of Charlotte's shine diminished, but she nodded. "Of course. I won't be late."

"And stick together. All of you." Sophie's voice had an edge. She paused, as if to let the gravity of her warning sink in. "You can't be too careful."

Charlotte nodded. "I know. I will, Mom."

"Char, wait up." Sareena Chamoun rushed past them, also dressed in zombie rags and face makeup. "I'm coming too."

The teens wandered off together while Fatima appeared at Sophie's elbow. She wore wide-legged purple pants with black cats embroidered around the hem.

"You do not fool me, Ms. Durand. You did not see one second of the performance."

The other book club members materialized around them, all garbed in varying degrees of witchiness. Brad swooped in, Merlin-style, his dark gray robes and wooden walking stick making him look like he'd just walked off the famous Led Zeppelin album.

"I invoke my Fifth Amendment right," Sophie told Fatima serenely. "Now, where are we headed?"

Destiny stepped forward to point the way toward a local landmark. She wore a silver crown with spikes and a high-necked cape over a purple dress like the evil queen from Snow White. "The Canfield Casino is open for another half hour. Let's grab drinks at the bar and then check out the band at Caroline Street Pub."

"Sounds like a plan." Kaitlin gave a thumbs-up before looping her arm through Mei's to start walking in that direction.

Mei's headless bride costume made her seem six and a half feet tall. She must have been looking out through the neck of the bridal dress while she held a doll's head under one arm.

Tara would have complimented the originality of the outfit if Mei hadn't immediately turned away from her. Clearly Mei was still nursing a grudge in the mistaken belief Tara had spent time with her husband. The rebuff hurt, but Tara knew she should be using this time to confront Sophie anyhow. She'd been too freaked out by seeing the damned dress in Sophie's closet to come up with a way to broach the subject on their ride over to the Witch Walk. But maybe now was the right time.

She hastened her step to catch up with Sophie as the group headed toward the three-story Renaissance Revival structure that had been a landmark since its construction over one hundred and fifty years ago. The building often appeared on ghosthunters' lists for one of the most haunted places in the

United States, which was probably why the city had opened the venue for the Witch Walk.

"Tara, I want you to meet someone." Fatima's voice halted her just before she reached Sophie.

Turning, Tara saw Fatima next to a pretty stranger, a petite blonde with brown eyes and elfin features, dressed like a steampunk witch. She wore a black top hat covered in black feathers with a band of silver gears around the brim. A velvet choker with a pendant shaped like an alarm clock hung around her throat.

"I love your outfit," Tara exclaimed, admiring the black gown that looked like it came out of an authentic Victorian dress shop as opposed to a fast-fashion factory. Belatedly she stuck out her hand and smiled. "I'm Tara Hughes."

"Gina Vallot." The other woman squeezed her hand briefly, her expression inscrutable. "It's really nice to meet you. I met Fatima at a 10K race a couple of weeks ago, and she invited me to your book club."

Something about her inflection hinted that she wasn't from New York. Not quite southern. Not quite northern either. But she spoke so softly it was hard to tell.

"Gina sacrificed her race time to help me when I turned my ankle," Fatima explained. "I would probably still be limping home, if she hadn't offered me an arm."

"That was good of you." Tara made idle chitchat for another few minutes, all the while keeping an eye on Sophie to see when she could corner her privately about that dress hidden in her closet. Gina spoke of being a Florida transplant and house hunting while renting a local condo. Apparently she worked as an independent stylist and had scored some jobs helping notable women in the area with their wardrobes.

Tara would have been more interested in talking fashion with her if she hadn't been stressing about the conversation with Sophie. Lately it seemed like relationship after relationship went up in flames for her because Tara avoided confrontation at all costs. She'd delayed questioning her mom about the events that had led to her dissociative episode because she'd known it would upset her. She hadn't stood up to Sophie about her questionable ethical decisions on *The Clean Break* for the same reason, and it had taken a significant toll on her relationship with Kaitlin after Sophie had cut her out of the show. She suspected Brad harbored ill will too, though he went through the outward motions of friendship with her.

Now, this thing with Mei.

So when Luke left Sophie's side, Tara spotted her chance.

"I can't wait to talk more at book club," she assured Gina, hoping Fatima didn't think she was being rude. "But I just remembered a business item I forgot to mention to Sophie earlier today. Will you excuse me?"

"Of course. No worries." Gina replied in her soft voice with a wave of her lace-gloved hand. "We'll be seeing a lot of each other in the coming year, I hope."

As Tara slipped away, she could hear Fatima explaining to Gina about the podcast, which Tara appreciated. At least with Gina, Tara would have a clean slate to try and forge a friendly relationship.

She caught up to Sophie while she stood in front of a book shop window strung with lights in the shape of skulls and pumpkins. As she reached her friend's side, Luke's words ran through her mind like a warning.

My wife is ten steps ahead of you.

"Hey, Soph, I wanted to ask you about something." Tara took the same approach now that she had with her parents. Dive right in. Don't give herself time to get even more nervous than she already felt. "Mei showed me a photograph of a woman with Nikolai who looked a little like me because of a dress she was wearing."

Sophie didn't even glance up from the display. She pointed toward a gray leather journal in the store window. "That one's pretty."

Irritation fired through her. "Mei is angry with me, even though the woman in the photograph wasn't me."

Now Sophie straightened from her scrutiny of the merchandise. She met Tara's gaze. "I'm sure she'll get over it. As you pointed out, that wasn't even you in the photo."

It took all her courage to continue.

"I have reason to believe *you're* the one in that photo, Sophie. I saw the same green dress in your closet tonight when I retrieved your cape for you." Relieved to have the accusation in the open, she braced herself for whatever excuse Sophie made.

She was not prepared for Sophie's amused laughter.

"As if I had any need of a man like Nikolai Moskol in my life. No offense to Mei, of course." Turning on her heel, she resumed walking.

Tara did too. She felt flustered and ill-equipped to deal with her friend. Or could she even call her that anymore? Maybe Luke had a point when he warned her that his wife was going to run Tara out of their shared business.

"Whether or not you need him is beside the point. Why would you dress up as me? Even your hair was the same color as mine."

"Women play dress up all the time." Sophie tugged on her cape to illustrate her point. "But I'll keep in mind that you have the market cornered on red hair and green dresses in the future, okay?"

Was that an admission?

Breathing deeply and exhaling slowly, Tara struggled to remain calm. She worked hard to channel the voice of her therapist before her anxiety turned to panic.

"It's far from okay. I don't understand why you would deliberately disguise yourself to look like me to spend time with a married man."

For a long moment, Sophie didn't respond. But when they came to the intersection with Caroline Street and the group ahead of them turned down it toward the pub, Sophie finally spoke.

"I'm not saying it was me. But given how inclined you are to toy with *other* women's husbands, perhaps you shouldn't be so quick to cast stones."

Tara's stomach dropped. Sophie knew about Luke? That kiss? The idea rattled her to her core. Especially since Sophie had just assumed that there was more to it than Luke making unwanted advances.

Tara wanted to explain herself, but Sophie had already walked away, calling to Fatima to wait for her.

In the meantime, Tara's knees felt like water. She couldn't have rejoined the group and made polite conversation with the others tonight if she tried. Not when she felt the physical symptoms of a panic attack coming on. She needed to leave now. First thing in the morning, she would talk to the attorney her father recommended. Find a way to protect her business interests in *The Clean Break* as soon as possible.

Because one thing had become crystal clear to her tonight.

Sophie Durand was no longer her friend.

Worse? Maybe she never had been.

CHAPTER

18

Jordyn

Present

AFTER WAKING UP before dawn to catch a train from Albany into Manhattan, Jordyn stepped off the platform into Moynihan Train Hall at Penn Station. Right into total sensory overload. The commuter hour Empire Service was touted as the fastest rail route of the day, which meant it had taken less than two and a half hours to make the trip to New York City. But it dumped her off into Midtown during the morning rush.

Being a New Yorker born and bred, Jordyn wasn't fazed by the sudden crush of coffee-carrying Bluetooth users walking at breakneck speed. Even though the crowds around Madison Square Garden weren't the kind of thing she encountered in the Crown Heights neighborhood in Brooklyn where she'd grown up. It would have been faster for her to take the subway straight from the train station to the Plaza Hotel where she was supposed to meet Lauren Hughes, but she figured the walk would do her good. She needed to shake off the queasy feeling caused by finding that note on her car the night before.

Had it been from Tara's killer?

The idea that someone knew who Jordyn was and why she was in town had made her triple-check the locks on the carriage house before going to bed. She'd also texted a photo of the note to Natalie, so maybe the PI could help her figure out who'd placed it on her windshield.

So with a new sense of danger looming around Saratoga, the walk in Manhattan among a million strangers helped Jordyn to relax a little. Plus, when she phoned Lauren half an hour ago to set up a time to meet today, Tara's mother had been insistent that she couldn't meet until after nine AM. The walk up Seventh Avenue would fill the minutes until then.

Maybe Jordyn could savor some happier memories while she was at it. She'd been here with Tara once. By the time Tara reached her second summer at the foster home, Jordyn had become an expert at working the system. Not for herself but for Tara, she'd made the extra effort. She'd been worried during the school year what the summer would be like for her friend since the lack of activities and structure left the kids in the home with too much time on their hands. Which might translate to harassment. Fights. Unfit parents showing up at the home trying to take back their kids.

So Jordyn had applied for two free spots at a YMCA summer camp, writing an essay with hand-drawn illustrations. She'd nabbed the slots for herself and Tara, which kept them out of the house every day that summer, taking swimming lessons, making crafts, playing games. Their age difference put them in separate groups, but at the end of the season, all the campers went to Central Park Zoo together. An outing Jordyn would never forget.

That day came back to her in vivid detail as she dodged stalled tourists taking photos in Times Square. She and Tara had petted baby goats and watched the sea lions sunning themselves. There'd been a grizzly bear and a polar bear, peacocks and parrots. Afterward, they ate lunch near a playground in the park where there were enough swings for everyone who wanted one. No squabbles over one ratty swing. The whole day had felt weirdly normal. Like if she closed her eyes, they could have been any two real, full-blooded sisters on a summer trip.

Later in life, she'd had a sunflower-covered swing tattooed on her shoulder. That one had been done by a professional with a machine, whereas the labyrinth on her forearm was something she'd created herself as a teen using the stick and poke technique with pen ink. The maze had been a promise to herself that she could navigate the foster system and be free of it one day. While the swing had been a reminder that there *had* been good moments in her childhood.

By the time she reached the southern edge of Central Park at Fifty-Ninth Street, Jordyn felt energized and ready to talk to Lauren Hughes. The memories had grounded her, reminding her why finding Tara's killer was so important. Jordyn might not have been able to protect her friend from whatever suburban danger had come for her on Halloween night. But she could still vindicate her.

She sidestepped the horse-drawn carriages lined up to give tours of the park and bypassed the side doors of the hotel so she could go through the famous front entrance by the fountain. Inside, the black, gold and white décor was every bit as swanky as she'd imagined with a champagne bar tucked in one corner.

Lauren had told her to go to the front desk to pick up an envelope with a keycard to access the guest floors. That accomplished, Jordyn strode directly to the elevators and hit the call button to head to the twentieth floor. Even the elevators were extra fancy, with ornate gold in front of narrow columns of mirror.

A moment later, she texted Lauren that she'd arrived, and by the time she reached the end of the corridor, Tara's stunning, intimidating mother was already standing in the open doorway.

"I didn't think you'd really come here," Lauren said by way of greeting, her long dark hair and model good looks giving her a Demi Moore vibe. She wore wide-legged ivory trousers and a long menswear blazer in the same shade.

Jordyn bristled at the toneless greeting.

"I didn't think you'd ever invite me."

They sized one another up for a moment, the silence stretching. At last, Lauren pulled the door open wider.

"Come on in."

Stepping across the threshold into the suite, Jordyn could see the view of Central Park through a window. A couch and two chairs were grouped nearby, a low table bearing sparkling waters and fruit in the center of the seating arrangement. The bedroom door was slightly open to one side, the visible king-sized bed already made.

"Have a seat." Lauren gestured to the chairs, but Jordyn took the corner of the couch, leaving her hostess with her choice of the less comfortable seats.

Petty. But Mrs. Hughes had been far from cooperative so far.

"Thanks. I was surprised to receive your call after all the times you refused to talk to me."

"That was Randall's doing, not mine." Lauren leaned forward to open one of the sparkling water bottles and filled the two glasses on the silver tray that held a basket of grapes and apples. "He worries about negative publicity hurting his businesses."

Jordyn had to swallow a bitter retort, knowing she needed this woman's cooperation if she wanted to wrest any meaningful information out of this visit.

"Do you see your daughter as a media liability as well?" That came out sharper than intended, but these entitled people looking out for their own interests to Tara's detriment made Jordyn every bit as feisty as when she'd punched Ronnie McRory in the face for secretly pouring grain alcohol into Tara's soda on her thirteenth birthday.

Jordyn couldn't figure out why her friend had been sick all night long until she heard Ronnie laughing about it with his friends at school the next day.

"I respect that my husband's ability to make sound business decisions has afforded me a very comfortable life. It gave Tara a good life too."

"Not anymore."

Lauren looked down at her hands in her lap. Her voice was softer when she spoke again. "No. Not anymore."

It was the first hint of emotion she'd witnessed from either of the Hughes since Tara's death. There certainly hadn't been any sense of remorse in the legalese-laden missives she'd received from their lawyers. Glimpsing the woman's grief now made Jordyn's defensiveness thaw a bit.

"I'm . . . um . . . sorry to be so blunt." She fumbled for words, uncomfortable in million-dollar suites with people who moved through worlds far different than her own. "I'm just eager for answers to Tara's death and I'm here because I really need to know if you have any insights into what might have happened. Or what her life was like in the weeks before she died."

Lauren met her gaze directly, any hint of softer emotions gone. "And I invited you here because I want answers too."

Well. All right then.

Jordyn straightened in her seat, sensing a potential ally in the very last place she'd expected to find one.

"Tara spent that last evening with her book club. Are you familiar with any of the people in that group?" Jordyn asked.

"Only in a peripheral sense. My daughter didn't confide a lot of the personal details of her life to me." She paused, a wistful expression briefly crossing her face. "Saratoga is small enough that the residents who live there year-round tend to run into one another."

"So you don't necessarily suspect anyone in particular from the book club?"

"Absolutely not." The woman practically vibrated with indignation. "If I had any concrete suspicions, I assure you, I would have voiced them to the police."

Jordyn tried to parse out the meaning behind the careful phrasing.

"Do you have suspicions that are less than concrete?"

Lauren scoffed. "When you're desperate to blame someone, everyone looks guilty. But I can tell you that Tara seemed nervous about her partnership with Sophie Durand in the weeks before her death."

"What do you mean 'nervous'?"

"She asked Randall to recommend an attorney to put together a partnership agreement for her work with Sophie." Lauren withdrew a business card from the pocket of her ivory-colored blazer and passed it to Jordyn. "I'm not sure if Arnie will tell you anything, but this is the lawyer Randall recommended."

Jordyn's thoughts fired fast, having learned that Tara had been trying to shore up her business agreement with Sophie so close to her death. Had Sophie bought out Tara rather than agree to the partnership terms?

"I'll look into that, thank you," Jordyn said as she pocketed the card. "But when you wanted to arrange a time to speak *confidentially*, I had the impression you had something specific you wanted to share."

Lauren lifted one of the water glasses and took a small sip before nodding. "Tara had been on a quest to recover her memories. You know that since she reached out to you after she remembered more about her time in foster care."

"She told me she had dissociative amnesia. Something happened to make her lose most of the details from two full years of her life."

Jordyn was not proud to admit that when Tara had first confided this the day they reconnected she had briefly wondered if Tara was trying to make excuses for the fact that she hadn't contacted her for a decade and a half. But the longer they spoke, the more Jordyn could hear the sincerity of the friend she'd once known beneath the more refined speech and pretty social manners. Tara wouldn't lie to her about forgetting a portion of her past.

"Precisely. She seemed to recover memories in the reverse order from the point of trauma. The oldest first, and then as time went by she gained more memories closer to the . . . episode."

Jordyn felt her eyebrows shoot up, surprised.

"Have you known all along what caused the memory loss?"

Lauren's chin notched up a fraction. "I did. And I honestly believed that allowing her to forget was the kindest possible way of dealing with a horrible, traumatic memory."

"What happened?"

Sighing deeply, Lauren closed her eyes for a moment. “When we first brought Tara home, my then eighteen-year-old stepson, Evander, attempted to touch her . . . inappropriately.”

A ringing started in Jordyn’s ears. A warning system that was useless now since she hadn’t been around to protect her friend.

“When she was fourteen?” Jordyn’s blood simmered, anger twisting her insides.

Why the hell was this the first she’d heard about it? She knew for a fact that Randall Hughes’s heir had no criminal record. Far from it. The articles she’d read about the family all said Evander Hughes was now the CEO of the pharmaceutical company his father had helped to grow.

“Yes. But before you get the wrong idea, he didn’t exactly get away with it.”

“That you know of.” Jordyn bolted upright out of her chair, unable to sit still to hear a story that made her want to punch a wall. “How many times do you think he assaulted her after that when you weren’t around to intervene? How could you—”

“Jordyn. Please.” Lauren stood too, inserting herself into the path that Jordyn was attempting to pace. “Listen to me. He didn’t get away with it because she . . . stabbed him.”

Jordyn’s feet stumbled to a faltering stop. “Excuse me?”

“It was awful.” Lauren stepped away from her and leaned a shoulder against the window looking out over the park. “She picked up a letter opener from Randall’s desk and stuck it right through the little shit’s hand. She cut herself too since Evander’s palm was on her leg when she stabbed him.”

“Oh my God.” Jordan struggled to take it in. This is what caused the dissociative episode. A horrific encounter with someone in her wealthy, glamorous adoptive family.

Nothing at all to do with her time in the foster home.

"She was traumatized. I knew it from the second I looked at her face that she was . . . I don't know. Going into shock maybe? Evander screamed like he was getting slaughtered, bleeding all over Tara. I had to . . ." She stopped. Her fingers went briefly to her mouth for a moment before she seemed to regain control again and continued. "I had to pry her fingers off the letter opener."

A string of soft curses floated from Jordyn's lips while she pictured her friend having to defend herself so brutally. Just when she must have thought she was finally going to have a happy, secure life. Her stepbrother had disabused her of any such notion.

"Poor, poor Tara." Jordyn let the revelation sink in, not quite ready to figure out how the incident connected to her friend's death. All she could do was empathize. Wish she'd been there to help. "But how could she possibly have forgotten it happened for all that time? Her bastard step sibling must have reminded her—"

"What kind of mother do you think I am? I never allowed him to be alone near my daughter again. That's what prompted my move out of the city to Saratoga, just a few weeks after we adopted her. I wouldn't let her in the same *zip code* as him without constant supervision."

But what about all the other girls he could have gone on to harm with predatory behavior? By not reporting him, Lauren had allowed him to continue endangering others. Jordyn stuffed down her anger, needing to keep Lauren talking.

"And in all those years, Evander never brought it up?"

"Randall made sure of that. While I lobbied for my husband to go to the police to file a complaint, that was never going to happen to his precious son. But Randall let Evander know his trust fund was contingent on staying away from

Tara." Lauren tore her attention from whatever she'd been staring at out the window. Her lips lifted slightly in a crooked smile. "The scar she gave him is something to behold. His grip never did return to normal."

Jordyn guessed that would have been a small consolation for what Tara had gone through, even if she had recalled inflicting that wound on him. Someone from her new, adoptive family tried to assault her. And she'd been so emotionally devastated that she'd had to block it out for nearly two decades.

"So did Tara ever remember what happened to her?" Jordyn recalled how hard her friend had worked with her therapist to regain her memories from the time she'd spent in the foster home. Unraveling her past had been important to her.

"She did. Just a day before her death." A visible shiver went through Lauren, her slender form shuddering.

"Do you think that's related in any way? Maybe she confronted her stepbrother. Could Evander have been the one behind the hit-and-run?"

"No. He and Randall were both on a flight to Singapore that night to meet with potential clients."

Jordyn made a mental note to verify that. She didn't trust Lauren to share the whole truth. Just because the woman seemed protective of her daughter didn't mean she'd made good choices.

"Then why do you think all of this is related to her death? How could recalling the truth about her past possibly get her killed, if her former tormentor had nothing to do with it?"

Jordyn felt like she'd been spinning in circles trying to figure out what had happened to her foster sister. It still amazed her that one of the kindest people she'd ever met could have so many potential enemies. For years before they'd reconnected, Jordyn had just assumed that Tara must have gone on to a great life after she left foster care. But if anything, being adopted by the Hughes had only landed her in a pit of vipers.

"I've thought about that a lot," Lauren admitted. "Tara called me after the therapy session that unlocked the memory for her and she sounded so . . . different."

"How? I don't understand." She needed to squeeze every possible detail from this woman, to absorb any maternal insight she had about what happened to Tara. Based on how long it had taken Lauren to come forward in the first place, Jordyn suspected today would be her one and only opportunity to glean information from the woman.

Lauren tapped a manicured fingernail on the windowsill. Tapping and thinking. "The news freed her somehow. She'd always been such a people pleaser and then, all of a sudden, she remembered this warrior side of herself. It was like it gave her permission to take on the world. Confront anyone and everyone who ever slighted her."

"Including you?" Jordyn wondered what kind of relationship Tara and her mother had really had.

She knew Tara had never felt like a full-fledged Hughes, but then again, she didn't seem to openly dislike her adoptive parents either.

"Hardly. Don't forget, I always knew that side of her was buried in her subconscious, and I respected it. I worked hard to make her feel safe under my roof. To give her a worry-free life." Lauren smiled sadly. "Looking back, I can see now that I tried to create a mini-me when I adopted her. She just wasn't interested in shopping and traveling the world. I thought briefly I might have influenced her decision to go to design school, but I think that was a direction she took just to please me because she never pursued fashion for a career."

Lauren spoke a little more about Tara's seemingly aimless career, taking marketing work and fashion merchandising jobs when she could have done "so much more." But Jordyn's focus remained firmly on what Lauren had said about Tara recovering the traumatic event that had caused dissociative amnesia.

A new picture of Tara's last days solidified in Jordyn's mind. Pieces of the murky puzzle began sliding into place, becoming clearer.

A very different Tara Hughes had attended that last book club meeting before her death. If what Lauren had said was true, then Tara hadn't been interested in people pleasing on that final night of her life. Far from it.

She'd gone to the meeting with scores to settle.

CHAPTER 19

Gina

Present

IN AN EFFORT to settle her heart rate after her morning run, Gina slowed her pace to a fast walk. The weather app on her phone had said the day would be warm for late October, almost sixty degrees. But right now, shortly after sunrise, a heavy mist shrouded Daybreak Hill in a veil of fog.

The school bus had already driven past, making the long trek up the hill daily even though Sophie's spoiled daughters usually caught a ride to class with friends or with their father. For now, Gina had the road to herself as she halted near Tara Hughes's memorial marker. As was her habit, she paused to clear away any fallen leaves from the site, ensuring the white cross remained visible.

The roadside marker served as a reminder to the community that life could change in an instant. Death. Divorce.

Revenge. Any of those destructive forces could rob an unsuspecting person of their dreams and illusions.

Gina was righting a fresh bouquet of daisies and sunflowers when her phone vibrated in the thigh pocket of her leggings. Dusting off her fingers before she checked the number, she recognized the law firm she could hardly afford.

"Please tell me you have good news," she said as she straightened. She continued walking toward her house, covering ground quickly.

"Mrs. Ribeki?" a man asked, his cultured tone betraying the slightest Louisiana accent.

The hint of Cajun made her homesick. She missed the bayou. Her family. The life she used to have.

"Yes, Denis. It's me," she clarified, glancing around as she reached her own driveway to ensure there were no cars parked there. That she was alone and wouldn't be overheard.

"I don't have any definitive news for you today. Our office received word that the Fourth Circuit Court of Appeal moved your case to next month after your ex-husband's attorney—"

"Next *month*?" She had been waiting for her appeal to be heard for eight months already.

Ever since she'd lost her initial civil suit protesting the arbitration agreement she'd signed when she went on Sophie's podcast.

"That's correct, ma'am. The court has a very full docket, and your ex-husband's attorney requested more time to gather supporting evidence—"

"Evidence of what? His infidelity? His need for twenty-five expensive sports cars so none of his mistresses ever have to ride in the same one?" The words fired out of her mouth before she could filter them, anger at the delay robbing her of all patience.

She recognized that she was being unfair. Unreasonable. But her fury had endless triggers these days. She'd actually thrown a glass at the television screen two nights ago when she'd witnessed a random couple speaking their vows in a sappy romantic movie. Hearing the promises to love forever—it still felt like a knife in her heart all this time after the fact. Thankfully only the drinking glass had broken and not the screen since she could hardly afford to replace the television.

"I realize this is frustrating, Mrs. Ribeki." The attorney's words were measured and he didn't seem surprised or offended by her outburst. "Delaying proceedings is, unfortunately, a common tactic in these kinds of cases."

"I'm sure Mark hopes that driving up my legal fees will make me back down." She paused beside an oak tree, leaning up against the stout trunk.

Was it foolish of her to pursue this? All of the lawyers she'd consulted with had discouraged her from moving forward with her lawsuit, pointing out that the whole point of arbitration was that it was binding.

Which she understood in theory.

Yet deep in her gut she believed that Sophie had betrayed the principles of being a good arbitrator by making her decision a popularity contest. It wasn't right, fair, or just. The woman had a legal obligation to make thoughtful and fair decisions to the best of her ability. If she couldn't do so, she didn't deserve to hold that license.

Denis Landry had at least agreed to take the case. They'd lost in the lower court, but she'd been waiting for months for the Court of Appeal to hear it. Now, she would be waiting for at least four more weeks.

Her lawyer's voice in her ear called her from her thoughts. "If that's all then, I'll be in touch next month—"

"Actually, I have one more question for you." She shoved away from the oak tree and headed toward the house, wanting to review the paperwork she'd discovered in Luke's office the night of the Witch Walk.

She'd used her phone to scan the documents and then printed off copies the next morning. Now, she punched in her door code and stepped through the front entrance into the foyer.

"Of course. How can I help?"

Gina didn't even bother toeing off her shoes since Denis seemed to bill her by the second. She moved toward the hutch and opened the drawer where she'd stashed the papers.

Her gaze scanned the insurance policy dated just this week. She'd highlighted the section that spelled out "immediate coverage."

"Is it legal to take out life insurance on a spouse without their knowledge?" When she'd researched the question online, the responses seemed to skirt the issue.

"That's not my area of the law," Denis demurred.

"I won't hold you to the answer. This isn't related to me personally." She tilted the papers toward a window nearby, her eyes still adjusting to the dimmer lighting indoors.

"If you're asking, I'm guessing you've already read the nebulous guidance about it online. Technically, you can buy insurance for someone if they agree and are aware of the policy."

Her heart rate quickened again. Not like when she'd been running. This thready pulse had more to do with the cold feeling in her gut.

"But unofficially, you've seen policies paid out even when the decedent was unaware?" The paper in her hand quivered. Making her realize she was trembling.

"Dead people can't exactly protest they were unaware of a life insurance policy that covers them. So there remains a chance that some policies are paid out that weren't obtained under the proper terms."

"I understand. Thank you, Denis." Gina's words came out in a breathless rush.

Before she could disconnect, the attorney added, "Are you concerned that your ex-husband still has a policy with coverage on you? Because if you have any reason to doubt your safety—"

"No. It's nothing like that," she assured him, even though she supposed Mark could have done exactly that without her knowing.

She seriously doubted it, however. Mark Ribeki may have proven himself an adulterous liar and a cheat. Yet his reputation seemed too important to him to risk his sports career for the sake of a life insurance payout.

"I'm glad to hear you say so." Denis sounded relieved as he gave a low chuckle. "It's never a good sign when someone takes out a life insurance policy in secret."

Gina didn't guess that it would be. Disconnecting the call, she set her phone aside.

In the dim light of the dining room, she ran a finger along the verbiage of a two-million-dollar life insurance policy that Luke Sideris had secured on his wife, Sophie Durand, pondering what had prompted Luke to purchase the coverage now.

Then, she shuffled that paper behind the second document she'd scanned that night in his office. A briefly worded consent form signed by Sophie.

Except that Gina knew there wasn't a chance in hell that the signature on the agreement had been penned by Sophie.

Because Gina had discovered yet another, third document right next to the other ones in Luke's office.

A notebook page full of penmanship attempts to recreate Sophie's distinctive scrawl.

Together, the papers were clear evidence that someone had worked to forge Sophie's signature on the consent form. Luke had purchased a high-paying insurance policy with immediate coverage on his wife's life. All of which made Gina realize that her lover was a far more dangerous man than she'd ever guessed.

What exactly did Luke have in store for Sophie?

CHAPTER

20

Tara

One Year Ago

"I WOULDN'T TRUST LUKE Sideris if my life depended on it." Tara adjusted her tablet in the stand on her dressing table, grateful for the chance to video chat with Jordyn before her meeting with the attorney her father had recommended. She ran an eyebrow brush through her lashes to separate them. "Why do you ask?"

She'd already put in a long day at the studio with Sophie, the air between them thick with tension as she tried not to recall their uncomfortable exchange at the Witch Walk. Sophie hadn't come out and accused her of anything inappropriate with Luke, but the implication had hung between them like a shadow all during the work day. Because of that new tension, Tara had no intention of confronting Sophie about *The Clean Break* partnership agreement without some counsel from a professional. Fortunately, Arnie had agreed to stop by her house to hammer out the details of an agreement that he would submit to Sophie on her behalf.

"Why do I ask?" Jordyn repeated, staring at Tara like she had two heads. "I guess because I was under the impression you liked him well enough. I thought maybe he could be a go-between for you and Sophie instead of you having to request her signature through legal channels. That's the whole reason you're meeting this lawyer tonight, right?"

On her end of the call, Jordyn sat in her pickup truck in a strip mall parking lot. A few businesses were visible in the background including something called "Third Eye Tattoos" and an herbalist with a storefront window covered in painted flowers. Jordyn sipped from a stainless steel to-go cup, the blue exterior covered in decals of anime characters and stickers of farm animals.

Tara felt a surge of affection for her foster sister who'd pulled off the road to fully focus on their conversation. With Tara's life in Saratoga Springs falling apart more every day, having somebody she could really count on meant the world to her. What might her life have been like if she'd recalled Jordyn sooner?

"That's true. The short answer is, yes, I used to like Luke well enough," Tara admitted, hedging a bit as she wondered just how much to impart. She hated to be that friend who was needy all the time, and she'd already dumped the Sophie situation into Jordyn's lap. She would save the full-blown Luke story for another time. For now, she shared just one crucial fact. "I recently learned he's not the loyal husband after all. It's tough to trust a guy who isn't forthright with his own spouse."

"Statistics show that's over half the population," said Jordyn, ever the cynic.

Tara didn't consider herself cynical so much as wary.

"I would actually consider myself fortunate if I could trust even half the people in my life." She searched her makeup drawer for a lip pencil she didn't need to use a sharpener on. She could only imagine her mother's horrified reaction to Tara's metric for choosing a lip color. "Even my mom is keeping secrets from me."

"It seems like things are getting complicated there," Jordyn observed, adjusting the visor in the vintage pickup truck. The movement cast her face in shadow. "You should consider another visit here to decompress. Or we could meet up somewhere between Saratoga and Austin. We could find a fun halfway point and have a friend weekend."

"That sounds really nice. Any other time, I'd be tempted to take you up on that." Tara blotted the lip liner. She wasn't normally super careful about her appearance, but right now it felt like one thing she could control in a world that seemed to be careening toward disaster. She couldn't have said why she had a nagging feeling of doom recently, but the sensation had been growing the last two weeks. "I'm a little hesitant to quit my therapy sessions right now, though. I feel like I'm close to a breakthrough."

"As in you're close to finding out what caused the dissociative amnesia?"

Tara realized Jordyn was the only person outside of her family who knew about her scrambled memories of the past. Because her parents had asked her not to contact anyone from her past or share her foster care experiences with her friends, Tara had only ever offered the simplest of adoption stories to people who asked about her past. Of course, that had been easier after the dissociative incident cast such a heavy cloud over much that followed. But now that she recalled that period of time, it seemed strange that no one else knew about it except for Jordyn.

Everything she'd recalled about her time in the foster home had been reasonably good. Sure, there'd been the occasional issue with a rough-around-the-edges kid, but Jordyn had always been by her side, sticking up for her. Assuring her she had a friend in her corner. It hadn't been the scary place that Lauren had allowed her to believe.

"I might be." Giving up on her makeup attempts, Tara shut the top drawer of her vanity and tucked one leg under the other to make herself more comfortable. She was better off confronting her problems head-on rather than facing them with the social mask in place. "When our last session ended, I felt close to capturing a memory but my therapist doesn't want to rush the process. She says it's important for me to have the tools to cope with whatever we uncover, so we're taking it slowly."

"That makes sense. I briefly worked with a mental health counselor who used EMDR therapy with me, and I found it really helpful."

Surprised to hear Jordyn's easy familiarity with the eye movement desensitization and reprocessing technique, Tara couldn't recall if she'd shared that's what her own therapist had been using to help her manage whatever trauma had caused the dissociation.

"You've never mentioned being in counseling before."

"My high school guidance office referred me for some free services a long time ago. Because I found it helpful, I've gone back every now and again, if I start feeling overwhelmed."

The vague response told her that Jordyn probably had no desire to speak about whatever personal demons she battled. Which Tara very much respected.

"I hope you know that if you ever want to talk, I'm here for you too." Tara cringed as she heard the words, realizing that it might sound like she was angling to hear more about something Jordyn didn't want to share. "Sorry that came out wrong. I just mean, I hope you think of me as part of your friend network."

Jordyn smiled as she settled her decal-covered travel mug into the truck console's cupholder. "I knew what you meant. Although you aren't really a *part* of my friend network so much as the network itself. As in, you're it."

That fit with her girlhood memories of Jordyn too. She had never seemed like the sort of person who needed a lot of confidantes in her life. Tara had been the sum total of people close to her back then as well. Maybe that had to do with Jordyn's parents dying young and leaving her to navigate foster care alone. Or maybe the tendency to be a loner was just Jordyn's innate personality.

"What about Ezra?" Tara asked, curious about their relationship.

Jordyn's live-in boyfriend had struck Tara as nice enough, but their personalities seemed like polar opposites. Ezra, the quiet numbers guy who drove a Texas-sized pickup truck, and Jordyn, the artsy graphic designer who'd tattooed her own skin with thousands of little cuts.

"I guess I've never mastered the art of turning a romantic relationship into a deeper bond. Have you?"

Something about the question, sincere and meaningful, underscored how different her rapport with Jordyn was from the other connections Tara had in her life. Despite the outward trappings of friendship she had with the book club, maybe her real friend network ran to just one person too.

"I suppose not," she replied, thinking of the handful of guys she'd allowed close to her over the years. "Do you think some of that is due to our experiences as orphans? You used to say the fewer people who are close to you, the fewer people there are to hurt you."

"Oh, yikes." Frowning, Jordyn shook her head. "Sorry if I heaped my own baggage on you back then."

"You didn't." Tara would have said more, but downstairs the doorbell rang. Arnie, the attorney her father recommended, must be here. Standing, she removed the tablet from its stand. "It was actually really good advice for that time period in my life when I needed to grow an extra layer of skin."

For that matter, maybe the advice was even more relevant now. She'd allowed too many people to get close to her, and she was paying a high price with companions who didn't have good intentions toward her.

Knowing what Sophie had done—dressing up like Tara to go out with another friend's husband in a mistaken belief that Tara had slept with Luke—still stunned her.

"Will you do me a favor and think about taking another trip here? Or meeting somewhere in between your place and mine?" Jordyn asked. "You might be glad for an outlet if you end up having that breakthrough in therapy."

Tara switched on the light over the stairway leading down to the foyer as she prepared to meet with the lawyer about the partnership agreement.

"I'll definitely give it some thought," she agreed. "But the attorney my father recommended is at the door now, so I'll check in with you soon."

Disconnecting the call, she took a deep breath, preparing to discuss business. To craft a detailed partnership agreement for the future of *The Clean Break*.

But when she pulled open the front door, the visitor standing in the gathering dusk was not the lawyer. At least, he sure didn't match up with the photo image that had been posted for Arnie on the legal firm's website. The picture had shown a slim, distinguished-looking older gentleman with silvering temples.

Instead, a tall, athletic-looking man stood on the step, his unruly curls still dark. He had muscles on top of muscles, apparent even through the canvas field coat he wore open over a white dress shirt. Despite his strong features and heavy eyebrows, there was something boyishly attractive about his ready smile.

"Tara Hughes?" The man glanced backward over his shoulder, almost as if he thought someone else might be out in the shadowed driveway. Watching them.

"Yes, I'm Tara." She wished she hadn't opened the door to a total stranger. Especially not one who looked strong enough to murder her *and* bury her body with one arm tied behind his back.

"Mark Ribeki." He thrust his hand out for her to shake. "I did *The Clean Break* podcast a few months ago. It's nice to finally meet you in person."

The cheating football player? The same one whose fans had voted for him to receive the lion's share of assets when he split with his ex-wife, Evangeline?

What the hell was he doing here?

"I'm sorry. I don't understand—"

"Would you mind if I come in?" He peered over his shoulder once more, his expression turning agitated. "There's something I really need to talk to you about."

CHAPTER 21

Jordyn

Present

Driving north from the Albany–Rensselaer train station after the day trip into Manhattan, Jordyn followed the directions in her GPS to the law office of Arnold Van Ness. She'd taken the first available Amtrak out of Penn Station for her return, but even so, she would barely make it to the legal firm before five PM. She hoped that Arnie kept regular hours or this visit to see him would be wasted.

And she really needed answers about Tara's appointment with him before her death. She remembered the video call with her friend the day Tara had planned to see him about the partnership agreement. She had seemed unusually down that day, making a comment about trusting fewer than half the people in her life.

If only Jordyn had known that danger had been lurking close to Tara.

She wished she could go back in time and ask her more questions. Find out all the reasons why she felt like she couldn't trust her own friends. Her own mother.

Although at least the meeting with Lauren had shed some light on that relationship.

"Your destination will be on the right," the GPS informed her belatedly, at the same moment she spotted the Van Ness Associates sign on Route 9.

Slamming on the brakes, she just barely made the turn into the parking area. The two-story commercial building seemed like an unusual spot for a law firm with a dry cleaner and a cupcake shop downstairs but what did she know? The address wasn't even technically Saratoga. Her location told her she was in a town called Malta.

As she locked up her vehicle, her cell phone vibrated with a call. She double-checked the caller ID since Ezra had stepped up his efforts to get in touch with her, leaving panicked warnings on her voicemail since he was convinced she'd somehow end up dead or jailed for her efforts to investigate Tara's death.

And maybe he had a point given the threatening note on her vehicle. She had no intention of sharing that with Ezra, but she would be more vigilant about her personal safety for sure.

This incoming call was from Natalie, however. She hit the button to accept even as she strode toward the office building.

"Hey there. Any news?"

"Not about the anonymous note," Natalie began. "And my official advice to you about that is to go to the police."

"I'm not ready to do that just yet." Jordyn had wrestled with the idea herself. But she also didn't want to blow her cover to the book club, and she worried that getting the cops involved would do just that. "What else do you have for me?"

"I spoke to a detective who was willing to share more about the paint chip the medical examiner found embedded . . ." Natalie paused a moment. "That is, the chip recovered from the hit-and-run scene. It's a very common black metallic paint used on two brands of luxury vehicles."

Jordyn swallowed hard, knowing that Natalie had tactfully refrained from referencing *where* the paint chip had been discovered on Tara's battered body. Her mangled legs? Her shattered hip? The visceral pain Jordyn felt in empathy for Tara's final minutes of life was very real, even if it didn't compare to what her friend had experienced.

Jordyn shivered from more than the brisk autumn wind.

"Have you checked the color against all the vehicles owned by book club members when Tara was killed?" She lowered her voice as she reached for the office door and found it unlocked. Stepping inside, she shrugged out of her jacket in the bright reception area with a couple of barrel chairs and a sleek front desk that remained vacant.

Behind the desk, the Van Ness name had been spelled out in large letters on a marble wall. Off to one side, an open door led to a connecting hall where she guessed the individual offices must be located.

"Three so far. Kaitlin Teal had an SUV that color then, although she did not renew the registration for it this year. And Fatima's daughter Sareena has one that's still on the road. I've seen that vehicle myself, and it doesn't show any signs of damage, but they could have had it fixed."

"You said there were three?"

"The motor vehicle department shows that Luke has two SUVs registered for commercial purposes by his business.

One of those is listed as having black paint, but I haven't actually seen either of them for myself to verify."

"Maybe because one of them was totaled when he hit Tara? Or he disposed of it afterward so the crime couldn't be traced to him?" The possibility that they were closing in on answers sent a zing of anticipation through her.

Then again, a vehicle registered to Luke's business didn't necessarily mean he'd used it himself. The driver could have been his wife or his lover. Had he been sleeping with Gina Vallot a year ago? Or someone else? Because once a cheater, always a cheater.

Either way, maybe the SUV that killed Tara had been sitting in Sophie Durand's garage all this time.

"Hello?" A man's voice called to Jordyn from the back of the building, reminding her of the business at hand. "Can I help you?"

Jordyn spoke quickly into her phone. "Gotta go, Natalie. I'll call you back in a few."

After she disconnected, she edged past the reception desk to search for the speaker.

"Hello? I'm looking for Mr. Van Ness?" She peered into the first empty office and then the second.

By the time she reached the third office, the voice sounded much closer.

"We close at five. It'll have to wait until morning."

Jordyn rapped her knuckles on the partially open door. Heard the heavy sigh before the voice spoke again.

"Come in, then."

She stepped inside the space where a live-edge slab conference table took up half the room while a heavy cherry-colored desk dominated the other. Bookcases stuffed full of volumes alternated between windows looking out on three sides of the building.

At the desk, a distinguished-looking man old enough to be a grandfather worked at a laptop, a pair of wire-rimmed glasses perched halfway down his nose. A gray suit jacket hung on a valet stand near the desk so the attorney could work in his shirt sleeves. Jordyn admired the fancy French cuffs on his shirt, the silver cuff links glinting in the overhead lights.

"I apologize for bothering you so late in the day," she began, waiting for him to look up or acknowledge her in any way. "But I hoped you could answer a couple of questions I have about a friend who used your services last year."

That finally snagged his interest. Glancing toward her, he tugged off the glasses and set them on the desk. His shrewd dark gaze took in her disheveled appearance from the long day of travel, her hair in a messy ponytail and her sweater sporting a coffee stain at the hem. She was pretty sure his assessment didn't miss the small divots above her top lip and near one eyebrow from healed-over piercings.

"I'm afraid that my business with other clients is protected by attorney-client privilege, Ms. . . ."

"Sorry. I'm Jordyn Lawson." Surging forward, she extended her hand. Arnie Van Ness's gaze dropped briefly to the labyrinth tattoo on her forearm before he stood to shake her hand. She'd been so careful to keep that hand-done tattoo covered by a sleeve whenever she was around the book club crew, but it had been such a long day, she'd grown careless. "I understand that you might not be able to share much, but the client in question was murdered a year ago, so there might be some leeway with the privacy expectation."

"Murdered?" The lawyer reached for his jacket and slid an arm into each sleeve, almost as if a lifetime of habit wouldn't allow him to take a meeting without being in the proper uniform. He sure wasn't showing any sloppy teenage tats. "I don't take those sorts of cases—"

"It was technically a hit-and-run that's still under investigation, so there has been some debate about whether or not the death was accidental. My friend had a meeting with you to set up a partnership agreement," she explained, hoping to jog his memory. Hoping he would feel compelled to answer her questions if he understood her desperation. "She was killed less than a week later."

The older man snapped his fingers. "You mean Randall Hughes's daughter. Tara. Please, have a seat." He gestured to the conference table.

"Yes. Tara called me shortly before she met with you." Jordyn lowered herself into one of the cushy chairs on wheels at the table. "Do you recall going to her home one evening last fall?"

"I did make the trip out there. I don't normally make house calls, but a request from Randall Hughes is an exception. I was happy to meet his daughter wherever she chose." Arnie took the spot at the head of the table, his expression lost in thought. "But you should know that meeting never happened."

"Excuse me?" Jordyn distinctly remembered Tara ending the call because her doorbell rang.

They had been on a video chat, so she had witnessed her friend descending the stairs to answer it.

"Yes, I recall it quite well, Ms. Lawson, since I'm rarely stood up these days, you see." He gave her a small smile, a hint of his charm from another era apparent as he winked at her. "When I arrived at the address Miss Hughes had given me for our meeting, Tara was not there."

CHAPTER 22

Tara

One Year Ago

POLITE MANNERS WARRED with personal safety in Tara's mind as she stared back at Mark Ribeki, the famous football player, on her front step.

Should she allow the star quarterback into her home when he hadn't even called her in advance to set up a time to meet? This was her home, after all. Not a place of business. It had been months since he'd been on *The Clean Break,* so it didn't seem like he could be here to speak to her about the show.

"I'd suggest a public meeting place," he began, seeming to read her mind. "Except that I get recognized and then it's tough to carry on a conversation."

Once again, he flashed that boyish smile, and she promptly recalled how many affairs he'd been rumored to have had over the years. His poor wife.

Ex-wife.

"Unfortunately, I'm expecting someone." She checked her watch, wondering how much time she might have before Arnold Van Ness arrived.

"This won't take long," he assured her, still glancing around the yard as if he expected someone to pop out of the hedges. "It's important, but I would hate for you to end up getting photographed with me by some long-distance telephoto lens if we keep standing outside. What if we took a ride for a few minutes? You could drive if that makes you more comfortable?"

At least that explained the guy's need to keep looking over his shoulder. Was he that concerned about her reputation? Or did he have a reason to be more careful about his own? She'd be willing to bet that most sports teams would find the Mark Ribeki-level of publicity to be a locker room distraction.

"The media really hound you that much?" She peered around her yard but saw only trees and lawn.

"It was bad enough before the podcast, but once the show aired, there seemed to be a bounty on my head every time I stepped out with a woman."

Tara struggled not to roll her eyes. Did he expect her to feel any sympathy that his serial cheating had caused him to be a paparazzi target?

"I suppose I could take a trip around the block," she agreed, hoping she'd be back in time for her meeting. It didn't seem like she was going to get rid of her guest without speaking to him privately, and she really didn't feel comfortable inviting him into the house while she was alone. Especially if he truly was stalked by photographers. Besides, her car had so many features she could ask it to call for help if she got into trouble. "I'll back my vehicle out of the garage and meet you there."

"I really appreciate that. Thanks."

Minutes later, she drove down Daybreak Hill toward the lake, with Mark in the passenger seat. Her attention wavered as she peered around for the attorney she'd been expecting.

"I'm sorry to just show up today." Her guest flipped down the sun visor and swiveled in the seat to face her, as if all the tricks to avoid being photographed were engrained habits. "You were so nice when we set up the dates for *The Clean Break* interview that I hoped you wouldn't mind—"

"You came to my home though. Not the office." She didn't appreciate being put on the spot. Especially at a time in her life when it seemed like everyone except for her foster sister was taking advantage of her in one way or another. How had she gotten the reputation for being such a pushover? "How did you unearth my home address?"

She made sure her Bluetooth connected to the car so that she could place a call quickly if necessary. For as long as she could remember, she'd had a deep-seated phobia about being alone with men she didn't know well. Even the thought made her skin go cold.

"My manager found out where you lived," he explained, oblivious to her discomfort. "He knows I need to conduct my business privately because of the attention I received from your show."

Unbelievable. Did he have any idea how self-absorbed he sounded?

"What was so important it couldn't wait?" She drove past Kaitlin's house, where her friend's lights were on, her front porch covered in seasonal mums and pumpkins.

"You know my ex-wife filed a lawsuit about the divorce arbitration."

"I'm aware." She didn't blame Evangeline Ribeki one bit for being furious with both the show and her ex-husband. Tara couldn't think overlong about it herself, or she would grow angry all over again at Sophie's high-handed maneuvering.

"Well, she seems to have disappeared because none of her friends have seen her for weeks. She didn't even show up at the court filing for the lawsuit."

"Maybe she's letting her legal team handle that. And I don't think it's unusual for people to take off in the wake of a divorce."

"Perhaps not." He scowled as he stared out the window at Saratoga Lake, the surface glinting in the moonlight. "But I'm not sure if she's stable, and I think you and Sophie should be on your guard."

"You think she could be *dangerous*?" Tara pulled into the parking area of a bar that served drinks on the small beach in warmer weather. "To Sophie and me?"

She would head back to her place in a minute, but she wanted to get a read on Mark's face, to gauge how seriously he took the allegations he was making. Did she really have reason to be worried, or was he the kind of person who enjoyed bad-mouthing a former partner and stirring up trouble?

"I can't say for sure." He held up his hands in a gesture of surrender. Which in this case, seemed to say, "don't hold me to it." "But I heard she bought a gun shortly before our divorce was finalized, and she never owned one before."

Tara's stomach sank. She didn't necessarily believe the athlete's ex-wife would make a cross-country trip to shoot her or Sophie. Tara simply hated that she'd been a part of ruining another woman's life so thoroughly. Evangeline Ribeki had bought a weapon and disappeared, all because of *The Clean Break*.

Well, also because of the man seated in the passenger seat.

"Maybe living alone just made her want the extra protection." Although now that she thought back on the aftermath of the Ribeki episode, she recalled a message that Evangeline had texted to Sophie saying that she would do whatever it took to get even. "But I'll certainly take extra care with my personal security. Is there anything else you wanted to tell me before I head back?"

"That's it. I owe you and Sophie a lot for all you did to help me through a rough time. If there's any chance that Evangeline has gone off the rails and hatched some revenge plot, you deserve to know about it. Since my legal team has forbidden me from commenting about my ex-wife in writing, I figured I'd tell you in person."

Shifting the car into gear, Tara ground her teeth to stifle her natural inclination to defend a wronged woman. Everything about this man irritated her, from his entitled arrogance to his legal team, while his traumatized—and broke—former partner had been cheated out of a fair divorce settlement thanks to Tara's show.

Thanks to Sophie's decision to screw over Evangeline for the sake of a ratings boost.

Driving faster up Daybreak Hill to await her attorney, she wondered if she would be better off letting Sophie buy her out of *The Clean Break* and ending the partnership for good. Because things seemed to be getting downright dangerous. A week ago, Tara had merely felt suffocated in the relationship with Sophie.

Now, she wondered if she also had reason to fear for her life.

CHAPTER 23

Gina

Present

SLIPPING HER 9MM into the glovebox of the odious little SUV that Luke had provided her, Gina fully recognized she was crossing a line today.

Unlike her home state of Louisiana, New York was not an open carry state. If she was pulled over and caught with the weapon, it could lead to a felony charge, since she didn't have a permit. Yet here she sat behind the wheel in her own driveway, waiting for Sophie to leave her house for the day so Gina could break into the other woman's home. The job seemed to call for a weapon because . . .

Well, she couldn't pinpoint exactly *why* she needed the reassurance of the gun close by.

She only knew that everyone around her seemed more dangerous the longer she spent among them. Every person in the book club or associated with it seemed to be plotting something. For starters, Luke's secret life insurance policy on his wife made Gina uneasy. But that was just the latest blip in a string of upsets ever since she first set foot in Saratoga.

First, her ex had made a trip to town, warning Tara and Sophie to be on the lookout for Evangeline. It had taken all her courage to face the podcasters in person after that, terrified they would recognize her. Then there'd been the incident with Tara last Halloween that had been utterly horrifying.

Not at all what Gina had intended for revenge.

Afterward, the police investigation had been brief but nerve-racking, and she'd waited every day for one of the cops to call her out as an imposter. Thankfully, they seemed convinced the hit-and-run was accidental and the case had quickly grown cold. She'd barely had time to catch her breath in the aftermath when Jordyn Lawson waltzed into town and infiltrated the book club, making Gina wonder about her motives. Was she in town for a piece of Sophie too? Then there was the obvious animosity between Kaitlin and Sophie. Brad's not-so-subtle digs. Destiny's money problems. Mei's suspicions of anyone female around her tomcat of a husband.

As for Fatima Chamoun, arguably Gina's closest companion in the group? The woman was cunning. With an IQ to rival her aerospace engineer husband's and an ambition to match, Fatima played her cards close to the vest despite her outwardly effusive friendship. Gina knew Fatima nursed a grudge against Sophie. Was it strictly because Sophie's daughters occasionally outshone her own? Gina couldn't pretend to understand the dynamics, but she knew better than to underestimate Fatima, which was why she'd chosen to stay close to her.

Gina could not afford the distractions of friends warring to take a shot at Sophie before her. Not when she was so close to realizing her vengeance.

In the book club group chat the night before, Sophie had mentioned she had a few errands to run this afternoon in order to prepare for the murder mystery game. With Sophie out of the house and Luke at work, Gina figured the time was right to do a little behind-the-scenes work at Sophie's place.

Her own preparation for the Halloween book club night.

Now, she sat in the SUV and waited for Sophie to drive past in her white Mercedes. Fortunately, Sophie's Type A personality kept her to a strict schedule, and she zipped by Gina's driveway within two minutes of the departure time she'd referenced in that group text. As soon as the Mercedes was out of sight, Gina opened a security camera app on her phone. Luke had shared access to his home system when they started seeing each other regularly, which gave Gina owner privileges to disable the recording devices at will. If Sophie happened to check her own app while she was out, she might think her Wi-Fi was down, but according to Luke it wouldn't trigger any warnings. Sophie had made home protection his domain.

With the security turned off, Gina drove the short distance up Daybreak Hill to Sophie and Luke's gargantuan home. She took the added precaution of parking on the far side of the pool house so that her vehicle wouldn't be visible to any delivery services.

Parked beneath an oak tree bare of almost all its leaves, she removed the gun from the glovebox. She checked the safety before sliding the 9mm into the holster at the small of her back, concealed by her high-waisted leggings. The long hoodie she wore hid all signs of the weapon. Then she grabbed the cloth sack she'd brought containing items to plant inside the home.

Items sure to stir a wife's concerns about her husband's fidelity.

Walking quickly across the yard, she unlocked the side door from her phone app, holding her breath until she closed it behind her again without tripping any alarms. Safely inside the mudroom the family used as their regular entryway, Gina slid off her canvas trainers and tucked them into the neat cubby space designated for one of the girls. That way, if anyone else entered the home while Gina was inside, the sight of extra shoes wouldn't immediately give her away.

Besides, she preferred the quiet stealth of her cotton socks on Sophie's white oak floors, the home so minimalist in décor that it echoed forlornly with only one person inside it, especially with ceilings over twenty-feet high. She'd been a guest of both Sophie's and Luke's at various times over the past year, so she was intimately familiar with the French country mansion. Yet there was something very different about being inside it alone, when she could really take in the details.

Gina had lived in a mammoth house once too, but she'd like to think she did a better job of turning it into a home than Sophie had done here. The house surrounded the pool deck on three sides, with huge sliding doors that could disappear into the walls on sunny days, allowing in tons of natural light. White couches and seagrass rugs made for a sterile family room. There were no personal touches here. No photos or memorabilia from family vacations. Not even a charge cord or a leftover school textbook.

Gina paused before entering the kitchen, double-checking her phone app to ensure the interior camera was off too. She happened to know there was a recording device above the side-by-side refrigerator, but the security dashboard showed that one was offline as well. Only then did she venture into Sophie's high-tech kitchen, where silver travertine countertops and white oak cabinetry complemented top-of-the-line appliances.

She didn't technically need to be in this room since she had no intention of planting items in common areas of the home. The couple's bedroom and Luke's office were her ultimate destinations. Still, she found herself lingering in the space that was predominantly Sophie's domain. For a year and a half she'd been fixated on vengeance, obsessed with delivering Sophie Durand the comeuppance she so well deserved. Now that Gina's hard work was so close to paying off, she found herself savoring every moment leading up to the implosion of this perfect world Sophie had built for herself at the expense of others.

Gina found the details of it all fairly delicious. Because having Sophie walk in on Gina and Luke in flagrante delicto wasn't nearly satisfying enough. To have Sophie confronted with the affair all at once robbed Gina of enjoying all of Sophie's gut-wrenching fears that would come before the confirmation that her husband was cheating on her.

A slow, dawning awareness that her life was falling apart would be much more in keeping with the horrors that Sophie had visited on her show guests. She had spoken to Gina—Evangeline—so warmly on the phone before the podcast had started recording. Sophie had assured her that listeners would be interested in hearing the details of how her marriage had crumbled and that sharing her experience would help the audience relate to her. Sophie waxed on and on about the way her podcast fostered a community for people going through difficult times and created a safe space to discuss the emotional injuries of troubled marriages.

Gina had been foolish enough to believe her. Drowning in her financial and marital problems, Gina had thought that Sophie really understood her. Worse, she had believed that Sophie cared.

Sophie reeled Gina in like a prized catch, positioning her perfectly before sending a harpoon through her world. Overnight, Gina and her deepest pain had been cast into a popularity contest against Mark's charm and ability to play to a crowd. The breakup of her marriage had become entertainment, with strangers on the streets of her hometown stopping her to talk about the podcast. Even the ones who sided with her were unbearable, their noxious interest often exploitative, since they usually posted about their interactions with her online.

After she first left New Orleans, she'd changed her look just to keep people from recognizing her. The nose job had been something she'd thought about for years, and she'd already made a downpayment to the surgeon when her husband sprang the divorce on her, so of course she went through with the procedure. When she'd seen with her own eyes what a difference the adjustment had made to her face, she'd gotten the idea of moving to Saratoga.

Right into Sophie's neighborhood.

Later, straight into the neighboring house on Daybreak Hill after it had been vacated by Tara Hughes, the previous renter.

Abandoning the kitchen for the primary suite, Gina removed a delicate pair of red silk panties from her bag and searched for the best spot to hide them in an incriminating fashion. As much as she hated to part with anything from La Perla now that her budget for the finer things was seriously limited, she needed lingerie that would communicate to Sophie her husband wasn't just banging a local waitress. He was having an affair with someone who circled in her same orbit. Someone who might have a chance of actually wooing him away.

La Perla panties with hand-stitched embroidery would get the job done. But where to hide them?

Gina stood at the foot of Luke and Sophie's California-king-sized bed, the white duvet and pillows perfectly arranged. Should she slip the underwear into the nightstand drawer on Luke's side of the bed? Or maybe somewhere in his closet? She wandered into the walk-in dressing area that looked like a personal boutique, complete with chandelier over a chaise lounge in the center. Sophie's clothes took up two of the three surrounding walls, while Luke's garments were arranged on one. Gina's gaze roamed the slide-out shelves that displayed ties and belts before idly pulling open the shelf below it.

Cuff links and tie pins were organized in a dark leather jewelry tray, but that wasn't what snagged her eye. At the back of the sliding drawer, two small glass vials sat side by side, each about half full of clear liquids. They were the kinds of vials a prescription like insulin might come in, except there were no pharmacy labels on them. Instead, they were roughly identified with sharpie marker.

One with a "G," the other a "K."

Special K? She'd heard of the street drug before but had never known Luke to use anything recreationally, though he'd asked her a couple of times to try Ecstasy with him. Did he have a more serious habit? Had those needles in his car been his? She'd never confronted him about them since she didn't want bad blood between them before she used their affair to taunt Sophie.

Unwilling to get distracted from the task at hand, she made a mental note to read more about the drugs and shoved the drawer closed, her gaze skipping over to the hanging rods.

Maybe she should hide the lingerie in the pocket of a jacket he'd worn recently?

Noticing the black sport coat he'd worn to the Witch Walk, she tucked the panties in the pocket, leaving a corner of red silk visible. She doubted Sophie would miss the flash of color if she were to walk into the closet. As long as Luke didn't see them first.

Next up was his office where she had another item to plant.

Except a sound somewhere in the house made her halt in her tracks.

Was Sophie home already? Had she forgotten something?

Gina listened with her whole body, every cell in her being on panicked, high alert.

She couldn't even check the security app on her phone to see if someone was entering the house since she'd disabled it. If she rearmed it now, the camera outside would capture her vehicle on the property.

Walking softly across the bedroom floor, she moved closer to the windows to see if she could look across the pool terrace into one of the other wings of the home.

There must have been a tint on the windows, however. No matter how clear they appeared while looking out of them, she didn't have a good view into the windows on the opposite wing that flanked the pool. The glass must be semi-reflective. Her gaze tracked upward to the second level where a big balcony jutted out over the pool area and a set of stairs led down to the main deck. All remained quiet there too.

The casita was dark at the far end of the deck.

Her heart pounded so hard the sound whooshed in her ears, making it even harder to hear as she strained to catch any noise. Should she hide?

A low rumble that sounded like a woman's voice reached her a moment before rock music boomed across the whole-home speaker system. The shock of sound made her jump.

Oh God.

How would she ever hear the person's movements now with the music blaring?

Then again, the sound should camouflage her movements too, right?

Quickly, she circled around the bed toward the exit into the corridor and peered down the sweeping main staircase. Seeing no one, she darted along the passageway to Luke's office. As quietly as possible, she withdrew the burner phone she'd loaded with texts and suggestive selfies from her own phone number. She slid the device into a drawer of his desk, once more hoping that Sophie would locate the evidence of an affair before Luke spotted it.

If Gina had to put money on the more observant of the pair, however, it would be Sophie all day long.

Now, how to get out of the house without being seen by whoever entered. The rock music was the kind Luke might listen to, yet she'd been certain it had been a woman's voice she heard earlier. Did one of Sophie's daughters like the same bands favored by her stepdad?

Or was there a chance Luke was in the house with another woman who wasn't Sophie or Gina?

Gina tiptoed toward the home's second, less grand staircase between the main and first floors. This one was more functional and less aesthetic, with walls to hide people trying to sneak up or down.

Under the cover of the music, she braved one foot on the main floor, peering down the hallway.

The rock 'n' roll ended as abruptly as it had begun.

Suddenly, the house was silent except for Gina's breathing.

Shit.

Caught on the main floor with only the stairwell as a place for cover, she tucked back into it. Held her breath.

Listened hard for the sound of footsteps heading her way.

Because if the unknown visitor had been in the kitchen, the person would have to walk within just a few feet of her to exit the home using the family-favored side entrance.

When the footsteps sounded, coming toward her, Gina's fingers found the gun at the small of her back. Taking comfort from the weapon, she drew it. Just in case. Breathing fast through her panic, she debated making a break for the second floor. But what if the stairs creaked beneath her feet?

Before she could decide, there was a rustling in the mudroom. Like a bag being picked up or put down. A jingle of keys.

A moment later, the door opened. Gina could feel the rush of cool autumn air as it shut behind the departing person. Were they really gone?

She counted to ten. Then counted to ten again before she moved.

Silently, she padded toward the mudroom, the 9mm still in her hand. When she reached the area with the cubbies, she took in the blank space where her shoes should have been.

The canvas trainers had vanished.

What the actual hell?

Stuffing the weapon back into the holster at her back, she rushed to the door to peer out one of the sidelight windows. In time to see Sophie's older daughter walking toward a convertible BMW, with a backpack slung over her shoulder, her phone in one hand and her keys in the other.

Charlotte Durand was wearing Gina's shoes.

Could the daughter be just as much of a manipulative mind-game player as her mom?

Gina didn't bother trying to make sense of it. Her mission complete, she needed to get out of the house fast before Sophie returned from her errands. So a moment later, she slid behind the wheel of her SUV and headed for home in her socks. Only once she was safely in her own driveway again did she rearm the security system at Luke and Sophie's place. All the camera feeds came back to life in a grid pattern on the app before she closed out of the program.

It had been a close call, and her heart still beat like a jackrabbit's half an hour later. The discovery of those vials in Luke's possession didn't sit well, and the fact that Charlotte had taken her shoes still messed with her mind. Gina had come out all right though. Evidence of her affair had been planted.

The deed was done.

Everything was in place for Halloween and her last book club with Sophie Durand.

CHAPTER 24

Jordyn

Present

JORDYN DIDN'T TRUST her lock-picking skills any more than she knew how to override a complicated home alarm system. Therefore, breaking and entering into the book club members' homes to search for the missing hit-and-run vehicle was not an option. Assuming Tara's killer had even kept the car used the night of her death.

She needed to see those three vehicles that Natalie referenced as potential matches to the paint chip. Maybe she'd get lucky and see evidence of repaired damage.

So instead of lock-picking, she found herself knocking on Kaitlin Teal's front door the day before Halloween, a hastily made miniloaf of pumpkin bread in her hand. Cooking and baking were activities that Jordyn normally enjoyed, but it wasn't the same baking for someone who might have killed her best friend. She'd put in just enough effort to gain admittance inside private homes to search the necessary garages.

With Natalie's help, Jordyn knew who owned vehicles with the same color paint as the hit and run SUV. But now she needed to look for signs of front-end damage, or repainting, or . . . well, anything. It seemed unlikely that the person who hit Tara would have kept the vehicle. Or if they had, they surely would have repaired it by now. But figuring out who killed her friend meant following every lead. Jordyn wanted to see those vehicles for herself.

Inside Kaitlin's house, Nala's face appeared in the sidelight as the dog barked happily. Jordyn waved at the Akita, grateful someone in the home was glad to see her. A moment later, Kaitlin pulled the door open.

Dressed in blue workout separates, Kaitlin wore her hair in a high ponytail, her phone in one hand still running the audio for what sounded like yoga instruction.

"What a fun surprise!" Kaitlin exclaimed, extending her arms for a hug even though her expression remained a little unsure.

"Sorry to show up unannounced." This method had worked for Brad that time he stopped by Jordyn's house, so she hoped that the homemade goods would do the trick here too. "But I fell victim to a baking mania and thought I'd better share the spoils so I can still fit into my costume tomorrow night."

She thrust the foil-wrapped package toward Kaitlin.

"Friends don't let friends eat all the sugar alone," Kaitlin swore solemnly, snatching the loaf from Jordyn's hand before turning off her phone's audio. "I will do my duty, but you have to come in and have a piece with me."

"Are you sure it's an okay time?" Jordyn asked, even as she stepped inside.

Nala jumped in frantic circles, butt wriggling with her tail wagging. At least Jordyn wasn't completely alone in the house with Kaitlin. Because ever since Jordyn had found that note on her windshield, she'd been thinking more about the risk she took with her own life to find Tara's killer. Someone knew her real reason for being in town.

Could it be Kaitlin?

"Seriously? Nala would pack her doggy luggage and revolt if I turned away her new favorite person." Kaitlin drew Jordyn into the kitchen with her, chastising Nala in the mildest of terms as the dog ran circles around them. "Besides, we can dish about the horror show that is Sophie's murder mystery game tomorrow night."

Jordyn told herself to maintain a neutral expression, but something about the way Kaitlin said it chilled her.

"Hmm. I was under the impression everyone wanted to be in this book club. Now you're making my first time sound scary." They stopped near the built-in banquette table where a café-style chair was already pulled up to one side.

The kitchen was white and gray with pops of pink in unexpected places—the heavy-duty mixer, a glass vase on the island, a few decorative dishes propped against a silvery quartz backsplash. And, of course, there were horses. A framed poster from an old Travers race with a chestnut-colored thoroughbred on a bright magenta background filled the space above the banquette.

A quick scan didn't reveal any security cameras, but that didn't mean there weren't any. No matter if there was one, Jordyn still planned to snoop if an opportunity presented itself. She couldn't say for sure why it seemed time was running out to catch a killer, but the book club murder mystery game felt like a macabre way to mark the anniversary of Tara's death.

She couldn't shake the feeling that the killer might strike again.

Would she be the next victim?

"Oh God, I'm sorry," Kaitlin said. "I'm talking to you as if you've been one of us forever, but in my defense, it seems like you're already kind of one of us after the block party and the Witch Walk." She set the pumpkin bread on the island then reached for two dessert plates in an upper cabinet near the sink. "Plus Brad told me the two of you hung out one night. You got his stamp of approval, by the way."

"Nice. He blew me away with the story about his appearance on *The Clean Break*." Jordyn kept an eye on Kaitlin to gauge her reaction.

Would she defend Sophie? Or Brad?

"Right?" Kaitlin shook her head as she reached for a knife to cut the bread. "Who would believe one of his closest friends would give his kids away to his ex?"

Jordyn's breath caught at the sight of the knife in Kaitlin's hand, the blade glinting in the pendant light for a moment while Kaitlin waited for an answer to her question.

"Doesn't it ever come up during book club?" Jordyn dragged her gaze from the stainless steel. "As in, do they really even get along? I can't imagine how I'd ever stay friends with someone who stole my parental rights."

Kaitlin paused to consider, returning her attention to the bread. "Brad seems cool about it for the most part, I guess. But every now and then I notice he gets a dig in at Sophie, so I'm sure it still rankles."

Jordyn had noticed the same thing at the Witch Walk. Brad had been quick to point out—loudly—that Luke had vanished from their group at the same time that Gina had gone missing.

"Maybe he blames Sophie's former partner for the decision to award the larger share of custody to Carlo."

She tried to say it very casually, but Kaitlin swung to face her abruptly.

"You mean Tara Hughes?"

The chill in Kaitlin's whole demeanor caught her off guard.

"I think so." Her heart hammered under Kaitlin's scrutiny. "Wasn't that the name of Sophie's partner? The same woman from your book club who died last year?"

"Yeah. That was her all right." Kaitlin slid a plate and fork toward Jordyn while keeping one for herself.

In the face of Kaitlin's obvious dislike, Jordyn felt all her hackles raise, the same way they had a lifetime ago when they'd been kids and anyone had dared to give Tara a hard time. Jordyn had never fully understood why she'd been so compelled to be her friend's defender from the moment they'd come into one another's orbit.

Even before she'd gotten to know Tara, Jordyn had gone to bat for her. Maybe it had something to do with recognizing a singular goodness in her friend, the rare sort of kindness and empathy that was too often scrubbed out of kids who spent too long in the system. Like Jordyn. But just because she didn't possess those qualities herself didn't mean she couldn't appreciate them in someone else.

"I take it you didn't like her?"

Kaitlin forked up a bite of the bread like it was a piece of cake, then pointed the fork at Jordyn.

"Let's just say I won't speak ill of the dead. To protect my mortal soul and all that." She took the bite and changed the subject. "This is so good."

Jordyn smiled her thanks and debated how to wrangle more answers out of her host.

"So Tara was more like Sophie's friend than anyone else's?" She quit petting Nala and the dog settled at her feet, wrapping her furry body around the base of the counter stool.

"Tara was my friend too, once upon a time. Back when the three of us came up with the idea for *The Clean Break*."

"You were involved in the podcast?" Jordyn was familiar with Tara's side of that story, but she needed to hear Kaitlin's take on the split.

She also wanted to get into Kaitlin's garage at the first possible opportunity since there had been no sign of a dark SUV in her driveway either of the times that Jordyn had been to this home. Has she sold it? Natalie had mentioned that Kaitlin hadn't renewed the registration on it, but the PI hadn't found a record of the vehicle being sold either.

"I was. And it just goes to show you need to be careful of your drinking partners." Kaitlin's joke fell flat since she was obviously angry as she said it. "Anyway, over a bottle of wine by Sophie's pool one day, I made the mistake of getting swept up in brainstorming about a celebrity break-up show, adding my own ideas and helping them come up with a killer format. But then, Tara and Sophie cut me out of the project like I'd never been a part of all those early planning conversations."

Jordyn longed to tell her that Tara hadn't thought it was fair to Kaitlin either. That Tara had always felt guilty about the way Sophie cut Kaitlin out of the show. But of course, that wasn't her place.

Besides, if Kaitlin had been the one behind the wheel the night of Tara's death, Jordyn had zero sympathy for her.

"You're still friends with Sophie though," Jordyn pointed out when Kaitlin had gone quiet for a moment. "You don't blame her as much as Tara?"

Kaitlin's brow wrinkled as she stared down at her plate.

"Maybe it's just easier to put more of the blame on Tara, since she's not here now." The answer sounded sincere enough. Was it the response of a therapist who understood the way grief worked? Or the reply of a killer who'd eliminated the source of her anger? "Either way," she continued a moment later, "Losing Tara took some of the edge off my resentment."

Was that practically a confession?

Jordyn's thoughts were too scrambled to decide. Instead, she focused on her need to search the garage and hoped she could convince Kaitlin to leave the room for at least a minute or two so Jordyn could do some serious spying.

"But I seem to recall you said Sophie's party would be a horror show. Is that because of a beef with the hostess or does it have more to do with the fact that we're dressing up as crazy characters in a murder mystery game?" Finishing the pumpkin bread that had definitely been too dry, Jordyn set aside her plate. "I will admit being wildly curious what everyone else is wearing after reading my character description."

Kaitlin grinned. "Didn't you see the note in that email that expressly forbid us from telling one another who we are dressing up as?"

"How can that rule possibly apply to the superintimidated new girl?" she pressed, needing Kaitlin to leave the room. "Did I mention that seeing your outfit was my not-so-secret reason for baking extra today?"

"All right. I give in." Laughing, Kaitlin set the empty dishes in the sink and then backed toward the stairs leading to the second level. Nala got up to follow her. "I'll go grab my costume. Come on, Nala."

As soon as Kaitlin disappeared up the steps, Jordyn dashed to the door on the opposite side of the kitchen that had to lead to the area where the cars were parked. Opening it, she passed briefly into a laundry area before reaching a heavier steel door. That one led into a neatly organized two-bay garage. The closer bay held a white Lexus coupe that definitely wasn't what she was looking for. But the second space was filled by a much bigger vehicle hidden under a silver custom car cover.

It was definitely the correct size.

Sprinting across the painted cement floor, Jordyn reached the nose of the tarped machine and lifted the canvas. Revealing the grill of a metallic black Range Rover Sport.

A luxury SUV.

What was more surprising was the obvious front-end damage. From the cracked right headlight to the dented fender and shattered front bumper, it was evident the vehicle had been in an accident.

"Oh my God. Oh my God. Omigod," she whispered to herself, hardly able to believe it.

Seeing it with her own eyes sent a wave of nausea through her so fierce she doubled over from it. The car cover fell from her fingers. Had this been the point of impact that killed her friend?

"Jordyn?" Kaitlin's voice called from the kitchen.

Fear of discovery steadied her churning gut a little bit. She would never get justice for her friend if she couldn't engage in better detective work than this.

Quickly, she withdrew her phone and snapped a photo of the damage before racing back to the laundry room.

Kaitlin stood near the island, brow furrowed. She had a bundle of green fabric draped over one arm. Nala stood beside her, tail wagging, looking decidedly less judgmental.

"Sorry! I thought I heard someone knocking on the exterior door, but I got confused where I came in." Jordyn smacked her head with the heel of her hand. "I must be losing my marbles. But is this your costume?"

Frowning, Kaitlin moved to shut the door to the laundry room. "Yeah, that's definitely not where you entered."

Her voice was so monotone—so off—that it sent a tremor of fear through Jordyn. If Kaitlin was the killer, what was to stop her from silencing Jordyn? Did she realize that Jordyn had just found evidence that made Kaitlin look guilty as hell? The reality of the danger she'd put herself in hammered home.

They were all alone in the house except for Nala.

Unsticking her dry lips with a swipe of her tongue, she forced herself to speak.

"So I discovered. It was probably just one of those annoying people trying to sell solar panels for your roof or something," Jordyn rambled, knowing her face must be pink. She couldn't believe she'd just found a vehicle with front-end damage in Kaitlin's garage.

With the correct color paint.

"Maybe so," Kaitlin conceded, even though she continued to stare at Jordyn oddly. "But this is what I'm wearing tomorrow. Run-of-the-mill doctor scrubs."

Relieved that Kaitlin seemed willing to change the topic, Jordyn gladly followed her conversational lead.

"Oh you got a much cooler character than me. I'm supposed to be a nerdy scientist, so I got some coke-bottle-type glasses and a lab coat, but I have no idea what else to do." She felt like her heart pumped so loudly it must be audible as she plotted a quick escape now that she had the information she'd come here for. "You should bring some Jell-O shots with you and pass them out, kind of like a Dr. Feelgood thing."

The longer she stood here, the more scared she grew. The weirder things she was certain to say. She needed to get out.

Now.

"That's not a bad idea," Kaitlin admitted. "We'll probably need some levity while we solve a two-hour murder mystery.

Did you catch that on the game notes? Game play is two to three hours?"

"I did." Jordyn had studied all of it at length, wondering if somehow Sophie Durand was using the game to reveal *another* murderer. Just how much did Sophie know about her friends? "But I'm going to run home and see if I can find anything else to add to my outfit. I'm a little more pumped up to go to my first book club now that we've talked."

She tried to smile as she backed up toward the foyer, where she remembered perfectly well she had entered the house.

"I guess I'll see you tomorrow night then." Kaitlin dumped the hospital scrubs on the kitchen island before walking with Jordyn to the front door. "Thanks for the bread and the visit."

Jordyn smiled inanely, her brain stripped of sensible speech. Unable to think of anything beyond her fear that Kaitlin was a killer. She gave Kaitlin a goofy wave and made a quick exit.

Relief shot through her as the door of the house closed behind her. She wanted to look at that photo again, to see if a more careful study would show evidence the damage had been caused by hitting a person.

The moment she was safely in her car, she called Natalie and asked to meet her later this afternoon. She wanted to bounce her new theory off the PI before tomorrow night. Of course, Jordyn first wanted to find the other vehicles belonging to Luke and the Chamoun family before she made up her mind about who killed Tara.

As she backed out of the driveway, she saw a curtain flutter at the window, as if Kaitlin Teal was still watching her. A chill went through her. Reminding her that she'd been lucky to escape in one piece. Because right now, it sure looked like Kaitlin was guilty as sin.

CHAPTER

25

Jordyn

Present

SHAKEN BY WHAT she'd unearthed in the last garage, Jordyn wasn't sure she had the stomach to check out the next vehicle on her list.

She drove toward Saratoga High School anyhow, knowing it had to be done. With any luck, Sareena Chamoun's SUV would be easily accessible in a student parking lot so that no subterfuge would be necessary to take a look. It was getting tougher to play the role of friendly new book club member around people she suspected of harming Tara. When she'd first started this journey, she'd imagined singling out one person with bad intent and making them the subject of her investigation. Instead, it seemed like everyone she met had a motive. Or, at very least, a ton of hidden ill will.

As challenging as her childhood had been, first with her parents and later adjusting to life without them, Jordyn preferred the certainty of those times for knowing who her enemies were. She could throw a punch when she had an adversary. Threats were overt. But in Saratoga, everyone wore the mask of a friend while carrying a figurative shiv in their back pocket. It was a whole lot creepier.

And yeah, more deadly.

She had almost reached the high school when a gray sedan in her rear-view mirror caught her eye. She felt like she'd seen it behind her the day she'd left the lawyer's office in Malta. It had stood out to her because a transponder hung on the inside of the windshield at an odd angle. Now, two vehicles back, the same sedan ran a red light.

To keep up with her? Was someone following her?

Ever since the note she'd found on her car the night of the Witch Walk, she'd experienced moments of feeling like she was being watched. She was so distracted by the idea that she almost missed the turn into Saratoga High. At the last minute, she slammed on her brakes for the access road.

Heart pounding, she noticed the gray car speed off in the opposite direction. Was she imagining things?

She told herself she was being paranoid. Or at least, she hoped so. Reaching the packed student parking area, she slid into an open patch of grass and hoped no one would ticket her in the handful of minutes she needed to find Sareena's car. She'd checked and rechecked the bell schedule that varied depending on the day of the week, timing her arrival ten minutes before the last bell of the afternoon.

Even so, the student lot wasn't empty. Who were these kids that eluded teachers at this hour? Jordyn walked purposefully up the first row of cars, noting how many were brands she'd never afford in this lifetime. There was a mix to be sure, but it spoke to the area's affluence that high end BMWs and Audis sat beside the kinds of cars she would have expected at a high school, like ten-year-old base models that had been cheaper even when they were new.

Another few minutes spent in the lot told her the vehicle she was looking for wasn't there. Natalie had gotten last year's plate numbers for all three of the vehicles with the incriminating paint, so Jordyn was certain Sareena's wasn't here.

Frustrated to strike out, she walked back to her vehicle. As much as she knew she needed to see all three of the potential SUVs, the fact that Kaitlin's had been in an obvious accident made her lean heavily toward her as the guilty driver. Or at least the owner of the vehicle that had hit Tara.

Just as she reached for the door of her coupe, a loud pop song blared out the open windows of a vehicle on the main road. When she glanced in the direction of the sound, she spotted what she'd been looking for.

Sareena Chamoun's black Infiniti SUV, with Sareena herself at the wheel, and Charlotte Durand riding shotgun. The volume on the music lowered as the blinker light came on and the girls turned into the parking lot. Too eager to inspect the vehicle for possible signs of repaired damage, Jordyn didn't think to look away or hide her face.

So it was no surprise that Charlotte's gaze met hers, lighting with recognition for a moment before she lifted her hand in an awkward acknowledgement.

Crap.

Jordyn debated just slipping into her car and driving away, pretending like the moment never happened. But she still needed to check out the SUV. Besides, what if Charlotte mentioned Jordyn being at the school to her mom? Better to just say a quick hello and take a cursory look at the Infiniti while she was here.

Her phone buzzed as she walked the short distance to where Sareena had parked. Seeing Ezra's number on the screen again, she declined the call and wished she'd never told him a single thing about her mission in Saratoga. Then again, who would get vengeance for *her* if she was the next victim of the book club killer? Maybe she should at least tell her ex-boyfriend who was on her list of suspects if she didn't make it home tomorrow night. Ezra might not make a good significant other, but she felt sure he could be counted on to report a crime.

Jordyn adjusted her path so that she would arrive at the SUV from the front. Taking out her phone, she pretended to read a text while snapping a covert photo. Her eyes locked on the air intake area of the black grill, roaming over the intricate pattern to see if there were any signs of repair. Natalie had assured her none of the vehicles on their list had been reported as having been in an accident, but no one with half a brain would call their insurance company to collect damages if they'd just killed someone.

Could Fatima have been so cagey that she'd used her teenage daughter's vehicle to take out an enemy? Or maybe she'd loaned it to Gina? Those two were certainly close. They'd taken that shopping trip into the city together the weekend of the block party.

"Hi, Miss Jordyn," Charlotte greeted her. She slammed the passenger side door of the SUV and hitched her pink leather backpack higher on her shoulder. She nibbled her glossy lip and looked decidedly nervous. "Do you have kids that go to school here too?"

Jordyn supposed it was a legitimate question, even if the idea of her own teenage children knocked her flat. She'd barely figured out how to navigate her own life as a thirty-six-year-old, let alone how to supervise anyone else's.

"I don't have any kids," she admitted, pretty sure no one had ever asked her that question before. "I just wanted to stop by the office and give them my name as a potential volunteer."

She forced herself not to blather needless details the way she had at Kaitlin's house after she'd been caught scouting around the garage.

Sareena slid out of the driver's side and gave a small smile, her expression pensive. Also worried?

All at once it hit Jordyn why they seemed on edge. She'd been so concerned with what they'd think of *her* appearance at the school, it hadn't occurred to her they might be equally afraid Jordyn would pass the sighting on to their mothers.

"But no telling that you saw me here, okay? I want my first appearance to be a surprise to everyone next spring." She didn't know if that made any sense, but she would guess the students knew less about parent volunteers than she did.

Like magic, the girls both beamed at the mention of secrecy.

"Of course," Sareena assured her at the same time Charlotte said, "We won't say a word."

At that moment, the school bell rang, an electronic chime that sounded over an outdoor PA system a split second before kids burst through the exits of both buildings near the parking lot.

"That's my cue to go," Jordyn announced, backing away. "See you!"

She hadn't noticed any outright damage on the Chamoun family's SUV. But was she just being paranoid, or did the paint job on the hood appear a little different—shinier—than the rest of the vehicle?

It frustrated her she couldn't have had a minute alone with the vehicle to look more carefully. But she would study that photo she'd taken and compare it to the one she had from Kaitlin's house. Jordyn sped home, confident Natalie would be there to meet her so they could debrief before the book club party tomorrow night.

When she pulled into her driveway, however, it wasn't the PI's Jeep that waited for her. A big gray F150 sat in her driveway, the Texas plates a dead giveaway even if there wasn't a gun rack visible through the rear window.

What had possessed her ex to drive half way across the country today of all days when she was so close to answers about Tara's death?

She didn't have time to deal with him now. What if he was here to try to stop her from investigating? Furthermore, he wasn't exactly being discreet by parking in her driveway. Thanks to the close proximity of Brad's house to hers, she had no doubt all of book club would know she'd had a guest from Texas by tomorrow. She cursed softly to get it out of her system. Then, taking a deep breath as she stepped out of her car, she prepared to face him.

Her former boyfriend had never been formally introduced to her scrappy side, the girl with an edge who would take all comers when backed against the wall.

But he was about to get acquainted.

CHAPTER

26

Tara

One Year Ago

THE THERAPY BREAKTHROUGH happened one day before Halloween.

Tara struggled to process it three hours after the milestone appointment, pouring more bath salts into the jetted tub in her primary suite while steam filled the bathroom. She still couldn't believe she'd finally recovered her memories.

The morning had started out just like any other day. Then, during her lunch break, she had been seated in her psychologist's office, answering the same kinds of questions she'd been fielding for years during bilateral stimulation. Basically, she and her therapist worked together to find an array of alternate activities and eye movements that helped remove the stress of recalling her past. In the breakthrough session, Tara had been playing with a bright pink fidget spinner while her therapist walked her through some vague memories about her homecoming day with the Hughes family.

Tara had been cautioned not to think too hard about that time on her own after recovering some of those memories the week before, and she trusted the process enough to do as she'd been told. She'd been eager to get back to work on those memories, however, feeling certain they were close to recovering everything.

Then, the next moment, when her therapist asked her to think about what she noticed about that homecoming day?

Memory deluge.

Now, Tara sank deeper into the small tub, punching the button that would add a blast of heat to the cooling water. Or at least, she thought the water had chilled. She'd been shivering nonstop since the memories of her adoption day had returned to her in vivid—terrifying—detail.

Thank God she'd scheduled herself to work from home that afternoon, telling Sophie she needed a few undisturbed hours to research potential new guests for the podcast. Because there was no way she could have performed any of her usual job tasks right now, when she couldn't quit trembling. It had required all of her acting skills to convince her therapist that she would be fine at home with an extra dose of Ativan.

A dose she had not taken.

Even now, as she closed her eyes and tipped her head against the tub's foam headrest, events from that day in the Hughes's historic Manhattan townhouse replayed over and over. One of her new half-brothers had offered to show her around the architectural masterpiece near Central Park West that spanned five floors plus a basement where the live-in nanny stayed.

The live-in nanny who had taken Evander's younger brother to a visitation with their mother that afternoon. A fact that Tara hadn't known until she found herself utterly alone with Evander, locked in his father's office, three floors away from her new parents.

Briefly, the shock of what he'd done silenced her. It was ironic really, considering all the stereotypes about the pitfalls of the foster system, that Tara had been that innocent before her arrogant, entitled new brother had put his hand up her dress.

It was almost like her brain refused to believe that this boy would hurt her when she had—against all odds—found a seemingly fairy tale family who wanted to make her one of their own. Oddly, it was her foster sister's voice in her head that had broken through the wall of disbelief in that critical moment when Evander began to unzip his pants.

While Tara struggled to make sense of what was happening, from the back of her stunned brain, Jordyn's voice screamed at her to take action. To do something. *Anything* to stop him.

And she had.

Brutally.

She'd seized a letter opener from the desk that he'd pinned her against. Jammed it into his roving hand. She recalled the hot rush of blood from Evander's hand onto her thigh. Although she'd punctured her own leg in the process, she couldn't remember feeling hurt in any way. She just had a vivid impression of his blood steaming over her skin where she'd stabbed the back of his hand. The aftermath of those moments were still a little hazy, but her counselor said that time might be lost forever since it was possible Tara had gone into shock afterward, making it impossible for her mind to absorb anymore.

At the end of the day's dramatic session, her therapist had given her extra prescriptions for more sedating medication, eliciting a promise from Tara that she would engage in protracted self-care for the next two weeks. All in all, the woman had made Tara feel like the walking wounded for recovering a traumatic memory.

Yet the anguish was only a small facet of what she felt now. Beneath the raw wound, a wellspring of anger bubbled up hotter than Evander's blood had been on that life-changing day. Fury that she'd blocked out the one time when she'd fought for herself. Rage that Evander's action and her lack of coping skills to deal with it resulted in over a decade of blank space in her brain where the memory of Jordyn should have been. Instead, her spineless stepmother had allowed Tara to believe there had been some scarring incident in the foster home that made her lose that chunk of time. But it hadn't been her foster family who had hurt her. It had been the overprivileged vipers who'd adopted her.

Far from wanting to forget it, Tara now wished to commemorate the moment when she'd possessed the inner strength to advocate for herself. She would claim ownership of that assertiveness, a quality she'd spent a lifetime believing that she lacked.

Now, staring at the untouched new prescription bottle near the tub, Tara turned down the hot tub heater and clicked off the jets. She didn't want to spend another moment of her life people-pleasing or making herself small so that those around her felt good about themselves.

Toweling off, she made a plan to print a boilerplate partnership agreement to bring to Sophie tomorrow. She might have missed her appointment with the attorney while she'd met with the too-full-of-himself football player, Mark Ribeki. But that didn't mean Tara needed to delay the conversation with Sophie about their partnership any longer. Her father was right that she'd made a huge mistake not hammering out something before now.

Tomorrow night at book club, she would show the agreement to Sophie and insist her partner sign it. She'd also refute Mei's outrageous claim that Tara was sleeping with Nikolai and, if necessary, point Mei in Sophie's direction. As for Luke?

If she saw him, she planned to settle that score too.

Because today's therapy appointment hadn't just helped Tara recover her past. It had freed her to find her voice. With it, she planned to make sure the rest of the world knew she was no longer anyone's doormat.

How fitting that she would be wearing the Maleficent costume for Halloween. She'd been overshadowed by villains wearing masks of social acceptability for too long. When she swept into Sophie's home tomorrow night all in black from her horned headpiece to her winged collar and long train, Tara would rewrite her whitewashed history and—finally—speak her truth.

CHAPTER 27

Jordyn

Present

JORDYN SPEED-WALKED TOWARD Ezra's pickup truck at the same time he clambered down from the driver's side.

He looked rougher than normal. Patchy stubble on his face said that he hadn't shaved in days, and his olive-colored T-shirt and faded jeans were rumpled. His light brown hair had grown long enough to hang in his hazel eyes, but he shoved it out of the way as he faced her.

"What are you doing here?" she asked, even as she nodded toward the carriage house. "Actually, don't answer that until we're inside, since I'd rather no one overhear us."

Ezra spread his arms wide. "That's the welcome I get?"

Irritation made her impatient, but she tamped down her frustration long enough to unlock the door and motion him inside. "I'm allowing you to come into my home, even after you kicked me out of yours. Consider yourself fortunate."

"I never—"

"*Inside* please," she repeated, gritting her teeth and hoping Natalie showed up soon so she had an excuse to send him packing. For now, however, she would at least make it clear that she was at a precarious moment of her investigation into Tara's death.

He huffed a long sigh and lumbered into the house, his boots echoing on the hardwood. When she'd closed the door behind them, she swung around to face her ex.

"Now. Care to tell me why you not only ignored my requests to leave me alone, but you travelled halfway across the country to stand in my driveway where anyone could have seen you?"

"You stopped answering my messages, Jordyn. I got worried about you." Shoving his hands in the pockets of his jeans, he glanced around the small living space. "God, this place is tiny."

Jordyn peered around the renovated carriage house, seeing it through his eyes. Small, yes. But there were deadbolts on both doors, and that was really all that mattered to her.

"You told me to choose you or Tara. I chose her." She enumerated the points on her fingers. "You told me we were done. I took you at your word and packed my things. Now here you are, slowing down my efforts to investigate Tara's death when I'm at a pivotal stage?"

He scrubbed a hand through his overgrown hair. "Can we just sit down for two minutes? I've been driving straight for the last sixteen hours."

Her annoyance dimmed a bit in the face of his obvious exhaustion. How ironic he'd finally chosen to put some work into their relationship after they were finished.

"A few minutes, but then I've got an appointment with my PI, and I can't reschedule." She gestured toward the stiff-backed couch that had come with the furnished space. "Have a seat. I'll get you something to drink."

Ezra lowered himself to the dark blue cushions while she grabbed a couple of waters out of the refrigerator. She couldn't help but glance out her front windows as she strode back into the living area, paranoid that Brad or one of Tara's other friends would choose this moment to drop by, and she'd be stuck trying to concoct a story about her guest. She took the time to pull the blinds.

When she passed one of the bottles to Ezra, she dragged over one of the dining table chairs and noticed him staring up at her.

"You look different." He studied her while he twisted off the cap and took a long swig. "Is it just the clothes?"

Jordyn glanced down at the gray Alo Yoga top and black Lululemon leggings that she'd chosen for her errands. She had no idea how out of date the styles were when she'd chosen them at a consignment shop, and she'd never been an athleisure fangirl before. But she couldn't deny they were the most comfortable things she'd ever put on her body.

"Does it matter?" She folded herself onto the wooden chair and sipped her water. "Can you please just tell me whatever it is you drove all this way to say?"

"Two things." Leaning forward, he set the water bottle onto the square coffee table between them. "First, I'm really worried that you're going to either end up dead or behind bars before this quest of yours is done."

She knew she'd already addressed this, but since it was obviously weighing on him, she tried to reframe her response to be as simple as possible.

"Thank you for your concern. Please recall I was taking care of myself well before you came into my life. I'm tougher than I look." She hadn't told him much about the years she'd been in the care of her addict parents before she'd gone into the foster system. She'd slept in abandoned houses among people so deeply under the haze of drugs they didn't have a clue what they were doing.

There'd been no need to dwell on it because she'd survived. In the end, she'd been stronger. Resolute.

Behind her, the old-fashioned kitchen clock ticked a loud countdown. One way or another, she had the feeling this whole drama would be over tomorrow after the book club.

"So let's say you're tough enough to take on a killer and live to tell the tale. Maybe you even exact the vengeance I know you want." He leaned forward to make his point, eyes locked on her. "Is it worth risking jail time after you've worked so hard to build a good life?"

Her heart slugged harder in her chest, his words making her uneasy in a way she couldn't immediately pinpoint. Was it just her imagination, or did it sound almost threatening?

"I'm here to expose a killer, not mete out vigilante justice." She held up her hands. "I'm not the criminal here."

"Maybe not yet. But you're disguising your identity and tricking a whole lot of people with wealth and influence."

"That's not a crime."

"Have you checked the stats about the number of innocent people behind bars?" He seemed agitated, his voice growing louder. "You think everyone in this wealthy enclave you're trying to infiltrate will just sell out one of their own when you point your finger at whoever you think is guilty?" His frustration had distorted his features.

Making her wonder for an instant how far he would go to make his point. To scare her away from her mission. But this was Ezra. She knew him better than that, didn't she?

"I guess I haven't thought that far ahead." She'd been too consumed with finding answers to consider the aftermath. "I assumed everyone except the killer would be grateful to know who among them was guilty. But maybe they already know and have been protecting that person this whole time."

"Jordyn, you don't know who you're dealing with." His voice had an edge.

She did not appreciate the scare tactics at a time in her life when someone was already threatening her. Perhaps following her.

"It's unfortunate you came all this way to warn me when I've already explained that I'm committed to finding Tara's killer I *need* to see this through."

He reached toward her, mouth opening as if he would interject, but she bolted up from her chair and paced the small living space.

Even Ezra was scaring her now. She needed him to leave.

"Look, you of all people understand that I don't have strong bonds with many people," she continued, trying to convey that she was done listening to him by moving closer to the door. "Do you know how many meaningful relationships I've managed to form in my life?"

He shook his head sadly. "I don't suppose you count me in that number?"

She stifled an exasperated sigh.

"This isn't about you. This is about what I owe to someone who loved me for myself at a time in my life when no one else did. The cops have admitted that Tara's case is cold. Even if it's not technically closed, they haven't done anything on it in months. So all that matters to me now is finding the truth. Getting justice for her."

As the words settled into the room, echoing in her ears, Jordyn acknowledged there might be more to it than that. Ezra hadn't been wrong about her wanting vengeance.

Slowly, he rose to his feet again. Something in his expression told her she might have finally gotten through to him. Still, she remained alert. Wary.

Before he reached the door, he turned back to ask, "What if I go to the police first? Tell them who you really are and what you're trying to do?"

"I would be angry with you, but in the end it won't make any difference." Except possibly slow her down. "I'm not going to quit until I have answers."

"Yeah. I figured. But it was worth a shot to keep you safe." This time he pulled open the door and stepped out into the night without looking back.

She followed him onto the small wooden steps, ignoring the niggle of guilt she experienced at making him leave again as the low rumble of thunder growled nearby. At the same time, the headlights from Natalie's Jeep swung across the front yard of the carriage house. Jordyn felt relieved to have the confrontation with her ex over with. And maybe she had him to thank for clarifying her purpose.

Reinforcing her resolve.

She watched as Ezra stepped back into his truck cab at the same time Natalie hopped out of the Jeep. Jordyn reached for the medallion she wore under her sweater and smoothed her fingers over the contours of the saint.

Whoever killed her friend would pay the price.

CHAPTER 28

Jordyn

Halloween Night, Present

THE FIRST DROPS of rain pelted Jordyn's silver coupe as she arrived at the book club meeting. Sophie Durand's expansive home loomed ahead, brightly lit and decorated with jack-o'-lanterns and skeletons.

Switching off the headlights, Jordyn stopped the car in the long, horseshoe-shaped driveway. Two other vehicles were already parked on the black and white bricks laid out in a herringbone pattern. One she recognized as the white Lexus she'd seen in Kaitlin Teal's garage. The other—a sleek blue Jaguar sports car—wasn't familiar to her.

The storm had been threatening since the night before, and trick-or-treaters were sure to be disappointed the nor'easter had waited until now to blow in, during what should have been prime time for candy collecting.

Gathering her umbrella, Jordyn felt the electric charge in the air even before opening the car door. Was it the change in barometric pressure from the rain? Or the uncanny sensation that she could be standing in the same exact spot that Tara had stood one year before, unaware that the night would end with her death?

A shiver crept up her spine as she headed toward the double doors of the grand front entrance. Never before had she felt the presence of her departed foster sister so keenly as she did at that moment. As if Tara were right behind her, urging her on. Which seemed funny, considering Jordyn had never needed any urging to speak up for her friend in the past. Jordyn hadn't once shied away from a fight.

Tonight was different, though.

How could she battle a danger that was so much tougher to see? A danger that hid behind social niceties, designer labels, and small talk? This was the complicated world Tara had navigated alone, and Jordyn appreciated feeling like her friend was somehow at her side tonight when she planned to expose everyone's secrets.

Including the killer's.

Jordyn adjusted the oversized glasses from her extremely stereotyped nerdy scientist costume, then checked her phone one final time. Natalie had been messaging her updates for the last hour as she checked into what Jordyn had learned about Kaitlin's car. Natalie had also learned from her PI colleague that Tara hadn't been the woman with Nikolai in the months before her death. It had been Sophie, dressed like Tara, a fact proven from video footage obtained from another hotel that same night, when the couple had been recorded walking into the lobby together, their faces clearly visible. The PI had eventually passed on that information to Mei—but not until *after* Tara had died. And according to the PI,

Mei had refused to believe it had been Sophie despite the video evidence.

What the hell did that mean?

Could Mei have killed Tara thinking she was the one having an affair with Nikolai? And what did that mean for Sophie's safety now? Maybe Sophie was in danger too. Jordyn couldn't shake the feeling that tonight's party could be dangerous. That the killer could strike again.

But it was tough to see quiet, unassuming Mei as the killer. Jordyn came back to Sophie's strange ruse. Why would she try to throw Tara into hot water in the first place? If Sophie disliked Tara enough to masquerade as her while out with another woman's husband, did that also mean Sophie had disliked Tara enough to kill her? If anything, it seemed like it would have given Tara motive to kill her business partner, not the other way around. Not that Tara would.

But right now, Jordyn's phone showed no new messages. Standing outside Sophie's home made her feel exposed. Too visible. Ever since she'd found the warning message on her car, she'd been plagued by the sense that someone was following her. Watching. So she pressed the front doorbell to get inside, hoping she could pull all the clues together to make sense of what had happened a year ago.

A seasonally-appropriate chime sounded on an outdoor speaker—the high cackle of a witch's laughter. A moment later, one of the dark double doors swung wide, and she was greeted by two woodland fairies wearing matching jeweled crowns with pale, glittery wings attached to their backs.

"Happy Halloween!" The fairies chorused together before parting to admit Jordyn into the house.

"Happy Halloween," Jordyn said, recognizing Charlotte first, and guessing her sister Amelia was the other fairy, though her face was distorted behind a pale stocking mask with bulging eyes like an insect.

While Jordyn stepped into the echoing foyer, Charlotte jingled a set of keys in her hand and called over her shoulder, "Mom, I'm leaving. I'll be back by ten."

The girls vanished out the front doors a moment later, leaving Jordyn to hang her coat on the rack. She followed the sounds of "Love Potion No. 9" coming from another room, along with feminine laughter. The scent of cinnamon and nutmeg hung in the air.

Reaching a state-of-the-art kitchen, Jordyn paused to take in what and who she saw. She recognized Kaitlin in the doctor's scrubs she'd shown Jordyn the day before. Her long hair was tucked under the surgical cap, and her curves were less obvious under the shapeless top, but otherwise, she looked the same as she fanned out a stack of cocktail napkins on the island filled with drinks and snacks.

The two other women in the kitchen had leaned into their costumes hard.

"Welcome to the Murder at Rookstone Manor game," said Sophie, dressed in a vampy red gown with a white fur stole around her shoulders. She had curled her hair into perfect waves, her lips flawlessly outlined in crimson. Straightening from the oven where she pulled a tray of spanakopita from one of the racks, she asked, "Can I get you a cocktail?"

Sophie made room on the island for the tray and tugged oven mitts from her hands.

"I can help myself," Jordyn assured her, reaching for a wine glass from the island. "Thank you."

"There is a white Sancerre that's already open," Fatima announced from the other end of the island, dressed in a black dress with tuxedo accents like a bow-tie collar and satin piping running from her hips to her ankles. She held an opera glass in one gloved hand. "But I brought a pinot noir if you prefer."

"I'll open the red," Jordyn announced, marveling at the lengths everyone went to for their outfits even as she wondered if there was a reason Fatima wore gloves. Had she been thinking about not leaving fingerprints? "I can't wait to find out more about everyone's character in the game tonight."

The doorbell rang while she used a corkscrew on the pinot noir, the music changing to "Highway to Hell." She preferred to drink a beverage that she opened herself since it just seemed safer when a murderer lurked.

She had a plan for tonight, of course, but she wouldn't implement it until deeper in the evening when the guests let their guards down. Until then, she'd keep taking everyone's measure. Keep testing her theories of the crime to see which one fit best.

To see who fit the killer profile.

As Jordyn tugged the cork free, Mei and Destiny swept into the kitchen together, already embroiled in laughter and conversation. Mei's hair was piled high like the bride of Frankenstein, and she strutted in a slinky purple slip dress with a matching pashmina held by a green butterfly clip. Destiny rocked a black sequined body suit and silver feathered headdress with fishnet stockings.

"Welcome to the Murder at Rookstone Manor game," Sophie repeated for the newcomers. She still buzzed about the kitchen, pulling a tray of fruit from the refrigerator and opening a jar of honey to add to a charcuterie board. Luke had joined her at some point, sticking toothpicks into melon balls wrapped with prosciutto. "We'll get started as soon as Brad and Gina arrive, but I can tell you that one of you may disappear from the game at some point because there *will* be a murder."

Jordyn paused in the middle of pouring her drink, red wine splashing onto the counter.

"During the game?" She'd read about these kinds of entertainments online, and she couldn't recall any of them saying that someone disappeared while playing. "I thought the murder was supposed to happen off-stage, so to speak. Then all of us try to solve the mystery?"

"Not with the Rookstone Manor game," Sophie assured her.

At the same moment, Gina Lawson stepped into the kitchen, wearing a Stetson and leather chaps with a turquoise fringed shirt like a rodeo queen.

She paused in the entrance to the room, her hand on a very convincing-looking prop revolver in her jeweled leather holster. Cocking her head to one side, she tipped back her cowboy hat before she spoke.

"Did someone say *murder*?"

CHAPTER 29

Gina

Present

THE BOOK CLUB group appreciated her entrance, and Gina appreciated the attention.

Fatima imitated the cowboy swagger. Jordyn compared it to some Bugs Bunny cartoon with Yosemite Sam (could Jordyn be any weirder?) and Sophie—that tee-total bitch—just laughed delightedly, as if the performance was all for the benefit of her party.

Gina wondered at what point in the evening these people would quit being amused and start recognizing the very real danger she represented. She couldn't wait.

All the times she'd been lambasted in the sports media for "distracting" her ex-husband's focus from football because of their split. All the nights she sacrificed her body to sleep with Sophie's man-whore of a husband as part of her bid for vengeance. It would be worth every unhappy moment of the last two years to watch Sophie's face drain of color when she finally recognized how thoroughly she'd been beaten by the woman whose life she had destroyed without a thought.

While the music switched to Rhianna's "Disturbia," Gina helped herself to a drink from the extensive offerings on Sophie's kitchen island, choosing a healthy splash of top shelf gin with a little tonic and lots of fresh lime slices and ice. Brad arrived a few moments after her, dressed in chef's whites complete with the signature toque. Fatima was regaling the group with a story about her daughter and Sophie's going out for spots on a competitive dance team when a bell began to chime incessantly.

Glancing up from her drink, Gina saw Sophie in her red slip dress, shaking a small silver handbell.

"Attention, friends." Sophie bared her teeth in what probably passed for a smile to everyone but Gina. "I'm so glad you could all be with me at Rookstone Manor tonight while we try to solve a murder."

Destiny and Kaitlin provided the requisite "oohs" and "aahs," clinking their glasses to toast the event, while everyone waited to see what else their host had to say. Gina noticed that Jordyn Lawson looked down at her feet, hiding her expression.

Gina never had learned anything useful about the book club newcomer. And now that Gina was in the homestretch of her plan to decimate *The Clean Break* podcast, she had decided it didn't matter. Jordyn would be a footnote in the night's events.

"A little housekeeping before we begin a get-to-know-you mixer for our characters," Sophie continued. She set aside the silver bell and lifted a dark wicker basket lined with a white linen tea towel. "Starting with the game rules. No cell phones allowed to ensure a level playing field. If everyone could please shut down their electronics, Luke will come around to collect your devices."

A small amount of grousing took place before a flash of lightning preceded a violent crack of thunder. The floor rumbled with the strike, and a moment later the rain picked up in force, loud enough to hammer the floor-to-ceiling glass doors that surrounded the pool deck and courtyard.

All around Gina, the partygoers added their cell phones to the basket as Luke walked from one person to the next, saving her for last. She met his gaze as she dropped her device into the bread basket with the others.

"I need to talk to you," Luke said quietly, his tone urgent.

Gina glanced around them, wondering who had spotted the by-play, but everyone seemed well on their way to an evening of tipsy frivolity, drinks in hand, conversation humming along.

"So talk," she answered at regular volume, shrugging a shoulder to let him know she had no intention of hiding their conversation.

"In private," he practically growled the words at her before pivoting on his heel and stalking from the room.

Gina followed more slowly, using a purple swizzle stick to stir through the ice she'd added to her drink.

By the time she entered an adjoining sitting room decorated in more shades of Sophie's unimaginative white, Luke had already stashed the basket of phones. He swung around to face her, the expression on his face tense, the tendons in his neck standing out.

"What the hell are you doing sneaking into my home when I'm not around?" His accusation was underscored by another loud crash of thunder.

"What are you talking about?" She swirled her drink again, unwilling to confess anything until she knew what she was being accused of.

Had he found the panties she'd hidden in his jacket pocket? Had his stepdaughter confronted him about finding a stranger's shoes in the house?

"Don't play games with me. You turned off the security system for twenty minutes while no one else was home." He took a menacing step toward her and for a split second, she wondered if she'd been foolish to goad him.

But then, she recalled what she held over his head.

A burst of laughter came from the kitchen at the same time the doorbell rang. Not that Luke moved to answer it. Maybe they were ignoring trick-or-treaters foolish enough to brave the storm.

"I assure you, I'm not the one playing games," she shot back. "You're the one who took out a life insurance policy on your wife without her knowledge. Care to explain that one?"

The anger slid from Luke's expression, his jaw dropping for an instant before he snapped it shut again.

"You broke in here to snoop through my things?" His lips curled.

She was grateful for the house full of people, or she might have been scared. As much as she hated her ex-husband for cheating on her and swindling her, she'd never feared for her physical safety. Luke was another story.

It was a relief that her costume had allowed her the opportunity to carry a shiny silver derringer that looked straight out of the Old West.

"I didn't have to. You left the policy in your office downtown the night of the Witch Walk. I practically had the ink tattooed on my ass after we had sex on the desk."

She moved to rejoin the group, but Luke grabbed her by the arm. He yanked her to a stop.

"That's a lie, and you know it. You had to search to find those papers."

"So what if I did?" she hissed at him, wrenching her arm free. "Maybe I wanted to know what your plan was for that insurance policy. Maybe I'm just trying to figure out if you really want your wife dead."

"Don't be ridiculous." He spat the words back automatically, but she didn't believe his denial for a second.

A rustling echoed from the far side of the room, and she lowered her voice even though she was pretty sure everyone else was in the kitchen behind them.

"You can insist you don't want her dead all day long, but that insurance policy says something different." Folding her arms, she took his measure, trying to figure out how close he was to implementing whatever plan he had in mind.

She didn't want Sophie to die before finding out that Evangeline Ribeki was sleeping with her husband.

Luke remained stubbornly silent.

"What's wrong, Luke?" She laid her hand on his chest and felt his heart pounding hard just beneath her fingertips. "Can't work up the nerve to do the deed?"

His eyes narrowed. Darkened.

Gina leaned closer to whisper in his ear. "Because I'd be happy to help you."

CHAPTER

30

Jordyn

Present

NERVES STRUNG TIGHT, Jordyn couldn't focus on the details of what Mei was saying about her game character. Mei was supposed to be a countess of a small European country, and she was visiting Rookstone Manor because—who knew? Jordyn didn't care. How messed up was it that this group was mingling to learn one another's fictional characters, when the real people beneath the costumes were the true mystery.

One year ago today, a book club member had been killed a stone's throw from where they all stood knocking back cocktails, and you'd never know it to hear them chatter away about Rookstone freaking Manor. Like Tara didn't matter. Like she didn't deserve to be remembered with even a toast in her honor.

"What about you?" Mei asked, sipping from a martini glass with little left in it besides two olives on a toothpick.

"What about me?" Jordyn asked, hauling her attention from the arched entryway to a sitting room where Gina and Luke were engaged in an intense conversation.

Their body language did not look like that of lovers.

Didn't anyone else feel the same tension in this house that she did? The sense of impending doom, like a killer might strike again at any minute? They were wasting time speculating about the characters in a game when someone in this house had run Tara down in cold blood.

"Um, we're supposed to be trading character backstories, right?" Mei lifted a censuring eyebrow. "I intend to be the one to solve this thing."

"Right. The murder that has yet to happen? That's not how these mystery games are supposed to work." Jordyn had researched the crime-solving party entertainments as soon as she'd received the invitation, and she'd never heard of a version where the dead person was unknown for a portion of the event.

The whole point was to find out who killed a character who was already dead.

Mei gave a knowing smile. "You're new to the book club, so you might not be aware of the group dynamics yet. But Sophie Durand knows what she's doing. I can guarantee she has planned this night down to the smallest detail."

The knots in Jordyn's stomach tightened. Agitation spilled over. "What about last year? Was last year's murder mystery perfectly planned too?"

She didn't realize that she had raised her voice until the kitchen quieted.

Heads swiveled toward her.

"Everything okay, Jordyn?" Destiny asked, a warning clear in her dark eyes.

Jordyn couldn't think of a better time to disclose her motives than right now when she had all of the potential suspects under one roof. The front doorbell rang again, but no one moved to answer it.

"Things are far from okay," Jordyn informed them, shoving her oversize costume glasses on top of her head so she could see everyone's faces more clearly. "Because I can't fathom why we'd spend tonight trying to crack a fictional mystery when a much more important *real* one remains unsolved."

"Oh honey," Kaitlin murmured, moving closer in her doctor scrubs. "Let's not go there, all right? We're trying to put the pain of that behind us."

When Kaitlin looped an arm around her, Jordyn shook her off.

"Maybe that's easy for you to say since one of *you* is her killer." She met Kaitlin's startled gaze, recalling the damage to the woman's SUV. "But Tara Hughes was more than a friend to me."

She could have heard a pin drop in the room. Even the Halloween playlist had been silenced.

"What are you trying to say?" Destiny pressed, giving her a hard stare.

In the quiet, Jordyn could hear her own ragged breathing. Her erratic heartbeat that warned her she was treading shaky ground. She hadn't planned to reveal her mission this early in the evening, but she couldn't continue the charade when Tara's killer might be ready to strike again. Someone was following her. Someone had guessed her real reason for being in Saratoga and wanted to silence her.

"I'm saying that Tara was my foster sister. The best friend I ever had." She paused to let that sink in. Wanting them to feel the strength of that bond and how much it meant to her. "And she deserves justice. So no one is leaving here until I find out what happened on the last night of her life."

There was a gasp. An outcry.

Before Jordyn could figure out where the sound came from, another flash of lightning sizzled through the sky. Lighting up the kitchen.

Thunder cracked.

Every single light in Sophie's house went out, plunging them all into inky darkness.

CHAPTER

31

Tara

Halloween One Year Ago

JUST A WEEK before, Tara would have been nervous about what she had planned for the Halloween book club at Sophie's house.

Scratch that.

The week before, she wouldn't have even *dreamed* of the standoff she envisioned for tonight. But now she had her recovered memories to remind her that she was strong. That she could stand up for herself. Tara's whole sense of self had shifted since then.

Now, seated in her car in Sophie's driveway, she hit the button on her phone to make a quick video call to Jordyn so she could show off her costume. While she waited for her foster sister to answer, Tara checked her makeup in the rear-view mirror.

"Happy Samhain," Jordyn's voice greeted her as the video connected. "I can't wait to see your costume."

"Happy Halloween!" Tara replied as she took in her friend's flour-covered apron while she stood in her Texas kitchen, surrounded by cookie cutouts in the shape of cats, ghosts, and jack-o-lanterns. Cooling racks held piles of baked cookies while Jordyn rolled out a fresh batch of dough to cut out more. "And I can't believe I caught you in the throes of domesticity like some kind of YouTuber homemaking goddess."

"We all have our secret sides." Jordyn set down a cookie cutter shaped like a spider and brought her phone closer to her face. "But let's see your outfit. It's a little dark wherever you are."

"I'm still in my car. Hang on a second." Tara had arrived a bit late to the book club, so it looked like most everyone else was already on the scene. Thankfully, the exterior of Sophie's house was bright with security and landscape lighting despite the inky darkness of a moonless night.

Stepping out onto the herringbone-patterned driveway behind Fatima's dark green Audi sports car, Tara adjusted her headpiece so that the Maleficent horns were positioned correctly. Then she held her phone above her head at arm's length.

"Oh wow, Tara, that looks amazing!" Jordyn squinted into her camera. "Is that train pleated in the back?"

"Yes, and it's detachable." Tara spun around to show off the Velcro tabs she'd used to hold the heavy black fabric in place. "I only just finished the staff today."

She brandished the five-foot staff painted to look like a gnarled tree branch wrapped around a reflective purple ball at the top.

"You are completely frightening," Jordyn assured her. "I hope you're going to cast some serious spells tonight."

"I might just do that." Tara laughed darkly as she retrieved her purse from the car and then slammed the door shut. "I'll have everyone I need to hex all in one room at least."

"I thought this book club was full of your friends?" Jordyn frowned, swiping her hair out of her eyes and leaving a flour smudge on her forehead. "Is everything going okay there?"

"Better than okay," Tara assured her. As much as she wanted to share everything she'd learned in her last therapy session with her foster sister, this wasn't the right time. "Or it will be after tonight."

"Everything you're saying has an ominous ring to it."

Behind Tara, another vehicle turned into the driveway and she recognized Kaitlin's dark SUV.

"It's probably just a side effect of the spooky costume," Tara hedged, knowing that her showdown with Luke and Sophie was only minutes away now. She pointed her long scepter at the phone. "I'll let you know how it all turns out the next time we talk."

Tara smiled, feeling every one of the heavy red lipstick layers in her makeup mask.

"All right. Knock 'em dead. Your costume rocks and so do you." Jordyn lifted a sugar cookie and took a bite before she disconnected her video.

Tara tucked her phone into her bag, double checking that the partnership agreement paperwork still rested inside. Then, after greeting Kaitlin and receiving a grudging, two-word response in return, they headed for Sophie's front door. In the entryway, a table full of prestuffed bags awaited trick-or-treaters while a life-sized witch cackled as she stirred a cauldron billowing red smoke.

After Tara skirted the treat table to ring the doorbell Amelia answered, wearing gray sweats and a T-shirt with a skull on the front. Her expression was surly until she saw who it was.

"Cool costume, Auntie T!" Grinning, Amelia hugged her before giving Kaitlin a tamer greeting. "Come in. Everyone else is already here, and Mom's just working on the appetizers."

"Darling, I'm well finished with the food prep," Sophie chided from deeper in the house. "Bring my guests in and then get back to your homework."

Amelia rolled her eyes, some of the surly expression returning. Tara had no idea why Sophie never allowed her daughters ten seconds of fun, but then, she didn't pretend to be an expert on parenting. Her first role model had been a struggling single mother who'd spent too much time working to really be a memorable presence in Tara's young life. Her next role model had been Lauren, who wanted a shopping partner who loved gossip and travel as much as she did.

"We'll catch up soon?" Tara asked Amelia quietly as they walked together toward the kitchen where the others congregated. "I have a bunch of good book recommendations for you."

Tara enjoyed both of Sophie's daughters, but she identified better with the younger one who was a little curvier, a little more rebellious, and never seemed to snag her mother's full approval the way her sister Charlotte often did.

"Awesome. I could use some reading material to lighten the hours spent behind my prison walls." Amelia stopped just short of the kitchen, waving Tara and Kaitlin forward before retreating toward the stairs.

While Amelia stomped back up to her room, making no attempt to hide her displeasure with her mom, Tara pulled her attention to the kitchen where Kaitlin had walked ahead of her to greet Sophie with only a fraction more warmth than she'd given Tara.

Their stilted interaction reminded Tara that even though half of their book club had misgivings about Tara, most of them had equal reason to distrust Sophie. From Tara's perspective, however, the main reason her friends had issues with Tara were all directly related to Sophie herself. Because of *The Clean Break*, mostly. Though in Mei's case, Sophie had deliberately masqueraded as Tara to deflect Mei's suspicions about her husband away from Sophie and toward Tara.

It had been a cold and calculated stab in the back from her business partner based on Sophie's suspicions about her own husband.

She would add it to the list of things she got off her chest tonight when she spoke to Sophie. For now, Tara would have followed Kaitlin into the kitchen to join the rest of the group, if a rough voice hadn't called her from the far side of the sitting room.

"Happy Halloween, Maleficent."

Tara's gut sank to hear Luke from the shadowed half of the room. She turned to see him clutching a glass of amber-colored liquid, dressed casually in jeans and a white button-down. Her heart pounded harder, even though she knew he couldn't do anything to her with Sophie one room away. Within hearing distance.

Or was that his aim? To make Sophie jealous by flirting with Tara? Which made her wonder if Luke had been the source of the unfounded rumor about himself.

Would he really plant seeds of doubt about his fidelity if he wanted to cast one of Sophie's friends in a negative light?

"Hello, Luke." She gripped the scepter tighter, remembering the feel of that letter opener in her hand on the day she'd shown her stepbrother that he had no right to touch her without her permission.

"You've been avoiding my calls," Luke accused, rattling the ice in his glass before taking a sip from his drink.

Tara glanced over her shoulder toward the bright kitchen, wondering if anyone was listening to them. Sophie had overheard her daughter all the way from the foyer. Tara took a step closer to him, unwilling to give anyone cause for gossip.

"Because it was a mistake for me to think you would ever give me useful information about my business." She regretted that she'd allowed him to play upon her fears. Her weaknesses. "I'll be better served working things out with my partner in the future."

Luke laughed, not bothering to hide his amusement.

"You'll be better served, will you? What about me?"

"What about you?" she snapped back, still keeping her voice low, but unable to hide her anger. "My work with Sophie doesn't have anything to do with you."

"Sweet, innocent Tara. Always so kind to everyone," he mocked her. "Yet you're not above using the promise of sex to get your own way, are you?"

Stunned, she could only blink in confusion.

This too, he mocked, imitating her by batting his eyelashes. "You sure did snag a good deal on the house you rent from me, but that didn't have anything to do with you flirting your ass off."

Tara glanced over her shoulder again, hating the thought of anyone hearing this conversation about behavior that had no basis in reality. She'd assumed the reasonable rent on the house down the street was because they were all friends, and Luke was a wealthy man.

"I'm happy to pay market value. I hardly need handouts."

"Did you believe you could just toy with me at that anniversary party for *The Clean Break*? Never make good on all the sexy insinuation?" He reached for her, and she scuttled back fast, bumping into the corner of a console table with a yelp.

While she steadied the lamp she'd almost knocked over, he came up behind her, caging her between his arms and speaking directly in her ear. "Maybe uptight Tara just needs a little chemical help delivering on her promises. Maybe we can try some Ecstasy?"

She reared back an elbow, intending to jab it into whatever she could hit, but when she wrenched it backward, she met only air.

Luke had vanished behind her as fast as he'd grabbed her. While in front of her, Sophie stepped into the sitting room, cold fire in her blue eyes.

"Come and join us, Tara." Sophie's voice was strangely soft. Her manner in direct opposition to the murderous look on her face. But then, no one else but Tara could witness the other woman's expression at that moment. "We're all waiting on you."

Tara's heart was in her throat from being cornered. From the threat of being drugged against her will. Holy hell, who were these people? She wanted to scream at Sophie.

At Luke.

But with Sophie's kitchen full of guests, Tara told herself to wait until later. She would make sure to be the last one to leave Sophie's house tonight. Once she had her conniving business partner to herself, she would demand Sophie sign the partnership agreement or risk a costly lawsuit.

Then, as soon as her former friend's signature had been secured, Tara would get the hell out of this house. She would jump in her car.

Drive to the closest police station.

And file sexual harassment charges against that bastard Luke Sideris. Because if he touched her again, there was another letter opener in her purse.

She damned well remembered how to use it.

CHAPTER 32

Jordyn

Present

"No worries. There are plenty of candles."

Sophie Durand's calm, disembodied voice spoke in the dark kitchen, making Jordyn's skin crawl with anxiety. Did their too-perfect hostess ever get rattled? Had she even heard Jordyn's announcement about hunting for Tara's killer tonight?

In the seconds of zero visibility, as the sound of drawers being opened and closed filled her ears, Jordyn tried to remember if everyone from book club had been in the same room when the lights went out. She'd been so focused on Kaitlin, convinced the therapist was Tara's most likely killer, that the other group members had been in the periphery of her focus.

"Here we go," Sophie continued speaking a moment before a battery-operated lighter sparked into a flame. She stood at the island, a handful of fat candles in varying sizes and colors perched on the granite. "Let's just light a few of these so we can see what we're doing."

Jordyn's heart skittered faster. She felt uneasy about the power going off right after the announcement of her real identity. Had the storm really knocked out the electricity? Or had someone cut it on purpose? Maybe her news had upset Tara's killer.

Would it drive that person to act again?

"I think we should all get comfortable while we figure out the real murder mystery," Jordyn reiterated as the candlelight began illuminating the faces of Tara's former friends.

Brad was still in the far corner by the sliders leading to the patio, though he looked a little unsteady on his feet. Gina stood close to him, cowboy hat covering her face while she stared down into her drink as if the conversation didn't concern her at all.

Destiny and Kaitlin perched on barstools at the island, while Mei and Fatima hovered behind them, their faces in shadow.

Sophie set down the lighter and lifted one of the candles. "While you hijack my gathering for your own agenda, I need to use the house phone to call a neighbor and check on Charlotte. She doesn't belong at a party if the electricity is out there too."

Jordyn watched her leave the room, wishing she had a way to keep everyone contained in one place while she confronted them with the evidence she had collected. Would they begin to turn on one another as they learned the truth about Tara's last book club?

A gust of wind howled around the house, the sound more pronounced in the silence of the kitchen.

Across the room, Brad cleared his throat. "Jordyn, I'm not clear why you think one of Tara's friends killed her?" He peered around at the others in a clear bid for support. "The police investigated the accident, so if there was any evidence against one of us . . ."

He wavered on his feet a little, his drink overflowing the rim of the glass as he seemed to lose his train of thought.

Gina reached for his elbow to steady him. "Let me get you a water."

Brad nodded gratefully, setting his drink on the edge of a sleek display cabinet.

"There is plenty of evidence," Jordyn shot back, thinking about all the notes Natalie had given her. All of the incriminating things she'd discovered for herself. "Against all of you. There are so many motives in this room, it might take some time to wade through them all."

"I had a motive," Gina admitted, lifting her hand to wave. "I admit it. But I'm not sharing it until Sophie returns. I need her to hear about it."

Jordyn frowned even as a wave of nausea threatened. How could the woman be so cavalier? She took a deep breath and told herself to keep pushing for answers.

"I'll hold you to that, *Gina*." She laid enough emphasis on the name to ensure Evangeline understood that Jordyn already knew her identity. "What about you, Brad? Where were you last year after the Halloween book club meeting?"

He shook his head, still wavering on his feet. "You know I had a motive, but that's not my style. Right now, though, I don't feel so well."

He staggered toward the sitting room, and while Jordyn was surprised he'd had enough time to drink to excess when it was still early, she didn't stand in his way. Instead, she turned toward the women gathered at the island, all of them surprisingly quiet.

"What about you, Mei?" Jordyn stalked closer, wanting to see her face more clearly when she made her accusation. "Did you hate Tara enough to kill her after you thought it was her at the Adelphi Hotel with your husband?"

Mei's lip curled as she spun the blue wine charm around the base of her glass.

"It *was* Tara at the Adelphi, but I didn't kill her. Nikolai would never leave me for a social parasite like Tara whose claim to fame was being Sophie's shadow."

Jordyn sucked in a breath at the venom in Mei's voice. She would never have suspected that anyone in Tara's circle would view her that way. But perhaps, if Mei truly believed that Tara had been the object of her husband's affections, she could be excused for thinking poorly of her.

Mei could not be excused for murder, however.

Jordyn leaned over the island to look Mei in the face. Up close, she could see where Mei had woven the bride of Frankenstein wig into her own dark hair.

"Newsflash. It was Sophie, not Tara, with Nikolai that night," Jordyn informed her, unable to let Tara's name be tarnished even now. "Where were you after book club last Halloween?"

Mei appeared a little less certain of herself. She lifted her chin. "I saw the photo of them together at the Adelphi. I know that was Tara."

More lightning lit up the room. The thunder rolled a moment afterward. Rain came down in sheets against the retracting glass pocket doors.

"But you also saw the photo evidence from another hotel where you can clearly see the woman wearing that dress was Sophie, not Tara. Why did you refuse to believe what your PI told you? Was it because you'd already killed Tara and didn't want to think you'd done it for nothing?" Jordyn glanced around the kitchen, hoping their two-faced hostess would return soon, but there was no sign of her yet. "Why don't you share with us your alibi for Tara's time of death?"

"If you were with the police department, *you'd* already know." Mei folded her arms across her purple slip dress and glared at Jordyn, but a line of perspiration dotted her forehead now. "I don't owe you any explanations."

"So much for sharing our character backstories." Jordyn eased away from her, putting a row of kitchen cabinets at her back. She didn't want anyone sneaking up behind her as she confronted these false-face friends who didn't hesitate to stab each other in the back. "Destiny, you owed Tara a boatload of money after she helped you get The Ascent off the ground. An investment you never repaid her estate, since Tara had been content with a handshake."

Destiny rose from her seat, her huge fan tail of feathers rising with her. "You think I would kill one of the few people in this town who always supported me?"

The anger in her voice seemed genuine. Then again, some people flipped into offensive mode when they felt defensive. Maybe Destiny was trying to deflect from her guilt.

When Jordyn didn't reply right away, Destiny huffed a frustrated sigh. "Besides, what start-up do you know that makes a profit in the first year? I told Tara I could have it repaid with interest in three years."

Fatima lifted her wine glass in a gloved hand, giving a general toast in Destiny's direction. "I believe you. Tara seemed upset that last night at book club, but not toward you."

Jordyn whirled to face Fatima, the movement of her body stirring the air enough to extinguish one of the candles Sophie had left burning on the island among the wine bottles. Jordyn's eyes had adjusted enough to the dark, however, that it hardly mattered. Especially since she could still see Fatima's face well enough.

"What do you mean, *upset*?" Jordyn had relived her last phone call from Tara over and over again.

I'll have everyone I need to hex all in one room, Tara had said as she stood in Sophie's driveway wearing her Maleficent costume one year ago. She hadn't sounded like she was joking either.

Tara had seemed on edge. Uneasy.

"Just that." Fatima reached for the pinot noir and topped off her drink. "If you were really such great friends with her, you know she was normally a little Miss Sunshine. Full of life and ready to engage with everyone. But that last night she seemed distracted and quiet. Moody, I guess?"

Destiny returned to the bar stool beside Fatima. "Agreed. She was out of sorts. I asked her about a romance book she'd recommended to me a few months before, and she *rolled her eyes* at me. That girl was *not* an eye roller. And I don't think it was about the book. I think it was the word 'romance' that got her twisted. Maybe you should be looking for a romance gone wrong."

Surprise, surprise if Tara found relationships challenging considering her past. Her adoptive brother had violated her the day he met her.

She wished she'd known more about Tara's state of mind in the last hours of her life before tonight. She wanted to share this new information with Natalie to discuss it, see how it fit with the rest of the puzzle. But there wasn't time. She was on her own to find this killer.

For all she knew, Destiny was trying to misdirect her with the whole romantic interest angle.

Jordyn turned toward Kaitlin, who twirled her surgical mask by the strings. "Or maybe I should be looking at the woman with an SUV with a damaged front-end that matches the description of the hit-and-run vehicle."

Swearing under her breath, Kaitlin tossed the mask on the island. "You little sneak. That's why you went into my garage?"

Jordyn's temper flared even as she hoped the other women would intervene if Kaitlin turned on her. "Why don't you tell everyone why you didn't take it into a mechanic to have it fixed? Worried someone would report the damage?"

Seeing the fury in Kaitlin's eyes made her wonder if that was the last thing Tara saw before she was struck. Before she landed on the pavement, her hip smashed and her leg crushed. The internal bleeding too severe to staunch.

"I hit a deer last fall, you numbskull. I haven't fixed the SUV because I needed a new roof this spring and—you know—*bills*? I'm a single-income household." Kaitlin chugged from her wine glass, clearly aggrieved or doing a good acting job. "And if you're looking for Tara's enemy number one, why don't you talk to our peerless hostess?"

Fatima let out a dark laugh that seemed to echo Kaitlin's view. Mei set down her drink at the edge of the countertop and almost missed the granite all together, dodging sideways to save the drink from spilling.

"Where is Sophie anyway?" Mei asked, using a few cocktail napkins to mop up some wine that sloshed onto the counter. "I have questions for her."

"She's taking forever to check on the girls," Destiny agreed before swiveling in her seat to see beyond her feathered fan tail. "For that matter, where did Brad and Gina go?"

The corner where the two of them had been standing was now vacant. Brad's half empty glass still rested on the ledge of the display cabinet, but he was nowhere to be seen. As for Gina, there was no sign she'd ever been there.

Was the real killer escaping even now?

"No way. No fucking way." Jordyn lifted one of the fat candles that Sophie had left on the island. "No one is leaving here until we figure this out. Otherwise, I will go to the police tomorrow with the dirt I have on every last one of you. So if you don't want that to happen, I suggest you help me nail the guilty party."

"Good luck with that, Gumshoe Girl." Destiny reached a hand into a bowl of popcorn. "I'll keep my front row seat to this shitshow, but I am *not* walking through a dark house with a killer on the loose."

Jordan opened her mouth to argue, but from somewhere in the house, a muffled scream sounded.

Jordyn's pulse accelerated. She was more scared of someone getting away than she was for her own safety. Especially when a sudden gust of cold breeze blew through the kitchen. As if a door was being opened somewhere.

Someone trying to leave?

The panicked thought got Jordyn's feet moving even as all of the candles flickered, then went out.

Through the dark, she raced in the direction of the front door.

CHAPTER

33

Gina

Present

ALL THE TALK about a killer was creeping her out. Especially since people kept disappearing from the kitchen.

First Sophie. And then, where the hell had Brad gone? After slipping out without anyone noticing her departure, Gina crept along the corridor leading to the primary suite, in search of Luke.

Or Sophie. At this point, she wasn't sure who she needed to confront more. Sophie, to finally reveal her identity as Evangeline and tell her about the affair? Or Luke, who had scarcely batted an eye when she'd offered to help him take out his wife?

He'd simply scoffed and shoved her back toward the kitchen, urging her to rejoin their friends. His reaction to her morbid proposal hadn't told her one way or the other if he had murder in mind for his spouse. Which had been her only reason for suggesting she would help him. She'd used her proposition as a litmus test to determine if he truly meant Sophie harm. At least, she hoped that had been her sole purpose for speaking aloud a desire to kill someone. She hadn't lost all of her humanity because of *The Clean Break* debacle, had she?

This night of revenge wasn't going to plan. At all.

She'd known these were bad people, yet she hadn't anticipated this level of malevolence. She feared Luke really was going to dispatch his wife. Then tonight she'd discovered Jordyn Lawson's secret. The woman was Tara Hughes's foster sister, convinced someone in book club had targeted Tara exactly one year ago.

While the news of Jordyn's identity had been a surprise, Gina hadn't found it at all difficult to believe that a member of this book group had killed before. Beneath their smiling socialite exteriors, every last one of these cultured Saratogians had a dark side.

"Luke? Are you here?" Gina called into the blackness of the cavernous home, her voice lost to the twenty-foot-high ceilings and the ambient noise of the storm outside.

Her eyes adjusted to the new level of darkness since she'd left the light from the candles behind in the kitchen. The double doors to the primary suite were closed, as was the door to Luke's office. Everything seemed quiet. Still.

But from some far corner of the house . . . a shout. Of pain? Surprise? Then, everything went silent again, but she felt a slight swirl of air past her chilled arms that warned her doors were being opened and closed somewhere.

She backtracked to the sweeping staircase that led to the upper rooms—two guest suites and the girls' bedrooms. Had everyone gone there?

Gina paused at the top of the landing. Strained her ears, listening. Her heart thudded hard enough to make her feel dizzy, and she wished she'd skipped the alcohol earlier. Was that what was making her feel woozy now? Or from holding her breath in apprehension? She forced herself to draw in long, slow gulps of air.

Here too, all the doors were closed. Softly, she walked to the first one and put her ear to the white oak. Nothing. At the second one, she did the same, and all seemed quiet within. But at the third—a room she was pretty sure belonged to either Charlotte or Amelia—she heard muted voices.

Or at least one voice.

A woman was ranting in an angry sort of raised whisper.

Gina pressed closer to the door.

"—was having an affair with her. Of course I had to confront her—"

Whatever else the woman—was it Sophie?—was saying got lost to a shout from the base of the main staircase.

"Brad? Gina? Are you up here?"

Gina recognized Jordyn's voice even as she cursed the woman for drowning out the whispered conversation. Making a split-second decision, Gina turned on her heel and fled for the back stairs that led to the mudroom, the same route she'd used when she'd sneaked into the house the day before. The steps were darker, and she slowed to navigate them. By the time she reached the bottom, she felt sure that she'd escaped Jordyn without being seen.

Flattening herself against the mudroom wall, Gina willed her erratic breathing to decelerate. Her tension to recede. But that proved impossible. Because at some point tonight she'd gone from wanting revenge to being quietly terrified.

Something dangerous was happening upstairs. Maybe downstairs, too. Because as she stood on shaking legs, she heard a door slam nearby. Followed by the unmistakable mechanical scrape of a deadbolt sliding into place.

The tension in Sophie's house was thick enough to choke on. Gina had the overwhelming sensation that she was just one cog in the bad vibes factory that was Sophie Durand's life.

Gina now understood there were far darker forces at work tonight than her plan for vengeance.

Silently, she crept along the downstairs corridor in the direction of the sound she'd heard. As she moved, she reached into the slim holster at her waist. Allowed her fingers to trail over the cold steel of the derringer she'd worn as part of her costume.

She hadn't come here with the intent to kill. But if it came down to her or someone else?

Gina wouldn't hesitate to fire.

CHAPTER

34

Tara

One Year Ago

NORMALLY, TARA LOVED the book club meetings.

Over the years that she'd been a member, they'd read mostly fiction with a little nonfiction mixed in to break things up. Tara had enjoyed classics like *The Great Gatsby* and *The Bluest Eye*, both Brad's picks since he was on an endless quest to improve their literary minds. Then there'd been more recent bestsellers like *Bel Canto* and *Demon Copperhead*.

But tonight, as half the group sat around Sophie's living room in costume and the other half hadn't bothered, Tara wanted to throw her copy of the self-help book selection in frustration. Would this meeting ever end?

Her anger toward Luke had built throughout the evening until it reached a boiling point. How dare he accuse her of being sexually manipulative? Of somehow cajoling him into giving her a good deal on rent with the promise of . . . *eww.*

She couldn't think back on that conversation without triggering all the newly rediscovered fury at her stepbrother Evander.

No wonder she had the urge to stab Luke Sideris. The man had played into her personal nightmare, an experience so traumatic she'd blocked it from her own mind for almost two decades.

Finally, *finally*, someone in the group said they needed to head home. Tara had been so tuned out that she couldn't have said who'd spoken, but suddenly everyone was on their feet, exchanging hugs and air kisses, draining their wine glasses and raving about what a fun evening they'd enjoyed.

Tara hung back, dully accepting a couple of hugs, but mostly waiting for her opportunity to confront Sophie about . . .

Everything.

She hunted around the living room for where she'd laid her handbag, finding it on an end table near someone's forgotten wineglass. Although, on second look, there was a pink wine charm around the stem, which normally indicated one of her drinks. The book club ladies were careful about maintaining the same charms from meeting to meeting. Sophie had given the group matching sets of stem tags two Christmases ago, and Tara had claimed the pink crystal for her own.

Someone must have refilled her glass without her noticing.

She lifted the wineglass, thinking a few sips might steel her for the confrontation that lay ahead. Except, just as she put it to her lips, Luke's taunts circled through her brain.

Maybe uptight Tara just needs a little chemical help delivering on her promises. Maybe we can try some Ecstasy?

Would the bastard try drugging her drink?

She set the red wine down with a clatter. She wouldn't put anything past him after that ugly encounter earlier.

"Tara? Are you heading home too?" Sophie turned toward her now, a questioning look on her preternaturally calm face. Was it Botox that made her skin appear so placid? Or was she simply that expressionless and unflappable?

"No, Sophie. I'm not going anywhere just yet." Tara reached into her purse. She withdrew a pen and the partnership agreement she'd printed off from a legal advice website, since she'd never been able to reschedule with Arnie Van Ness. "We have some unfinished business to address."

"Is that so?" Sophie didn't so much as glance at the sheaf of papers. "I thought we'd agreed business is for workdays and book club nights are for fun?"

"I think you've put off this discussion long enough," Tara informed her evenly. She unfolded the printouts and passed them to Sophie. "It's past time that we formalize our business arrangement."

A small smile curved Sophie's mouth.

"I see. At least allow me to change out of my costume first." She smoothed a hand over the long crimson gown she wore, then set the papers down. "It's hard enough to think about work when you're dressed as Maleficent. But maybe if I at least change out of the *Hocus Pocus* clothes, I'll be able to concentrate on this."

Sophie moved toward the door.

Tara sidestepped into her path.

"I don't think that will be necessary. I just require a signature, Sophie." She handed her the pen. "That's all."

"Excuse me?" Sophie ignored the pen and folded her arms, using her greater height to look down her nose. "I don't know what's gotten into you tonight, but I'm not going to sign anything I haven't read carefully. I think you'd better leave, and we'll revisit this at the office."

"That's unacceptable to me. I no longer trust you to honor a handshake agreement. So either sign the papers tonight or buy me out of my half of *The Clean Break,* and you can go your own way with the business." Tara tucked the pen between Sophie's folded arms. "How about that?"

"Not on your fucking life." Sophie grabbed the pen and hurled it across the room, never taking her eyes off Tara. "Now, gather your things and scuttle back home before I run out of patience."

Tara pulled her lips into what she hoped constituted a Sophie-style polite smile.

"You're not understanding me," she began again, remembering all of the times she'd caved to Sophie's big personality and iron will. All the times Tara hadn't made waves in the name of a civil partnership. "You have two options tonight. Sign the papers that outline the terms we agreed on verbally a long time ago. Or write me a check."

"You're not understanding *me,*" Sophie parroted, lifting the partnership agreement and slowly tearing it in half. "I'm not doing either of those things tonight."

Tara hung on to her patience by a thread. "You do know I have other copies? In fact, I already emailed you an electronic version so you can sign digitally."

"But I won't sign any such thing," Sophie assured her.

A fresh wave of anger rolled through Tara. Up until now, she'd been trying to channel her father, the powerhouse businessman Randall Hughes. But seeing that agreement ripped in two fueled a new level of animosity. So instead of letting Randall Hughes's business acumen guide her actions, she dredged up her old memories of Jordyn Lawson in action.

Her kick-ass friend never backed down from a fight.

"You really want to pick what's behind door number three without knowing what you'll find?" Tara taunted, recalling with perfect clarity a time Jordyn had gone toe-to-toe with two older kids—man-size kids—at a playground after they cornered Tara on a swing.

Jordyn hadn't flinched. She'd picked up two fistfuls of dirt. Then, screaming like a Viking warrior, she'd flung sandy gravel in each of their faces, grabbed Tara's hand, and ran sprinting for six city blocks without pause.

Tara had a different kind of dirt.

"Tara." Sophie shook her head, her expression grave. "You're so overmatched, it's frankly pathetic."

"You think so?" Anxiety strung her shoulders tight, but she didn't give ground. "Because from my perspective, I'm about to play my ace."

Sophie's expression wavered. A hint of worry showed in her blue eyes before that placid mask was back in place.

"You're bluffing. How quaint." Sophie turned from her with a sweep of her long red gown. "Stay if you want, but I really do need to clean up before I can retire for the evening."

"I'll go to the police tomorrow."

Tara's words had the desired effect.

Sophie stopped. Turned to take her measure.

"What are you talking about?"

"Your husband," she said pointedly, enunciating with precision. "The sexual predator. Looks like I'll be filing my harassment claim in the morning."

Sophie's color drained a little. She hadn't been expecting that.

"What proof do you have?" Her voice had a strangled sound, as if the words cost her.

Tara picked up her purse and her scepter.

"Wouldn't you love to know?" Tara asked before she walked out of the living room, opened the front door, and stepped out into the night.

Breathing deeply of the crisp fall air, she savored the memory of the look on Sophie's face. The fear in her eyes when she'd realized Tara had not, in fact, been bluffing.

Tara hadn't gotten what she wanted tonight. Not by a long shot.

But she also hadn't backed down.

Sophie would come around and sign the papers. Maybe even before morning. She would see reason when she thought about the scandal Luke's behavior would create for her. For her family.

Tara felt a pang about the way that kind of news would affect Charlotte and Amelia. Yet she knew Sophie, for all her faults, loved her girls. She would protect them.

Reassured, Tara still felt wired as she made the short drive home through the darkened street, careful of the straggling older trick-or-treaters out long past curfew. Maybe she needed to go for a run before bed.

Pound out her frustration with some cardio.

Within fifteen minutes, she had her face washed and her running clothes on. At one point she thought she'd heard some shouting from her neighbors' home. Could it be the unflappable Sophie had decided to confront her bastard second husband about his behavior?

By the time Tara returned outside and jogged up the street, Sophie's house remained quiet. She popped in her earbuds for workout music, still buzzing with adrenaline from her argument with Sophie.

She never heard the vehicle approach until it was too late.

Out of nowhere, the headlights all but blinded her. Only at the last minute did she glimpse who was behind the wheel. Someone who looked almost surprised to see her.

A face she recognized all too well.

When the crash came, the flash of excruciating pain, Tara didn't bother to guess if the driver had hit her purposely or if there was a small chance the collision had been accidental.

Instead, with the clarity of a woman who knows death has come for her, Tara hoped Jordyn would somehow figure out what had happened. That Jordyn would work her fearless friendship magic for Tara's sake.

One last time.

CHAPTER

35

Jordyn

Present

SHE WAS IN over her head.

Jordyn cursed herself for her attempts at playing Poirot as she ran around the house in the dark, stubbing her toes, banging her hips on unseen furniture, and toppling over one piece that had resulted in glass breaking. Noisy. Dangerously so. Still, she searched the house in vain for the exit that had been opened somewhere.

Her efforts to draw a confession from someone in the kitchen had been laughable. No one was admitting to killing Tara. Worse, two of her suspects had vanished without her ever noticing. Where the hell had Brad and Gina gone?

And why hadn't Sophie ever returned?

Jordyn had been so dismissive of law enforcement's struggles to solve this case, but she hadn't done much better. She didn't care about endangering her own life per se, but she definitely didn't want to give up the ghost before she pointed a finger at Tara's killer.

Amid the din of the storm, Jordyn hadn't heard any doors opening or cars departing. Not finding evidence of a defection downstairs, she moved to check out the second floor.

"Brad? Gina? Are you up here?" She climbed the steps when no one answered, careful not to trip in the dark.

She wouldn't be doing Tara's memory any favors if Jordyn was found at the base of the staircase with a broken neck. The book club would close ranks, shrug their collective well-toned shoulders, and move on as if nothing had ever interrupted their charmed lives.

A rustling noise emanated at the far end of the upstairs corridor. The ceilings weren't as high on the second level, making sounds easier to pinpoint than on the echoing first floor.

Jordyn rushed forward, determined not to let anyone leave the house. But as she passed one of the closed doors along the hallway, a rush of cold air blew in from the threshold.

Could this be the source of the gust that had blown through the kitchen? Maybe someone had opened a window, not a door.

"Hello?" She knocked on the panel of polished white oak. "Anyone in here?"

When no one responded, she turned the heavy handle and pushed her way into a freezing, darkened bedroom. Cold air lifted her hair from her neck, and she moved toward an open set of French doors where a tall, slender woman stood silhouetted against the rainy night. The exterior landscape lighting was extinguished when the electricity cut out. But there must be a few solar lights dotted among the others outside because a dull glow made the storm and the woman just barely visible.

"Sophie?" Squinting into the shadowed dimness, Jordyn stepped deeper into the room. "What are you doing?"

"The girls are both fine," Sophie informed her, her voice sounding a bit uneven. Remote, actually. Detached. "Charlotte is back home now. The party she was going to was cancelled when the power went out."

A rustling noise sounded from the other end of the room. Was it just the wind?

"Glad they're safe." Jordyn glanced around, trying to determine if this was one of the daughters' rooms, but the shadowed suite seemed as minimalist and bland as every other vanilla nightmare in the house. Either this was a space for guests or else one of Sophie's offspring had inherited her mother's spare style. "Why are you up here alone? Letting all the rain in?"

"We're alone?" Sophie glanced back, her eyes scanning the room as if searching for someone else. Then, not seeing anyone else in the shadowed corners, she turned away from Jordyn to step through the open French doors out onto the balcony. "The deck is covered, so it's a good place to watch the rain."

How weird was that?

Something was off about her words. Even her walk seemed wobbly. Maybe she'd started drinking before her guests had even arrived.

"You want to enjoy the rainstorm during book club with a house full of guests while we're all downstairs trying to solve a murder?" Jordyn's eyes narrowed as she followed Sophie outside.

There were a couple of low loveseats and some tall plants that probably made the space feel more private, but Jordyn could see the outline of the pool area below. A waist-high railing wrapped around the deck, save for the space where a wide stairwell led down to the pool.

"I think you came here tonight believing you already knew who the killer was, didn't you?"

It was the first thing Sophie had said that made some sense. Even if she was way off base.

"No. I have a lot of suspicions, but I'm still not sure." Jordyn studied her in the gloom that was only a tiny bit brighter outdoors thanks to the occasional streak of lightning and a few solar lights in the garden between the pool house and the main structure. "Do you know who killed Tara?"

Sophie walked toward the stairs as if she planned to leave the shelter of the balcony for the pool deck. In the rain.

The storm had slowed from a sheeting downpour to a steady, cold shower. That didn't mean a sane person would want to stroll through it without a coat.

"Do you know what she threatened to do on her last night here?" Sophie asked instead, turning unsteadily to face her.

Jordyn wished she would come back inside. Or at least away from the wide outdoor steps that were sure to be slippery. But she wasn't about to lose the thread of this conversation. A discussion of Tara's killer was what had brought her here after all.

"Tara? Threatening?" Jordyn shook her head. "What happened to her having a generous heart and absolutely no agenda?"

She hadn't forgotten Sophie's description of her friend at the Witch Walk.

"She changed," Sophie said simply. She stuck her hand out beyond the roofline so that the rain fell freely on her skin. Her moves seemed to be in slow motion. "That last evening, she was like a totally different person."

Jordyn remembered the phone conversation they'd had that night. Tara had been dressed as Maleficent, telling Jordyn that everyone she wanted to hex would be at the book club meeting.

Sophie wasn't wrong. Tara had seemed different. Still, she needed to keep the woman talking. Find out what had happened.

"How did she change? Why would you say that?" Jordyn felt the old defensiveness flare. Her need to protect her friend.

Only now, she protected the memory of her. The legacy of kindness Tara had left behind.

"She tried to blackmail me into—" Sophie swung around to look at Jordyn and seemed to change whatever she'd been about to say. "She threatened to tell the police that Luke was some kind of . . . that he was harassing her."

Sophie's words were sluggish. Maybe a guilty conscience driven her to drink too much.

Perhaps the anniversary of killing her friend weighed on her?

"Was he?" Jordyn swiped rain from her face as she recalled the way Tara had avoided talking about Luke. "Harassing her?"

"Don't be ridiculous. If anything, she would have been the one to harass him. I saw her hanging all over him at *The Clean Break* anniversary party months before her death. She made a spectacle of herself. It was an embarrassment."

There was a venom in her tone that Jordyn hadn't heard before from perpetually composed Sophie. A flash of anger and, perhaps, jealousy toward Tara.

"And no one is allowed to embarrass you, are they Sophie?" Jordyn strode closer, ready to ratchet up the verbal pressure if it meant rattling this woman. Squeezing a confession from her. "Not your husband. Not your daughters, who you make sure never quite earn your approval."

"I'd be careful if I were you," Sophie said, pointing a finger at her. "That's my family you're talking about."

"And Tara is *my* family," Jordyn reminded her, not caring for the finger in her face. She knocked it away. "So you be careful too."

Sophie sucked in a hiss. Her eyes went wider at the physical contact, the whites of her eyes momentarily visible.

"Your *family* was a spineless orphan who could only find success in life when attached to other people," Sophie spat out, leaning forward to make her point. "She either fluttered her eyelashes to get what she wanted, or she insinuated herself into your world so thoroughly you couldn't scrape her off."

Jordyn's heart slammed against her ribs. She saw red. A roar sounded in her ears like a rogue wave. Or like the storm had picked up.

Only, she was pretty sure *she* was the storm.

"Did you *kill* her for that?" Jordyn asked, remembering that Natalie had told her one of Luke Sideris's vehicles had paint that matched the hit-and-run vehicle. "Did you run down your friend because of some petty business bullshit? Or jealousy?"

She had shouted her way closer to Sophie so that they were practically nose to nose. Both angry. Breathing hard.

"I didn't run her down! And I saw her flirt with my husband with my own eyes at a work party." Sophie put a hand to her neck, wincing. She patted the area, as if searching for the source of the pain. As if something had stung her? Her brows furrowed as she seemed to struggle to think. She spoke slowly. Deliberately. "Yet Tara had the audacity to then threaten me with going to the police to claim Luke had sexually harassed her."

"She confided in you, and you didn't believe her." Jordyn heard a rustling noise behind her again, but she barely paid any heed, her brain overrun with images of Sophie gunning the engine to hit Tara.

"It wasn't true!" Sophie insisted, backing up another step, wavering on her feet as she gesticulated. "She tried to use it as a bargaining chip so I'd sign some partnership agreement. I drove over to her house later that night to talk to her. And I didn't even see her in the dark until—"

Jordyn's gut dropped to her toes.

"You hit her," Jordyn finished, the pieces coming together in a final picture. "You were angry with her, and you hit her."

"I was on my way to talk sense into her!" Sophie insisted, her voice wracked with emotion.

It sounded like guilt.

But Jordyn didn't care about Sophie's feelings. She only cared about the admission. Because Sophie had absolutely done the crime even if she couldn't bring herself to say the words.

* * *

"You never confessed though. All this time you've left Tara's real friends to worry and wonder. Worst, you just left her there, on the cold pavement in the dark to die alone." Anger vibrated through her. "You cold-hearted, conscienceless *bitch*."

She wanted to throttle the woman, but she settled for shoving her with both hands, the fury in her body needing an outlet. Also needing to get a killer out of her face. Just a small shove.

Except Sophie reeled backward, still unsteady.

The moment played out in horrible slow motion. Sophie standing at the top of a stairwell slippery from rain. Scrambling back made her lose her footing. Her arms pinwheeling as she tried to find her balance.

The scream she made as she fell would be something Jordyn would never, ever forget.

C H A P T E R

36

Gina

Present

THE SCREAM FROZE Gina in place.

She'd heard the term "bloodcurdling" before. Not until this moment did she understand that it was a real phenomenon. Like every one of her red blood cells halted in her veins and shriveled.

In the awful, haunting silence afterward, Gina thought her knees might give out. A shriek like that meant something horrible had happened. That all her fears had been well founded. That a murderer lurked among them.

Drawing her gun, she took small reassurance from its cool weight in her palm. Gina refused to be the next one screaming.

Should she call out for the others? Or would that only allow a potential killer to find her? She thought she heard feet pounding on the main staircase. Or maybe down the back steps. Gina had ventured too far from both of them to be sure.

The kitchen ahead remained quiet. Where had everyone gone? From upstairs came high, panicked voices. Sophie's daughters? Book club members?

Some instinct drew her toward the huge glass doors as the rain slowed. Had the sound emanated from out there? The house was well insulated, muting most of the external noise. Yet that scream seemed loud enough to hear for miles.

She tugged on the handle, rolling the pocket glass window aside just enough to squeeze through. Outside, there was a sheltered patio table and enough overhang to protect her from the rain. Breathing in the earthy scent of the air, she scanned the pool deck, searching for any movement. The source of the scream or the person who'd caused it. All was still save the falling rain and the wind stirring the ties of cushions on some chaise loungers.

Then her gaze snagged on an oddly shaped shadow. A lumpy pile near the steps into the pool.

Behind her, Gina heard stirring in the kitchen through the door she'd left cracked. But her focus remained on that misshapen heap. Wet clothes?

Stepping closer, out into the rain, she peered down into the pool. Distinguished a body partially submerged. Recognized the seaweed-like strands floating in the water's edge that was actually long blond hair.

Marine-blue eyes stared back at her. Open, but unseeing.

Sophie Durand lay along the watery steps, a dark stain around her head clouding the water.

Fear bubbled free. Gina screamed.

She scuttled backward, almost slipping. Catching herself on the table because no way was she falling into that water with . . . a body.

People came pouring out of the house and onto the pool deck. Some from the kitchen. Others from another set of doors. Gina vaguely registered Fatima and Kaitlin. Destiny and Mei. Another group rushed down the stairs from the second-floor balcony—Charlotte and Amelia, with Jordyn two steps behind.

Then, a horrible cry from Charlotte as she and Amelia saw their mother. The girls clung to one another, Amelia hiding her face against her sister's shoulder while Charlotte couldn't seem to drag her eyes away from Sophie's lifeless body.

Arms extended, Jordyn moved to comfort the girls, ushering them out of the rain toward the shelter of the first-floor overhang with the others.

"Where is Luke?" Gina asked, her throat raw after her terrified scream.

It had been the first cohesive sentence to come out of her mouth even though her brain ran a mile a minute trying to put together what had happened here.

Only murmurs in reply. Someone behind her sobbed quietly.

In the meantime, fury simmered inside her. Rage that she'd *known* Luke could be a murderer, and she'd done nothing. She'd been too focused on revenge that now she'd never have the chance to deliver.

All that hard work had been for nothing.

Sophie had been a horrible, horrible person. But justice should have meant taking her down a few pegs. Humiliating her. Making her regret her life choices. Not . . . *this*.

"Where. Is. *Luke*?" Gina shouted, turning toward the women gathered around the pool deck.

Jordyn and the girls stopped in their tracks. The rest of them huddled together under the overhang close to the house. Only Gina stood fully in the rain near Sophie's body.

"Gina," Destiny said gently. "Put the gun down."

Lowering her gaze, Gina saw she still had the small derringer drawn. Raindrops slid along the steel onto her shaking hands. Nausea clawed at her gut.

"I . . . Oh. Sorry." Fumbling to click the safety into place, Gina lowered the weapon.

As she did, the others began to speak.

"We need to call 911."

"I don't know where the phones are."

"Did anyone find Brad?"

Gina didn't know who said what as the words circled her adrenaline-fogged brain. Or maybe it was shock acting like a barrier between her and the rest of the world. Then, three words blasted into her consciousness and detonated.

"Was Sophie shot?"

Mei had been the one to voice the very reasonable question. A question that told Gina how much trouble she could be in.

"It wasn't me," Gina assured them, spinning to face the book club members and Sophie's daughters. As the adrenaline wore off, her teeth started chattering and she trembled all over. "I swear."

Even in the shadows of the rainy night she could see them take a collective step back. Did they think Gina would start firing on them? Oh God. Did these people really think her capable of murder?

Jordyn cleared her throat, shoulders back. "I think we should have the girls look for our cell phones. Is that okay with everyone?"

While the others agreed that would be best, Gina took the opportunity to slide her weapon into the holster. No way was she relinquishing it until she figured out what the hell was going on. Only Destiny seemed to have noticed. The woman's eyes tracked her every move.

"I never fired the gun," Gina informed Destiny as she stepped under the overhang out of the rain. She needed to tell her story so they could find the real culprit. "It's Luke we should be looking for. He's the one who wanted to kill her."

Destiny looked her up and down. "We all came out here to find you standing over her with a weapon in hand."

"But did you hear a shot fired?" Gina asked, still shaking from the cold and the shock of finding a body. "I only drew the gun because I heard a godawful scream."

Fatima fidgeted with the opera glasses that were part of her costume. "And you make it a habit to come to book club armed?"

"I didn't see any bullet wounds on Sophie," Mei observed, her voice more measured than the others. "But there is a lot of blood around her head."

"Mei, you had a good reason to kill her," Kaitlin announced flatly, her mascara smeared from rain or maybe tears. "You just found out it was Sophie and not Tara who slept with Nikolai. Maybe you ran over Tara last year when you thought *she* was the guilty one, then decided to exact revenge on Sophie tonight."

"That's preposterous," Mei scoffed, moving farther from the body toward the house. "And I'm going inside. I'm not going to catch pneumonia defending myself against baseless accusations."

"I second the going indoors part," Destiny added. "But I'd like Gina to come in where we can see her since my money's still on her."

"I could use a hand over here." Brad limped out from the shadows at the far end of the pool deck. He held an arm at an awkward angle.

Wounded?

Mei and Kaitlin rushed forward to help. Then, before they reached him, Luke ran up from behind him as if trying to catch up. He reared back for a moment at the sight of the guests outside. Then he rushed toward Brad to lend him an arm.

"Are you okay, man?" he asked. "What's going on?"

Gina thought he sounded strange. Had he killed his wife and was trying to pretend like he didn't know about it?

Brad visibly shook off the help, muttering, "Get away from me."

But they'd just neared Sophie's body and Luke's attention shifted. With a choked gasp at the sight of his wife, Luke moved toward her, falling to his knees.

"Sophie!" His shout sounded raw. Wretched.

But was his reaction genuine? No one else knew what Gina did about Luke. That he was a serial cheater who took out a fat insurance policy on his wife without her knowledge. Destiny moved toward Luke, laying a hand on his shaking shoulders while he hung his head.

As Brad moved nearer to them, Gina could see his wrists were duct-taped together. He looked unsteady on his feet, each step faltering.

"Brad what happened to you?" Kaitlin asked as the same time Fatima pushed her way to the front of the group and asked him, "Where have you been?"

"I don't remember so well," Brad admitted with a hesitant glance back at Luke. His gaze dipped toward the body briefly before he refocused on the others. "But *someone* bound and gagged me and put me in the basement. I think I was drugged."

That caught Gina's attention. Made sense considering his delayed reactions.

Moreover, the only person in this group that she knew enjoyed recreational drug use was Luke. Not often. But he'd asked her twice if she wanted to try Ecstasy, supposedly to make sex all the hotter. She'd refused both times.

"Luke," Fatima called to him where he leaned over Sophie. "I don't think you should touch her. The cops will want us to preserve any evidence."

"She's my wife, goddammit," he barked back. "I'm entitled to see if she's really gone or if there's any chance—"

His voice broke, and it was all Gina could do not to run screaming at him. To call him out for faking his grief.

"You did this," she accused him in front of everyone. "I saw the life insurance policy you took out on her last week. I know you wanted her dead."

At the back of the group she heard a soft gasp. Turning, she realized Charlotte and Amelia had returned with the basket of cellphones in Charlotte's hands. Jordyn stood behind them.

"Girls, that's not true." Luke straightened from the body, seeming to pull himself together as he reached a pleading hand toward them. "Let's go inside and we can—"

"Call the police," Fatima finished for him as she dug in the basket for her device. "I'm going inside, and I'm reporting this right now."

"Wait. *Please*, Ms. Fatima." Charlotte passed the basket of phones to her sister, gesturing for Amelia to make the rounds with it. "Can we just hear what Mr. Brad has to say first? I don't understand who could have done this to him."

"Smart girl." Gina nodded her satisfaction as she found her phone in the jumble of devices that Amelia gave her. "Who else but Luke is strong enough to restrain Brad and maneuver a drugged man into the basement?"

"Oh please," Destiny scoffed. "Someone with a gun doesn't need to be strong to do either of those things."

Gina's stomach pitched at a possibility she hadn't considered. What if Luke had framed her for this murder? Everyone already looked at her as if she was guilty.

"I do remember something now," Brad said, supporting himself against the wall of glass doors leading into the kitchen. "I overheard an argument. And then someone hit me on the back of the head."

"Who was arguing?" Kaitlin prodded him, her fists on her hips. "Luke and Gina?"

Gina trembled with the realization that could have happened. She *had* fought with Luke tonight.

In a flash, she recalled all the things she'd done to plot against Sophie in the last year. Breaking into Sophie's house. Planting evidence of her affair with a dead woman's husband. Putting GPS trackers on her lover's vehicle. An ambitious prosecutor could make a case against Gina even without physical evidence. The circumstantial would be damning.

Was it too late to start bargaining with God for some help?

She vowed to do better. Be better.

She would leave Saratoga and never come back.

"No, it wasn't Luke and Gina," Brad answered, rubbing his forehead with his still bound wrists. "I heard Sophie. And . . ." He swallowed visibly as he glanced around at the group. "And Amelia."

CHAPTER

37

Jordyn

Present

OBVIOUSLY, SHE WOULD have to come clean. Even though it had been an accident. A terrible, terrible accident.

Jordyn kept hearing that final scream over and over in her brain as she mindlessly wiped up some spilled wine from Sophie's normally pristine countertops. She couldn't believe what had happened. How had a shouting match turned deadly so fast? Sophie had gone down like a ton of bricks, never even putting out a hand to stop herself.

And Jordyn would tell everyone what happened soon. Of course she would. She'd been a scrappy kid who turned into a scrappy adult. While she may have been a hard luck case no one had wanted as a kid, she had built a sense of self around the character principles she found important. Standing up for what she believed in. Not backing down.

And, yeah, facing up to the consequences of her actions.

Yet as the bedraggled group filed into the kitchen, tracking damp footprints all over Sophie's floor, Jordyn couldn't bring herself to confess the events from the balcony just yet. No matter how horrible she felt about the argument upstairs with Sophie—the push that had turned deadly. She'd come here tonight with a singular mission. To catch Tara's killer.

And even though Sophie had been the one to run Tara down, there were still too many unanswered questions. Too many weird things coming to light. Luke taking out the insurance policy on his wife. Someone drugging Brad and tying him up. There were missing pieces to this puzzle, making the picture fractured and out of focus. Sophie had admitted that Tara threatened to out Luke for sexual harassment. Could he have had a hand in covering up Sophie's crime? If Luke had played any role in Tara's death, Jordyn could hardly just quietly turn herself into the police for what happened to Sophie, leaving Luke free as a bird.

Jordyn's fingers went to the St. Rita medallion. She tugged it from under the white T-shirt she wore beneath the costume lab coat and brushed over the familiar worn ridges of the saint's outline.

Rita? Tara? If anyone was listening, she sure hoped they'd guide her toward more concrete answers about Tara's death before she had to fess up to what happened on the balcony. She felt so jittery inside she was surprised everyone didn't spot her guilt scrawled over her face.

But she needed more answers first.

"The longer we wait to call 911 the worse it looks for all of us," Fatima reminded the group, still brandishing her cell. "Charlotte, we need to report this."

"My mother is gone." Charlotte opened a long drawer and scooped out half of the identical white dish towels. She flung them unceremoniously on the island while keeping one to wrap around the ends of her damp hair. "And once the police arrive, I will forever lose my chance to ask questions about what the hell happened here tonight."

The older Durand daughter glared at them, her unnatural calm reminding Jordyn eerily of her mother. Other than that initial cry of surprise, Charlotte hadn't shown much reaction to Sophie's death. Maybe she was just in shock.

"I give up." Fatima slid her device onto the island. "We'll just wait for the killer to take out more of us while we square up our stories."

"Innocent people don't need to worry about getting their stories straight," Kaitlin huffed as she wiped tears and makeup from her cheek. "But Charlotte, think of Amelia. If she was the one arguing with your mother, the police might have questions about that."

"Thanks for that resounding endorsement of my character." Amelia still wore the woodland fairy costume from earlier in the evening, though the stocking mask and bug eyes were long gone. Unlike her sibling's cool façade, Amelia's expression moved readily from sneer to scowl. "Is anyone surprised I argued with my mother on a regular basis? I'm virtually surrounded by people who hated her, whether any of you admit it or not, so let's not rush to judgment that I found her *overbearing* and occasionally called her out on it."

The accusation seemed to quiet the book club members, but Charlotte didn't appear surprised by the outburst. She squeezed the dishtowel around her hair before returning it to the counter, then turned to where Brad was seated at a small table off to one side of the kitchen.

"Mr. Brad, did you hear what they were arguing about?"

Amelia shook her head, muttering, "Jesus, Charlotte."

Brad hedged, looking uncomfortable. "Things are still a little foggy."

"Because Luke drugged you," Gina shouted, slapping her hand on the counter, her whole body seeming to vibrate. "He keeps illegal shit in this house." She swung to face Luke. "I looked up G and K, by the way. Date rape drugs can make you forget things."

Luke sagged against one of the closed glass doors. "You're out of your mind, Gina. Get a grip."

"You've seen that stuff?" Destiny asked, sounding skeptical. She'd pulled off her feather fan tail so that she walked around in a rhinestone bodysuit. "With your own eyes?"

"Yes I did," Gina snapped, leaning into a Cajun accent that Jordyn had never heard her use before. "And it's Evangeline, from now on. I only came here to wreck Sophie's life the way she wrecked mine with her stupid podcast. I never planned to kill her. But in my haste for revenge, I ended up sleeping with a *murderer*."

Someone made a soft whistling sound of surprise while eyebrows raised around the room. Jordyn, of course, wasn't surprised by the admission. But hearing Gina's vehement denial of coming to town with murderous intent made Jordyn less inclined to think she'd had any role in Tara's death.

"*You're* the woman who's suing Sophie?" Luke scrubbed a hand over his face as he stared at his lover. Then, he turned to stepdaughter. "Charlotte, we need to call the police."

Somehow Sophie's older daughter had taken command of the room. But she also seemed to have stepped into her mother's role with ease. All of the book club members looked to her, waiting. Maybe they were *all* in shock by now.

Charlotte didn't answer. She moved toward the kitchen table where Brad Reynolds still sat. Lowered herself into a chair across from him.

"I'm sorry about the duct tape," she told him softly. "But if there are fingerprints on it, we need to preserve them until the police arrive."

Jordyn blinked at Charlotte's matter-of-fact thinking in the aftermath of her mother's traumatic death. It seemed strange. Almost frightening. Could she be in denial?

"That's fine." Brad nodded. "If my drink is around, someone should test it."

From the back of the room, Mei said, "I'm on it."

Kaitlin almost knocked over her counter stool to stand in a hurry. "We should work in pairs. You know, keep an eye on one another until we know who killed Sophie and drugged Brad."

They weren't seriously suggesting that this murder mystery evening play out for real?

Jordyn couldn't smother a surprised laugh. "I spent my childhood surrounded by drug dealers and addicts, and my teen years in and out of foster homes with more than a few criminals in the making. Yet my Saratoga book club knows more about crime than any of them."

"We've read a few police procedurals," Fatima admitted.

Amelia stepped forward, her eyes on her lit phone screen. She laid the device on the table near her sister to share it. "K is ketamine, an anesthetic that can cause dissociative episodes."

Charlotte didn't look at the device, keeping her attention on Brad. "I know what it is. Mr. Brad, what were my mother and sister arguing about?"

"Amelia said she wished her mother was dead."

A chorus of startled gasps from the book club seemed hypocritical considering the way this group all trash-talked one another. Maybe they didn't realize how much the younger generation mirrored the older one.

Jordyn saw the way the group looked at Amelia now, and knew she needed to speak up soon. She wouldn't let an innocent teen go down for a crime Jordyn had committed, no matter that it had been an accident. Unlike Tara's killer, she wouldn't hide her actions behind a false façade.

For now, she said, "Ninety percent of teenagers have said that to their parents at one time or another. It proves nothing."

Jordyn was more interested in what happened to Brad. Did the person who accosted him have any role in Tara's death?

"I agree," Brad said tiredly. "And I wouldn't have thought anything of it until . . ." He swung to look at Luke. "Luke tackled me and tossed me in the basement."

"I knew it!" Gina screeched, picking up her phone. "He drugged Brad and then killed Sophie."

As she tapped the screen to life, Fatima put her hand over the device. "Or Luke drugged Brad to protect Amelia. The real killer."

Heads swung in Amelia's direction. The girl looked ready to sink through the floor. Making Jordyn recall exactly how it felt to lose everything—her parents and her freedom—the day she'd been carted off to foster care. She felt Amelia's hurt keenly, and she hated that she'd been the cause for her grief.

She sure as hell wouldn't be the cause of Amelia being subjected to false allegations too.

"Amelia didn't kill her mother." Jordyn stepped forward, hoping Charlotte and Amelia would forgive her one day. The time had come to pay the price for something she'd never meant to do. "I did."

CHAPTER

38

Jordyn

Ten months later

JORDYN WALKED OUT of court on a blistering hot August day as a free woman.

Not a felon. And not even guilty of aggravated assault, the least of the charges the district attorney had initially considered bringing. Turned out the judge in Jordyn's case had been on the zoning committee the year Sophie Durand had successfully pushed through the plans for her over-the-top house, and the woman was still salty about it.

At least, that's what the book club gossips had decided.

Kaitlin had taken to visiting Jordyn once a month since the new year when Jordyn had been officially charged, and Kaitlin shared the latest opinions of the group along with a copy of whatever book they'd decided to read next. Jordyn had no idea whether the zoning committee rumor was true or not. She knew better than to quibble about the gift of a second chance.

Jordyn had an excellent lawyer thanks to Lauren Hughes. Arnie Van Ness had offered his services when he'd read about Sophie's death and Jordyn's involvement. But Tara's mother had insisted on paying for the best possible legal counsel, sending a top tier criminal defense attorney to represent Jordyn within forty-eight hours of her arrest. Jordyn hadn't realized she'd made a decent impression on the woman on that trip to Manhattan, but Lauren had been staunchly supportive. Jordyn suspected her loyalty had more to do with guilt over not making better choices to support Tara.

Either way, Jordyn planned to pay the woman a visit to thank her for everything she'd done. Offer free graphic art services for life. Because the lawyer that Lauren had sent to represent Jordyn had been a legal genius, finagling with the county prosecutor long before the trial began to ensure murder or even manslaughter was never on the table.

Which had been a shocker at first. But then, Jordyn hadn't known what the attorney had. The county coroner had discovered a needle mark in Sophie's neck and the toxicology report had said she had enough ketamine in her system to render her close to a state of paralysis at the time of her death.

Jordyn hated to think about that. She'd suspected Sophie had been intoxicated at the time of their argument, but apparently the woman had been under the influence of something far more powerful. The injection she'd received had taken hold during that argument so that by the time Jordyn shoved her, Sophie had no way to stop herself. She'd never put a hand out to break her fall.

The police had only recently charged Luke Sideris with drugging Sophie. Gina Vallot—who had gone back to using her real name, Evangeline Jameson—had told police that she'd seen vials of illegal substances in his closet during the course of their affair. Plus, Brad Reynolds had gone on record saying that Luke had injected him with something that night too. He hadn't recalled the injection at first, but Kaitlin had noticed the needle mark on his neck shortly after the cops arrived at Sophie's house on Halloween night. So even though Brad's memories were somewhat suspect due to the drug he'd had in his system, there was proof he'd been injected.

Luke's trial still loomed. Jordyn would be following it to see if anything ever came out about his role in what happened to Tara. Briefly, she thought maybe he'd been the one responsible for leaving the threatening note on her car and had reported it to the cops. But later, the investigating officer had told her that Ezra had actually been the culprit. According to the officer, Ezra had claimed to be so worried about Jordyn's safety, he'd left the note hoping it would scare her into returning home. The dolt.

At least the police were investigating Luke now. If he'd helped Sophie to cover up what had happened to Tara, there would be accessory charges to come.

Kaitlin had told her that Charlotte and Amelia had been allowed to remain in their family home. Charlotte had turned eighteen before Luke had been arrested, so there'd never been a time when guardianship was a cause for concern. Neither of the girls cared to live with their birth father, so they'd remained in Saratoga with Charlotte planning to attend college locally while Amelia finished high school. It came as no surprise that wealthy, historic Saratoga was home to a college considered a "Hidden Ivy." Charlotte would go to Skidmore as a prelaw student.

Now, Jordyn left court and the ordeal behind her. She smiled to see a familiar white Jeep at the back of the court parking lot. Natalie Ramos, her PI friend, leaned against the spare tire mounted to the bumper, shading her eyes with one hand.

"Welcome back." Grinning, Natalie leaned in to give her a hug.

"My head is still spinning that it's over." Jordyn glanced back at the courthouse and shuddered. "Thanks for the lift. And for packing up my rental and—everything."

Natalie had stepped up in a way that had been wholly unexpected, offering to box up Jordyn's things from the carriage house so she didn't owe rent for the months she'd been in custody awaiting trial. Natalie had put everything in storage for her. But then, Natalie knew a lot about handling things like that from her line of work.

"My pleasure. I think my bill will be decidedly smaller than that attorney your friend hired for you." Natalie whistled appreciatively as she slid behind the wheel. "Pretty sure she eats prosecutors for breakfast. Do you mind if we keep the top down?"

She pointed through the roll cage to the blue sky overhead.

Jordyn laughed. "I think the wind in my hair is going to feel pretty nice for a change."

On cue, Natalie popped the vehicle into gear and took off with a flourish, fishtailing just enough to make it fun.

Clutching the door in one hand, Jordyn sucked in the fresh air, promising herself she was going to exercise a little more caution in life going forward. A little restraint.

Kaitlin had spoken to her at length about developing a podcast of her own, something about foster families and the unique bonds that resulted from those relationships. *The Clean Break* may have ended, but Kaitlin still had the podcast bug after being shut out of Sophie and Tara's brainchild. Kaitlin had a lot of contacts in the foster system from her work in counseling, but she wanted to use Jordyn and Tara's story as her first episode.

Jordyn had agreed, mostly so she had a chance to talk about Tara. Honor her friend, who had been a better person than she could ever hope to be.

Her one request? Kaitlin would have to come to her in Austin, because there wasn't a chance in hell she would be setting foot in Saratoga again.

Epilogue

Present

AMELIA DURAND WAS a free woman these days too.

Seated on a chaise lounge by the pool, just a few feet from where her mother's legs had crumpled at an unnatural angle in death, Amelia scrolled through the local news videos on her phone. Because she'd followed the legal case closely, her feed was full of reels of Jordyn Lawson walking out of the courtroom today after her release.

Later, Amelia would revisit her favorite Reddit page where people weighed in on the case. Some lauding Jordyn as a hero for trying to find a killer in the hit-and-run police had all but given up on solving. Others villainized Jordyn for her vigilante role in something that should have been left to law enforcement. Amelia enjoyed their comments and wild speculations about what had really happened that Halloween night.

Especially since she was the only one who actually knew.

"Come on, Hazel," Amelia called to her Great Pyrenees, the white fluffy dog still growing into her massive paws. She didn't want to keep the furball out in the heat for too long. "Let's go inside and cool off."

Hazel leapt from her chaise, following Amelia into the casita through the French doors before she closed them behind them to keep in the air conditioning. Not all of the lessons her mother had taught her were lost. Amelia did still remember to shut a door behind her. But the rule against animals in the house had been well and thoroughly broken almost immediately following Sophie's death.

Amelia had brought the Pyrenees pup home from the shelter the next week. Even ten months later, Amelia still enjoyed having parties at the house with all her friends. And all their pets.

Setting her half-finished soda on the small kitchen counter, Amelia breezed through the empty pool house while Charlotte attended her college orientation. This year, with Charlotte out of high school and occupied with her course work, promised to be epic. With their mother gone, Amelia could finally breathe freely.

If Luke got out of jail and came home?

Amelia wasn't worried. She could handle her stepfather. He knew enough about what had really happened on Halloween night to give Amelia some space.

Some respect.

Opening the door that led into Sophie's personal office space, Amelia lowered herself into the pale gray leather chair. She ran her hands over the mahogany desktop, smiling to herself as she remembered how perfectly everything had worked out.

She'd fought viciously with her mother, of course. But that was nothing new because Amelia had despised her mother ever since Auntie T had been killed. Amelia had known in her gut as soon as it happened that her mother had been the guilty party. She'd overheard Tara and her mother arguing that night about ownership of *The Clean Break*. Then, after Tara had left the house, Sophie and Luke had gotten in a heated argument about whether or not Luke was sleeping with Tara. Her mother had been literally spitting with rage. Sophie had left the house in a fury, saying she'd find out the truth from Tara once and for all.

When Sophie returned to the house, her face had been chalk white. Luke's SUV that she'd driven had been dinged up. By morning, Sophie had behaved as if she had no idea what had happened, but Amelia knew. It had been just one more reason to hate the mother who rode her constantly for not being smart enough, not putting in enough effort on her school work, not excelling in sports to the same degree as Charlotte did.

Those jabs still hurt Amelia sometimes. Even with Sophie gone. She held out a hand to Hazel, who padded over to offer her comfort, putting her huge furry head on Amelia's lap. Amelia had named the dog for that crazy costume Auntie T had worn at the Witch Walk, when she'd tried to thumb her nose at the sexy witch costumes with her Witch Hazel outfit. That memory still made her smile.

Made her remember there were good people in the world.

People different from her. Different from her mom.

"You're the best girl," she crooned to the dog, petting the dog's fluff for a minute before she searched her mother's desk drawer for some stationery.

Finding the heavy linen stock Sophie had bought home from Italy, Amelia smoothed her fingers over the paper, her mind fast-forwarding from one Halloween to the next. She'd bided her time with her mother. Tried to forgive her for running down one of Amelia's favorite people. But things came to a head last Halloween when her mother had been livid that Amelia had "snuck out" of the house with Charlotte to try and attend a friend's party. Amelia had finally had enough. She told her mother that she would reveal to the world that she'd killed Tara if she didn't back off. She hated Sophie.

Then Luke intervened, trying to calm them down. Which would have been fine, until Brad Reynolds had overheard them. Luke had been scared that Brad might have unwittingly heard details about Tara's death. So he'd tackled him, jabbed him with a needle that seemed to appear out of nowhere.

Amelia had known her stepfather had a little drug habit, but not that it had escalated to the point where he'd just happened to have a needle on him. The sight of it had given her an idea. In the darkened house, it had been simple to retrieve the needle while her mother resumed berating her. There had been a little liquid left in it.

Amelia didn't even know for certain what it was at that time, but she was only too happy to steal up behind her mother from the shadows and inject her too. The effects had been speedy. But even if they hadn't been, Amelia had been too far beyond worrying about repercussions to care. Something about Sophie trying to jail her in the house again, and on a night when all her friends were out, had been the final straw for her.

Still, their unhappy little dysfunction would have surely just gone on another day if Jordyn hadn't wandered into the room then. Amelia had hidden quickly, jumping into a darkened closet. And she'd been able to witness the whole encounter between Jordyn and Sophie while the drug Amelia had injected into her mom was taking hold. Later, after the toxicology report had been released, Amelia learned the drug had been ketamine, shutting down her mother's thoughts and reactions. For all Amelia knew, Sophie had never taken it before. She wouldn't have any tolerance for it.

With fascinated delight, she watched Jordyn go toe-to-toe with her mother. Taking her to task for the murder that Sophie had never paid for.

Even then, her mother had been a coldhearted bitch, taunting Jordyn. Revealing her dark side openly. That was how Amelia knew that the drug was really affecting her. Wiping away her boundaries and her control. Sophie usually saved her deepest evil for behind closed doors.

So when Jordyn shoved Sophie in anger, Sophie reeled back with no way to stop herself, her body in the grip of a powerful anesthetic. The fall had been sickening. The scream terrifying.

But then . . . it was over. Jordyn had killed the wicked witch who had kept Amelia's household under a suffocating dark spell. Freeing her.

For weeks, she'd tried to pick through her feelings. Overwhelming relief. A little grief. A pinch of wistful nostalgia, although less for her mom than for what a mother–daughter relationship should have looked like. Amelia had enough friends to know that normal moms expressed pride or joy in their kids, at least occasionally.

Though her older sister didn't know what had really happened that night, Amelia could tell Charlotte was not really grieving for the loss of a woman who had made them work on ballet moves until their toes bled. The woman who signed them up for so many sports, mentoring sessions, and volunteer activities that they routinely managed five hours of sleep a night.

They'd never been good enough to merit their mother's love.

But Amelia was done looking backward.

Jordyn had gone free today, and tomorrow Charlotte would begin her college program. A page had turned for Amelia.

She decided to celebrate with a party. Not a pool party, or a pet party. Nothing lame and high school like that. She would celebrate the new school year with something more elegant. High class.

Maybe something that looked to the rest of the world like a nod to her accomplished mother?

"Oh Hazel, this is going to be good." The idea came to her fully formed and perfect. She withdrew a heavy Montblanc pen from the middle drawer and uncapped it.

Then, setting the pen to paper, she used her best penmanship to craft a special invitation to her very own themed book club event. Taking care not to smudge the ink, she wrote:

Can you find the killer before another murder is committed?

ACKNOWLEDGMENTS

To the team at Crooked Lane Books for believing in *The Last Book Club*. Thank you for championing this story throughout the editorial process and helping me to fine-tune my vision for Jordyn's journey.

For my agent, Barbara Collins Rosenberg, for never batting an eyelash at a new storytelling direction. Thank you for helping me find a wonderful home for a story that means so much to me.

This story would not exist without the many wonderful suspense authors whose works inspired me. After years of devouring novels by Loreth Anne White, Teresa Driscoll, Kendra Elliot, Lisa Jewell, Lisa Unger, and so many others, I found the courage to write my own. Thank you for the hours of wonderful reading, and for transporting me to new places.

To my twenty-plus-year critique partner, Catherine Mann, for reading every word I've ever written. Where would I be without your brilliant storytelling sense, your unerring ability to know what I *meant* to say, even if I didn't quite say it the right way, and your reassurance that I know what I'm doing even on days where I'm pretty sure I have no idea? This story is so much better for your insights.

And to my sister, Linda Watson, for being my first reader. It was a testament to how much I believed in *The Last Book Club* that I wanted to share it with my *extraordinarily* well-read sibling right out of the gate. Thank you, Linda, for helping me re-see this story as a reader.

Also, with love to my supportive family for your understanding on the days when I'm so deep in the writing cave that I have no idea what anyone is saying to me. Thank you for your patience, and for repeating yourselves to bring me up to speed!